bad boys

After Dark

–Brett–

EVERYTHING'S NAUGHTIER AFTER DARK...

Billionaires After Dark Series

Melissa Foster

D1067148

ISBN-13: 978-1941480793
ISBN-10: 1941480799

Cover Design: Elizabeth Mackey Designs
Cover Photography: Sara Eirew

WORLD LITERARY PRESS
PRINTED IN THE UNITED STATES OF AMERICA

A Note to Readers

When I first met Sophie and Brett in Mick Bad's book, their connection was immediate and intense, and I have been excited to write their story ever since. It's amazing how well Sophie knows exactly what Brett needs. Equally as astonishing is how she knows him better than he knows himself. I adore these two lovers, and I hope you do, too! If you're new to the Billionaires After Dark series, you have plenty of other Bad and Wild brothers to catch up with. Each book is written to stand alone, so dive right in! For my avid fans, don't worry; this is not the last you'll see of the Billionaires After Dark.

You'll find previews of more upcoming publications at the end of their story, but the best way to keep up to date with releases is to sign up for my newsletter. Plus, you'll receive a free short story just for signing up.
www.melissafoster.com/newsletter

—Download free Love in Bloom ebooks:
www.melissafoster.com/LIBFree

—Download free reader goodies, including family trees, series order, and more:
www.melissafoster.com/RG

Happy reading! ~ Melissa

Chapter One

BRETT BAD HATED to be *subdued*, in bed or in social situations, and he'd just about hit his limit. But he cherished his family, which explained why he was standing in the middle of a Manhattan perfumery at nine thirty on a Friday night, celebrating the grand opening of Cashmere, his sister-in-law's new boutique, instead of seeking relief in the arms of a beautiful woman. He was happy for her, but as he downed a second glass of champagne, he itched to get the hell out of the refined event.

His brother Dylan sidled up to him, his eyes locked on his wife, Tiffany, standing across the room. There was a time when Dylan would be eyeing the skirts in the room, playing wingman for Brett. But like Carson and their oldest brother, Mick, Dylan had recently fallen in love, leaving Brett as the last bachelor.

A position he planned to hold on to for a very long time.

Brett might look like his brothers—tall, dark, and athletic—but that was about as far as their similarities went. He couldn't imagine coming home to the same woman every night. Hell, he couldn't imagine *kissing* the same woman every night. Although, he had to admit, after spending time with his brothers and their wives, who were so swept up in each other they practically oozed love, he could no longer stomach the meaningless talk he'd once endured when he hooked up with random women. His brothers were so happy, Brett sometimes wondered if he was missing out on some magnificent world he hadn't been clued into. But that thought was usually followed by a laugh, a drink, and a fuck.

At least it had been, until a couple months ago.

He picked up another flute of champagne, and as he brought it to his lips, he noticed a brunette flashing a flirtatious smile in his direction. He took in her perfectly applied makeup, the practiced come-hither smile, and obviously fake breasts and waited for a pang of appreciation to hit him, for his cock to take notice, or the heat of lust to simmer inside him. A minute later, as she nudged the blonde standing beside her and the two of them headed his way, he was still waiting. Ever since Carson and Dylan's double wedding two months ago, the desire that had once come so easily for ready and willing women had taken a decisive step back, and it was starting to piss him off.

He downed the drink and set the empty flute on the buffet table, his gaze catching on the perfect heart-shaped ass of a sexier, *curvier* brunette. The Magnum in his pants twitched. *That's more like it.*

"Is she beautiful, or what?" Dylan said.

He knew his brother was talking about Tiffany, a tall blond sports agent who was as fierce in business as she was *in love* with Dylan. But as Brett said, "A stunner," there was only one woman on his mind. The feisty one who had starred in every goddamn fantasy he'd had since he'd met her and whose sassy retorts never failed to turn him on. The one leaning closer to her friend to sniff a bottle of perfume. Sophie Roberts, his brother Mick's legal assistant, and the beautiful temptress who blew him off every chance she got—including at his brothers' wedding, when she'd flipped some sort of switch inside him.

The other two women neared with hopeful seduction sparkling in their eyes, and Brett planned his escape. Dylan seemed oblivious to anyone other than Tiffany, so he clued him in. "Trouble at two o'clock."

"Aw, hell. Thanks, man."

As Dylan headed for Tiffany, Brett set his sights on Sophie, who was being ogled by a blond dude with *let's fuck* in his eyes. Brett rolled his shoulders back, sizing up the competition as he crossed the room. *Competition my ass.* The douche bag was definitely barking up the wrong tree. Then again, any man trying to hook up with Sophie in front of Brett was in for trouble. She may not be *his*, but he was bound and determined to change that. *At least for one night.* It was time to reset his interest meter, and he was pretty sure the only way to do that was to finally have Sophie Roberts.

Sophie bent at the waist to smell another fragrance, and Brett came up behind her, leaning in close enough to feel her softness against him, and said, "I'd know that fine ass anywhere."

Without missing a beat, Sophie straightened her spine. Her electric-blue eyes slid down his frame, alighting every greedy ion inside him. A confident smile lifted her full lips as she met his gaze and said, "I thought I smelled cocky ex-cop."

As an international security expert, Brett knew how to read people, and no matter how many times Sophie turned him down, the desire in her eyes gave away what she really wanted.

"What was that? You want to smell my cock?" He paused long enough to notice, and appreciate, the effect he had on her. Her nipples strained against her curve-hugging gray dress. Stepping closer, he took in the flecks of silver in her eyes and the slight hitch in her breathing. He'd propositioned her more times than he cared to admit, and he loved each reaction more than the last. "*Smelling* isn't really my thing, but if you want to get up close and personal, I can be persuaded."

"Hey," her friend said with a scowl.

Sophie touched the brunette's arm, never taking her eyes off Brett. "It's okay, Grace. You know how some guys buy cars to make up for their"—she lowered her gaze to his groin, stoking the fire inside him, and arched a brow before meeting his stare again—"*deficits*? Brett is a master at it. Grace Montgomery, meet Brett Bad, Mick's youngest brother."

"And his *biggest*," Brett added with a smirk.

Now it was Grace's turn to size him up, and she did so with a jut of her hip, a crossing of her arms, and a long, slow leer from his head to his toes, which had zero effect on him, other than amusement.

"*This* is Brett? The one who wants to install monkey bars in the conference room for his after-hour fantasies?" Grace reached out and lifted his chin with her index finger, making a dramatic show of assessing his features.

He got a kick out of her brazenness, but an even bigger high knowing that Sophie had talked about him.

"He's definitely hot, Soph," Grace said. "You sure he's packing a minibike in there and not a Harley?"

Brett chuckled. Holding Sophie's gaze, he said, "How about we ditch this place, have a few drinks, and maybe you can find out?"

"I'm not sure that's a good idea," Sophie said.

It wasn't a *no*, which was more than he usually got out of her. "Since when has that stopped me from anything?"

"Probably never." Sophie lifted her chin with a sassy smile.

"And this is a *very* good idea," he assured her. Sophie was good friends with his brothers' wives, and because of that she was often included in their outings, which meant she and Brett were together a lot. But not *alone*. He'd give anything to get her alone, and getting her to go for drinks with him and her friend was one step closer. "We even have a chaperone, right, Grace?"

"You are good, aren't you?" Grace looked at Sophie. "Actually, I could use a little fun. I've been working like mad."

Sophie shifted her weight from one high heel to the other. "It's getting late."

"We'll only have a few drinks, not stay out all night." *That is, unless you want to.*

"I'm game," Grace said. "If for no other reason than so I can be entertained by Brett tossing out his fishing line. It's my only night off in weeks, and *I'm* the one who has to work in the morning."

Sophie bit nervously at her lip.

"Come on," Grace coaxed. "Stop being such a Girl Scout. Besides, what do you have waiting at home? The next Kurt Remington novel?"

Kurt Remington wrote thrillers, and Brett knew the author well. When Kurt was in town, he and his siblings hung out at NightCaps, the bar Dylan owned. But this new information about Sophie surprised him. He'd always pictured her reading romance novels and watching the Hallmark Channel, dreaming of finding Mr. White Picket Fence, which, according to Mick, was why she wouldn't give Brett the time of day.

"You read thrillers?" he asked, in case Grace had been kidding.

"Read them?" Grace laughed. "She's devoured them since we were kids. That's about all she does in her free time. That and dreaming about Kurt Remington, the very hot, very *married*, author."

"Grace!" Sophie tried to suppress her smile. "That's not *all* I do, and I don't dream about him. I just like his writing and the way his mind works."

"Well, Sexy Sophie, you've clearly got the wrong man starring in your fantasies. If thrills are what you're into, you're looking at the king of them."

Sophie laughed. "You never give up, do you?"

"Not easily," Brett admitted.

Her expression softened, and her gorgeous blue eyes moved between him and Grace. She exhaled loudly and said, "*Fine.* But I'm *not* sleeping with you."

"You keep telling yourself that, sweetheart."

AFTER CONGRATULATING TAWNY and assuring her that despite Brett's assertions, she did *not* need a perfume that smelled like him, Sophie headed to NightCaps with Brett and Grace. An hour, and two glasses of wine later, she sat at a table in the back of the bar as Brett got up to order another round of drinks. His piercing honey-brown eyes locked on her as he tossed his sport coat over the back of the booth and unbuttoned the top two buttons on his shirt, revealing a delicious path of olive skin and a dusting of chest hair. Damn, the man had cornered the market on hot bodies. She absently licked her lips, tasting the sweetness of the alcohol and wondering what Brett's lips tasted like. Were they sweet from the liquor, or spicy from his virility? She bet they held a hint of both. Little did he know it wasn't Kurt Remington she dreamed about, at least not in the ways Grace thought she did. It was *Brett*, the most arrogant, aggressive man she knew. She usually found those traits so annoying she never gave guys who displayed them a second thought. But Brett was a beast of a different kind. He had a way of looking at her that made her feel like there was more behind his hungry stare, which might be ridiculous since he'd never even asked her out on a real date, but still, that feeling lingered.

Brett leaned into the booth beside Sophie and said, "Don't get too hot and bothered watching my ass as I walk away."

His snarky comment snapped her out of her reverie. What on earth was she doing there? She knew better than to test her willpower around him. She watched him walk away, trying to ignore the familiar stirring low in her belly.

"I can't believe I let you talk me into this," she hissed at Grace. She and Grace had grown up together in their small hometown of Oak Falls, Virginia. Grace looked like a young Andie MacDowell, with wild dark hair and mossy green eyes. She was as fun as she was cautious, and Sophie loved her to pieces. They'd both had big dreams of living in New York City, and after attending college there, they'd remained. Grace was living her dream, writing and producing off-Broadway plays, and Sophie loved her job as Mick Bad's legal assistant.

"Are you kidding me? Sophie, he is totally into you."

"Yeah, and anyone else in a skirt." She glanced at Mr. Sexual Energy, with his brassy swagger and expensive slacks that hugged him in all the best places, and couldn't deny the heat streaming through her.

"Um, *no*, he's not." Grace stepped from the booth and wiggled her hips, reminding Sophie she was wearing a skirt and Brett wasn't hitting on *her*. She slid back into the booth and said, "I'm telling you, that man is all about *you*, babe. He hasn't taken his eyes off you the whole time we've been here."

She watched Brett lean across the bar beside a gorgeous blonde who was clearly pleased with his proximity. He said something to the woman, and in her mind Sophie imagined him saying, *What are you doing later, sweetheart?*

Brett glanced over his shoulder at Sophie, and the blonde followed his gaze, her smile wilting a little. *Ugh.* Grace was so wrong. The man was definitely not marriage material, and she had never been, and had no intention of becoming, a one-night stand.

"He only wants sex," Sophie said, turning her attention back to Grace. She didn't need to watch him in action. "And you of all people know what I want out of life."

"Okay, I totally get what you're saying. But you've got to hand it to him. The guy doesn't try to hide his intentions. On some level that's admirable." Grace glanced in Brett's direction. "Besides, you've been talking about him for the past few years like you *could* be interested."

"More like I'm *frustrated.*"

Grace lowered her voice and said, "It's been almost a year since you got laid. Of course you're frustrated."

Sophie rolled her eyes. "Not *sexually* frustrated, and I don't *get laid.* You're confusing me with Lindsay." Lindsay was Sophie's carefree younger sister who did not believe in long-term relationships or marriage. Sophie loved her dearly, but she had no idea how two sisters could be brought up under the same roof and have totally different ideals.

"Well, I personally think you should consider the very available option you have before you tonight. Because I have to tell you, with how lonely I've been lately, even *I'm* wondering just how *good* Mr. Bad can be."

Sophie's stomach pitched. "You cannot be serious. You

can't go after him."

"Careful, sweetheart. Your interest is showing," Grace whispered as Brett returned with their drinks.

"Let's see, we have one white zinfandel." He placed a wineglass in front of Grace, and then he set a drink in front of Sophie. "And one Dirty Girl Scout."

Grace laughed. "This guy doesn't miss a beat."

Sophie downed half her drink, trying to ignore the thrum of desire coursing through her as Brett waggled his brows.

"In your dreams," she said as he slid into the booth beside her, bringing his warm, masculine scent with him. She reminded herself that she was strong-willed and Brett was just like the dark chocolate cake she adored but knew she shouldn't eat too much of. She could handle him for a little while. But Grace was giving her the go-for-it look, and she couldn't deny that spending one night with Brett might *finally* put out the torch she'd been carrying for him.

That's a very bad idea.

She guzzled the rest of her drink. If her brain refused to cooperate, maybe she could dull her senses until she no longer felt the heat between them.

Brett put his hand on her leg and leaned closer, his fingers skimming her inner thigh. "How about we make those dreams come true?"

Sophie peeled his hand from her leg and set it on his own.

"Now, there's an idea," Grace said.

Sophie glared at her. She needed a lifeline, not encouragement. It was hard enough resisting Brett when they were in the office, surrounded by reminders of why she *shouldn't* be with him. Mick was an entertainment attorney, and more often than not he was cleaning up celebrities' messes, playing damage control. Those situations served as bright red flags. Sophie didn't need to play damage control with her own life or career because of one night with her boss's brother. But here in the bar, where couples were practically having sex on the dance floor and too much alcohol was wreaking havoc with her ability to think rationally, she was having trouble holding on to the reasons she should deny her sinfully hot pursuer.

They talked about the perfumery opening and made small talk. Just when Sophie thought she might be able to handle this night after all, Grace drained her drink and climbed from the booth, thumbing something into her phone.

Panic fluttered in Sophie's chest. "Where are you going?"

"I have to work in the morning, remember?" Grace dropped her phone into her purse and said, "I've got an Uber. You two kids have fun. I'll see you Sunday morning at the gym, Sophie."

"Wait—" *I cannot be trusted alone in a bar with Brett.* Even though she had never *been* alone in a bar with Brett, she somehow knew that about herself. She'd been careful about where and when she was with him since the first time they'd met, because she'd been *that* attracted to him, and lately her thoughts about him had become *relentless*. It had never been a problem before Mick and Amanda had gotten married. But Sophie was good friends with Amanda, who worked as a paralegal in their office, and what had once been girls' nights out had become get-togethers with a mix of friends, the Bads, *and Sophie.*

That was the problem.

If she wanted to stop thinking about Brett, she had to stop hanging out with her friends. The truth was, she didn't want to do either.

"I'll walk Grace out and make sure she gets into her car

safely. Be right back." Brett started to slide out of the booth, but Grace stopped him with a hand on his shoulder.

"I'm perfectly capable of leaving a bar, but I'm not sure Sophie is safe alone in here. Look at all the guys checking her out." Grace winked at Sophie and headed for the door.

Sophie was going to kill her. She wasn't used to having more than a drink or two, and between the champagne at the grand opening and the drinks she'd had at the bar, she was definitely buzzed.

Brett's eyes narrowed as he surveyed the people around them. Sophie couldn't help but laugh. *Like anyone's looking at me?* She glanced around them and noticed the blonde Brett had been talking to at the bar *was* looking at her.

"I think blondie is waiting for your date." She tried to scoot out of the booth, but Brett wasn't budging.

His brows slanted angrily. "What blonde?"

"The one at the bar. Don't even try to pretend you didn't see her. She's giving me the stink eye."

He glanced over his shoulder and scoffed. "She hit on me and I told her we were married."

"Married?" *Yeah, right.*

He shrugged. "I told her I wasn't interested, but she was pushy. So I pointed you out and said, 'See that gorgeous woman in the gray dress?'" His tone turned serious. "She's my wife, and there's not a woman on earth who could make me cheat on her.'"

Shivers ran down her spine. "You expect me to believe that a guy who is afraid of committing to second dates told a beautiful woman he was married?"

"I don't lie, Sophie. *Ever.*" His lips tipped up in an insanely sexy smile, as if he were proud of that fact.

"Um, you just did. To the blonde."

"Christ," he muttered. "That doesn't count. Some women don't know how to take no for an answer."

She laughed softly. "I know a guy like that."

"I would never make a woman do anything she didn't want to."

She leaned back with a deadpan stare.

He chuckled. "Sophie, you *want* to be here with me. You just don't want to admit it." He didn't give her time to respond, which was good, because she was pretty sure the response "so" wouldn't have driven home the point she was trying to make. "How many times have I gotten you alone?"

"None. But we're not alone now." She waved her hand toward the dance floor. "There are *dozens* of people around us."

He draped his arm around her shoulder, drawing her to him. "I only see you, Sophie. Let's stop playing these games. You know I want you."

Gulp. "You've made that pretty obvious."

"And I know you want a piece of me."

"A *piece*?" She laughed softly. "That's about all any girl gets of you. I'm not a *piece* girl."

Brett's expression turned serious, as if he was thinking about what she'd said. He stepped from the booth and offered her his hand.

"What are you doing?" she asked skeptically as he lifted her to her feet.

"*We* are dancing."

He gathered her in his arms right there beside the booth, which was across the room from the dance floor. She was vaguely aware of a few curious glances, but Brett was gazing into her eyes, his dark eyes as compelling as summer lightning. His hand covered the expanse of her back, so hot it felt like he was branding her through her dress. She'd never danced with him, had never embraced him before. As she put her arms around his neck, he felt broader and stronger than he looked. Even in her tipsy state, she was acutely aware of every place their bodies touched. His hand slipped to the curve at the base of her spine, and she knew she should stop him, draw a much-needed boundary line, but she didn't want to. Just this once she allowed herself to enjoy the feel of his hard frame pressing into her.

"This is a piece of me other women don't get," he said in a voice full of sensual promise.

"Then why me?"

"Because you've gotten under my skin, Sophie. I think it's time we explore whatever this is between us."

"It's...*nothing.*" The lie tasted horrible, but she couldn't say *lust.*

His hand moved up her back, holding her tighter. His heart thundered against her chest, and she felt the unmistakable hardness of his arousal.

"Feel that?" His eyes brimmed with passion. "That's not *nothing.*"

She was sure he was talking about his erection and not his erratic heartbeat. *After all,* she reminded herself, *sex is all he thinks about.* Even with that reminder, as their bodies moved in perfect sync, she couldn't escape the desire mounting inside her. She'd never *seen* Brett dance before. Not one single time at any of his brothers' weddings or at clubs when they were all out for a drink. He was a large man, with bulging muscles akin to a bodybuilder's, but despite his size he was an enticing mix of fluid grace and power. She found herself wondering if that grace and power would carry into the bedroom. When his hand slid lower, cupping her ass, and he pushed his other hand into her hair, she closed her eyes, allowing herself to soak him in. The sting of her scalp and the heat of his hand on her bottom crashed through her like a tornado, and her eyes flew open, meeting his hungry stare.

"Tell me you want me, Sophie."

Don't do it. Do not admit it.

She opened her mouth to speak, and he dipped his head, his lips hovering just above hers. His warm breath sank into her mouth, stealing her ability to speak.

"Tell me to kiss you," he said so firmly it bordered on a demand, but there was also something tethered about it, smooth and seductive.

Dangerously alluring.

She swallowed hard, breathed even harder, as Grace's words came back to her. *Careful, sweetheart, your interest is showing.*

"I'd better go," she finally managed.

"No, babe, don't run away. Not this time." His eyes bored into her. "Dance with me. We don't have to do anything more. Just be with me, alone."

He gathered her closer, and she rested her cheek on his chest, trying to calm her racing heart at the emotions she'd seen in his eyes. Maybe she was imagining it, but she swore beneath the storm, beneath all that heat, there was more. He might be made of hot steel and desire, but he was also a caring brother who made the time for family, who babysat for Carson and Tawny's little girl. He was the guy who offered to walk Grace outside and had often walked Sophie to a cab so no harm would come to her. It was that man she kept getting glimpses of, and as they danced late into the night, those glimpses stacked up like steps. What would she find at the top? A locked door keeping the world at bay? Or would it be ajar, just waiting for the right person to slip through?

They danced with few words passing between them, and those wordless hours moved by too quickly. She was enjoying this quiet part of him that she'd never been privy to. *Has anyone?*

When Brett stopped dancing she realized she hadn't noticed the bar clearing out. *Whoa*, she'd been completely lost in him.

He reached for his jacket and her clutch. "Come on, I'll walk you home."

When they hit the street, the cool night air brought a dose of reality. Brett put his jacket over her shoulders as they headed in the direction of her apartment building.

"Thank you," she said, wondering when he'd become a gentleman.

He flashed a smile, uncharacteristically quiet as they walked along the busy sidewalk.

"You're a good dancer," she said to try to quell her nerves. She was letting Brett walk her home, and she knew that sent a signal, but she felt things changing between them, like she was getting another glimpse of a side of him not many got to see.

"I'm good at a lot of things." He flashed a cocky grin.

"And here I was thinking that you'd turned into a gentleman."

"I can be anything you want, Sophie."

His smile softened, and she found herself wanting to believe him.

"Tell me, Sexy Sophie, what do you want? What do you dream about late at night?" he asked carefully, not aggressively, which took her by surprise. "And don't tell me Kurt Remington, because you're far more interesting than that."

She mulled over his question as they turned down her street. "I dream about things that aren't even on your radar screen," she said honestly.

"You might be surprised." He thanked the doorman, putting a hand at her back as they crossed the lobby. As they waited for the elevator, he said, "My radar is set to pick up *lots* of different stimuli."

When the elevator arrived, they stepped inside, and she hit the button for her floor. His gaze raked boldly over her, and her traitorous heart thumped harder. As the elevator climbed slowly to her floor, he swept his arm around her waist, drawing her closer.

"Seriously," he said as he gazed into her eyes. "I want to know. Do you ever dream of me? Do you wonder what it would be like to kiss me?"

Yes. She turned her face away, and her hair fell over her eye. Brett tucked it behind her ear, and with his fingers at her chin, he gently guided her face back toward him, until she had no choice but to see him. A long, silent moment stretched between them, anticipation building inside her. He was so handsome, gazing at her with a thoughtful, and also somehow seductive, expression.

"I dream about you, Sophie," he said just above a whisper. "I dream about your smile." He touched her cheek, his expression softening. "And the way it lights up your eyes. I dream about the way you lick your lips and how much I want to feel your mouth on me."

Every sentence brought a thrum of heat. She tried to swallow, but her mouth was dry. She felt herself breathing harder, *wanting* him to kiss her. Wanting to fulfill both of their fantasies, and finally get her mouth on him, too.

The elevator doors opened, and for a moment neither one moved.

Kiss me.

His brows twitched, a strange expression filling his eyes. He stepped aside, slid his hand to her lower back, and they stepped into the hallway. She kept her eyes trained on the carpet, trying to wrap her head around what just happened, and fished out her keys from her purse.

He took the keys from her hand and unlocked the door, opening it just a crack before handing them back to her. Their eyes locked, the air between them sizzled, and when he leaned in, she closed her eyes, preparing for a kiss.

His lips touched her cheek, and he said, "Sleep well, Sexy Sophie. Thanks for an unforgettable night."

Chapter Two

FOR THE FIRST time in as long as Brett could remember, Saturday sucked. Carson and Dylan both blew him off for their morning run, so he pushed through six miles on his own. Usually that was no big deal, but without his brothers to distract him, he was stuck listening to his own thoughts, which all revolved around Sophie. He'd finally broken through her barriers, finally had her in his arms, and he'd seen—*felt*—her resolve to keep her distance withering away. He'd gotten so lost in her, the restlessness that had been his constant companion since he was a kid had lifted. He had it all within his grasp— one night with Sophie—and he'd blown it. He'd relived those last moments at her door a thousand times as he'd pounded out a grueling two-hour workout following his run, and he'd given himself shit for not taking the kiss he'd been dying for. The gleam of interest in her eyes had never wavered, but something strange had lodged in his chest when he stood at her door and she blinked up at him with her trusting blue eyes. Or maybe it was in his head. He couldn't be sure, because it felt a hell of a lot like it had taken up residence in both areas. Whatever it was had kept him from pushing her toward what he knew they both wanted, and he'd spent all damn day trying to figure out why.

Now, as the evening rolled in, he sat at the bar in Night-Caps, and the irritation still clung to him like a second skin.

A host of beautiful women slinked around the bar, fluttering their lashes and thrusting out their assets, some probably hoping for free drinks, others hoping for a hookup, while still others, like the redhead at the end of the bar sizing up all the guys in suits, were probably hoping for a diamond ring. Not one woman piqued his interest.

How could they when Sophie has imprinted herself in my fucking mind?

If he didn't get Sophie out of his head he was going to lose his shit. He took a long pull of his beer, then rubbed his hand against his thigh, trying to forget the lingering feel of Sophie's softness against it.

"You look like hell," Dylan said as he pushed a beer across the bar. "Tiffany said she saw you leave with Sophie last night. Did you two finally get together?"

"We had a good time," he answered vaguely.

"Seriously? I guess I just lost ten bucks." Dylan wiped down the bar with a concerned look on his face.

"Who'd you bet? Carson?"

"No, Tiff. She was sure you'd sway Sophie to the sinful side. My money was on Sophie. I can't believe she finally gave in to you. I guess I'm happy for you, because you've been trying to get with her for so long, but don't hurt her, man. She's Mick's assistant, and neither he nor Sophie need trouble."

"Fuck, Dyl. I'm not a dick." A stab of guilt sliced through him. Whether that guilt was caused by Dylan believing they'd hooked up when they hadn't, or because Dylan knew that when it came to women, Brett was a once-and-done type of guy, he didn't know or care. The guilt lodged in his chest, digging deeper with every thought of her.

Dylan cocked a brow.

"Okay, I *can* be a dick, but I wasn't. Sophie and I had a good time, but we didn't hook up."

"That's probably a good thing, considering you're working in Mick's office Monday," Dylan reminded him. There had been a rash of hacks into celebrity cell phones and computers, including two of Mick's clients. Even though Brett and Carson's company, Elite Security, had ensured Mick's proprietary data was locked down tighter than Fort Knox and none of Mick's files had been hacked, they were testing the systems just to be sure.

"I wouldn't call it a 'good thing,' but whatever." He didn't want to think about seeing Sophie dressed in tight skirts and low-cut blouses. He'd been drawn to her incredible figure since the first time he'd set his eyes on her, but it was her intelligence and quick wit that had kept his interest. Sophie had it all—brains, beauty, humor, and those insightful, sexy blue eyes that stuck with him long after she turned him down. *Or I walked away. Goddamn fool.*

Dylan went to tend to a customer and Brett pulled out his phone, debating sending Sophie a text. They'd long ago exchanged numbers, but he'd always held back from using hers. It was one thing to tempt her when the opportunity arose in person, but he knew himself well enough to realize that once he opened the door to twenty-four-hour access, he'd have a hard time holding back until he got what he wanted.

Fuck it. He was done pissing and moaning about not taking his chance when he'd had it. He wasn't a sit-around-and-wait type of guy. He was ready to play with fire. As he typed a text to Sophie—*Miss me yet?*—he told himself it was to get her out of his system once and for all.

He took another swig of his beer, and his phone vibrated.

His heart leapt at the sight of Sophie's name on the screen. He couldn't open and read the message fast enough. *I'm surrounded by a bunch of stuffy people at a wine tasting. Even your come-ons would be better than this.*

As he conjured a host of dirty responses, a vision of Sophie as they'd said good night floated into his mind. He clenched his teeth against the squirrely feeling in his gut and typed, *I've got a bottle of red from France with your name on it.*

Her response was immediate. *Did you have to erase someone else's name to write mine in?*

He hated the sting that accompanied her jibe. Before he could type a response, "Thrive!" rang through the bar. The cheer pulled Brett's attention from his thoughts. He spotted his buddy Dex Remington, founder of Thrive Entertainment, one of the country's leading PC game design firms, moving through the crowd. Dex waved to the people in the back of the bar who had called out the cheer. It was how his employees had greeted him since they began hanging out there.

Dex sidled up beside Brett at the bar.

"How's it going?" Brett asked as Dylan came to take Dex's order.

"Can't complain." Dex slapped Brett on the shoulder, then reached across the bar and tapped fists with Dylan. "Can I get a round of our usual?"

Brett's phone vibrated again, and he glanced at the text from Sophie. *99 bottles of wine on the wall...* He could think of ninety-nine ways he'd like to help alleviate her boredom.

"Coming right up," Dylan said. "Where's Ellie tonight?"

"She and Siena went shopping. Did I tell you Ellie's three months pregnant?" Ellie was Dex's wife, and Siena was his twin sister.

"Man, that's awesome," Brett said. "Congratulations."

"Congrats, man," Dylan said.

"Thanks. We're stoked," Dex said as Dylan filled his order. "We just had dinner with Kurt. He's heading over to Pages bookstore, so I stopped by to have a drink with Mitch and Regina." Mitch and Regina worked for Dex.

"Kurt's at Pages tonight?" Brett asked as he typed a text to Sophie. *Where are you?*

"Yeah. Ellie's friend works there, and when she found out he was in town, she asked him to do an impromptu reading. Want to join us for a drink?"

Brett's phone vibrated, and a quick glance told him where to find Sophie. "I've got to run, but thanks. Good seeing you. And congrats." He patted Dex on the back and headed for the door.

IF SOPHIE HAD to listen to one more stuffed shirt talk about bouquets and aeration she was going to lose her mind. She'd hoped the plethora of well-dressed, handsome men and wine would offer a much-needed distraction from the brazen man who had kept her up all night—or rather, had left her reeling and wondering why he *hadn't* tried to keep her up all night. But the minute these guys opened their mouths, all that came out was pretentiousness. Sophie knew how to dress the part of high-fashion city girl, and she enjoyed living in the Big Apple, but she was still a small-town girl at heart. She didn't give two hoots about summering in Italy, and she didn't have a love affair with wine. If it tasted good, she'd drink it. And if not, she'd choose something else.

Like a Dirty Girl Scout.

Her mouth watered with the thought of that delicious drink, but her body heated up with the memory of the *dirty playboy* who had bought it for her.

And danced with me.

And walked me home.

And didn't kiss me.

She'd felt her biggest distraction's touch long after he'd dropped her off last night, and it had been *his* voice whispering in her ear as she'd pleasured herself in an effort to stop thinking about him. The short-lived relief had only left her wishing it had been him doing the deed.

She glanced down at her phone. She'd been shocked, and delighted, when she'd received Brett's text, but now a wave of disappointment washed through her at the sight of the blank screen.

She'd spent half the night dissecting their interactions, wondering if there was something wrong with her, and the other half thankful that he hadn't pushed her to sleep with him. She'd hoped the morning would bring clarity to her lust-addled brain. After all, she had no one-night stand to regret. But after hours of remembering how he'd held her, how tempting his body had felt, and the sensual way he'd spoken, when the sun rose, she was still muddled with confusion. As if that wasn't enough to turn her inside out, the look in his eyes when they'd stood outside her apartment last night, when he'd said, *Sleep well, Sexy Sophie. Thanks for an incredible night,* had only made her want him more.

Great. Now she'd never stop thinking about him.

She closed her eyes, telling herself to focus on the boring

conversations going on around her. The ones that made her want to gouge her eyes out. *That might be better than fantasizing about a man who admittedly is allergic to commitment.*

"There you are, Pookie Bear."

Sophie's eyes flew open at the sound of Brett's deep voice. Holy cow. What was he doing there? And who the hell was Pookie Bear? He stood at the far side of the room, devilishly handsome in a black dress shirt and slacks, and so focused on her, she wanted to *be* his Pookie Bear.

He wasted no time eating up the distance between them, carrying himself with such a commanding air of self-confidence he drew the attention of the women *and* men in the room. His arm swept around Sophie's waist, and he grinned at her. "I have been looking all over for you. Are you ready to go, Pooks?"

Go? Pooks? "What are you doing here?" she whispered.

He pressed his cheek to hers as he led her toward the door and said, "Saving your fine ass from the worst night of your life."

Ten minutes later they were laughing in the back of a cab. "I can't believe you did that! I'd been trying to figure out a way to leave for an hour, but every time I started to, someone would rope me into a conversation. I swear, if I had to watch one more person swish wine around their mouth before swallowing, I would have lost my mind."

His lips curved up in a lustful grin. "I think you'd better not use words like *swallow* around me right now."

"Right now, or *ever?*"

"How about we say right now." He put his arm around her and pulled her closer. "I've got a surprise for you."

She tried to move out from under his arm, but he held on tight. "Does this surprise have anything to do with us being naked?"

"Oh, baby, you know how to make me crazy."

"No. I just know what you're really like."

"Do you?" His expression turned serious. "Why don't you tell me what I'm *really* like?"

"Seriously?" She stared out the window at the passing lights of the city, turning over responses in her mind. It was Saturday night. Shouldn't he have moved on to a *sure thing* by now?

"Yes."

He curled his hand around her shoulder, and when she turned toward him, he was *right there*, as close as he'd been last night when they were dancing. His breath carried the faint scent of spearmint, and she had the urge to taste it. She really needed to get over this infatuation before she got herself in trouble.

He raised his brows expectantly, and she realized he was still waiting for an answer.

"Okay, *fine*. What are you like? You're funny, smart, you love your family, and you are hotter than any man I've ever known." The words fell fast and easy from her lips, but they were the truth, and she didn't want to take them back.

"I think I misjudged you," he said indulgently. "You've got an excellent handle on me."

"I wasn't finished," she said, as much to herself as to him, because the way he'd danced with her last night, and swooped in tonight and saved her, made her heart take note, and that was not a good thing. It was dangerous, because if he'd pushed last night, she was pretty sure she would have finally given in. And then this morning would have brought a whole different type of worrying.

She forced that realization aside and said, "You're all those things, which makes you very tempting, but you're also arrogant, a shameless flirt, and you collect one-night stands like other people collect stamps or baseball cards."

He winced. "Stamps or baseball cards?"

"It was the only thing I could think of under pressure." She smiled, thinking she saw a flash of sorrow in his eyes, but that might have been wishful thinking, because when she looked closer, it was gone. "The truth is, you're a great guy in many ways, and I've been into you for a long time. But we're on opposite ends of the life-goal spectrum. Call me old-fashioned, but I don't ever want to feel like I need to compete for someone's affection. I still hold out hope that one day I'll meet a special man who wants the same things as I do."

He reached up and caressed her cheek. "And what do you want, Soph?"

She sighed at the intimate touch. It would be so much easier if he wore dark sunglasses so she didn't have to see that look in his eyes. The one that told her he really wanted to hear her answers.

"I want all the things you don't. Marriage, babies, to look in to the same man's eyes for all my years and know I'll love him more with every passing second. And that those feelings will be reciprocated, no matter what temptations come his way."

"You deserve all those things." The honesty in his eyes had her anxiously awaiting his next words. His gaze moved slowly over her face, lingering on her mouth. "But before you *settle* for any man"—he brushed his thumb over her lower lip—"it's only right that you experience the *best* man, the *only* man, who can exceed your darkest fantasies and pleasure you so thoroughly, you'll hear my voice in the wind, feel my touch when we're miles apart."

The cab pulled over, but Sophie was too stunned to respond, much less move. How did he make her want to experience him like that? Knowing he was offering only one night of pleasure? *Ugh.* She'd probably go straight to hell, but she wanted that one night.

She tried to pull herself together as Brett paid the driver. He stepped from the cab, offering her his hand with a pleased-with-himself smile. "Come on, sweet stuff. Let's go check out your surprise."

As he brought her to her feet she said, "You mean there's more than just blowing me away in the back of a cab?"

He chuckled. "If you call that being blown away, your bar is set way too low. I'm going to take great pleasure in fixing that so you don't end up short-changing yourself."

"Oh my, isn't that gracious of you?" she said sarcastically. "Where are we going?"

"The bookstore." He pulled open the door to Pages and motioned for her to walk through.

"Brett Bad is taking me to a bookstore? What's *really* going on?" She reached up and felt his forehead. "No fever. Are they having *Fifty Shades* night or something?"

"Jesus, Soph. I'm not one-dimensional."

Brett took her hand and led her toward a crowd in the back of the store. She loved Pages because it was not only the largest bookstore in the city, but it wasn't all vamped up the way most big outlets were. The floors were scuffed hardwood, like they'd been there forever, and antique velvet sofas and chairs were placed at odd angles and in nooks throughout the store. Simple wooden tables lined the front windows like a coffee shop, even though they offered no food or beverages. The chemical scent of new books and what Sophie thought of as the aura of happy readers hung in the air. Just walking into bookstores lifted her spirits, but walking into a bookstore with Brett was like walking into a sex shop with a nun. They didn't fit together.

"Brett, what's going on?" she asked quietly.

Brett winked, guiding her around the perimeter of the crowd, until he found a gap and then he moved behind her, holding her by the shoulders as he steered her toward the front of the group. She peered around a gray-haired man and gasped at the sight of Kurt Remington standing at a podium reading from one of his books.

She spun around, feeling light-headed. "It's Kurt Remington!" she whispered excitedly. "You brought me to see Kurt Remington!"

A collective "Shh" brought her hand over her mouth. She dropped her hand and mouthed, *Thank you,* to Brett.

His smile radiated all the way up to his eyes, softening his rough edges and making him even more handsome, but it was the genuine nature of the smile that captivated her. Gone was the player mask that threw sparks and seemed to always be planning his next move. He gently turned her by the hips so she was facing Kurt, but she looked over her shoulder at Brett, wanting to savor the sight of this side of him, for fear she might never get another glimpse.

He wrapped his arms around her from behind and whispered, "Surprise, Sexy Sophie."

Brett's voice didn't carry its usual illicitness of sexual promiscuity he used when trying to railroad her into the bedroom. She didn't step away, because suddenly everything felt different, as it had last night when they were dancing. She tried to concentrate on Kurt as he eloquently conveyed the emotions of his characters, but she was having trouble reconciling the man who had tracked her down and surprised her with this incredible event with the one who made nonstop sexual innuendos.

Brett held her during the entire reading, making it tough for her to let go of the hope that maybe there truly was another side of him. His touch was warm and comfortable, as if they had been a couple forever, and he wasn't groping or whispering propositions. Was this the man she saw lingering beneath the lust in his eyes? She told herself not to pick it apart, just to enjoy the moment, because *this* Brett, this thoughtful, not-on-a-sexual-mission man, would have long ago won her over.

After the reading, as the crowd applauded, Sophie turned to thank Brett and found him gazing at her entrancingly. Neither one said a word, and the magnetism of the moment amplified. He took both her hands in his, and she readied for the kiss she'd missed out on last night. She didn't care that they were in the middle of a bookstore, or that it would be a kiss from a man who might be incapable of ever giving her more. She *wanted* that kiss, and this time she wasn't going to spend the night wondering why she didn't get it. She went up on her toes as he pushed a hand beneath her hair, drawing her forward. Spearmint and the unique scent of Brett coalesced, and she closed her eyes. Someone brushed against her shoulder, and her eyes flew open as she stumbled sideways. In the blink of an eye, Brett's gaze turned sharp and threatening, as impressive as it was intimidating.

"Hey," Brett snapped at the offender as he caught Sophie around the waist and held her against him.

"Sorry," the guy said, and joined the line of people waiting to meet Kurt.

She turned back to Brett, hating that their connection had been interrupted, but she was too nervous to try to find her way back to it. She waved awkwardly toward the line and said, "We should…Would you mind if I got an autograph?"

"That's why we're here." Brett's gaze flicked to the guy again as they stepped into line. His jaw was clenched, and his gaze moved over the room as if he expected there to be trouble at any minute. That aggression, and his sexual bravado, were part of what set him apart from any other man.

Sophie realized with surprise that she was as attracted to those parts of him as she was to the side that had brought her here tonight.

Kurt took the time to chat with each and every person who had come out to see him. He spoke quietly, as if he were more comfortable reading in character than absorbing the attention of fans. The pictures in the back of his books didn't do him justice. His blue eyes were set off by thick dark hair and refined features. He was handsome, as the women in front of them were remarking, but he didn't hold a candle to Brett. She stole another glance at Brett. The sharpness she'd seen had softened. He smiled and brushed his fingers over hers. It was such a gentle touch, it took her off guard, and her pulse quickened again.

When it was their turn, Kurt looked up and his eyes widened. "Brett. I didn't expect to see you here." Kurt's smile was open and friendly as he came around the table and embraced him.

He turned that disarming smile to Sophie, and when she opened her mouth to greet him, her fangirl slipped out. "Wow. Kurt Remington. Ohmygod. I can't…Your books…"

He and Brett both laughed.

"I think what Sophie is trying to say is that she adores your books." Brett put his hand on the small of Sophie's back as if he knew she needed grounding. His touch helped bring her down from the clouds, and she managed what she hoped was a normal, not a fangirl, smile.

"Yeah, I got that." Kurt smiled. "Don't worry. It happens a lot. But what readers don't realize is that I'm just as nervous as you are. Even after years of meeting fans, I still get a thrill when someone tells me, or *can't* tell me," he said with an appreciative glimmer in his eyes, "how much they love my books. Thank you for reading them. It means the world to me."

"I really love your books. The way you build suspense is incredible. I have to keep all the lights on in my apartment while I read."

Kurt laughed and glanced at Brett. "At least you can take it. This guy can't handle thrillers."

"Maybe all his bravado is just for show," Sophie teased.

Brett scoffed. "She loves my bravado."

They talked for a few minutes, and when Kurt signed a copy of his most recent release, Brett took a picture with his phone. "Let me get a picture of the two of you." Brett motioned to Kurt and Sophie. After he took the picture, he asked a salesperson to take a picture of the three of them. He put his arm around Sophie. "A Sophie sandwich," he whispered in her ear. "Mm. I sure am hungry."

Quintessential Brett. She had a huge smile in that picture, and she knew she'd treasure it even more than the signed book and photograph with Kurt.

As they left the bookstore, Sophie was on cloud nine again. The fact that Brett had brought her to see not just her favorite author, but the man Grace had told him she dreamed about, underscored just how confident Brett really was, which made him even more appealing.

"Thank you," she said. "That was incredible."

He put an arm around her and said, "You can thank me properly later."

And just like that, the Brett she knew so well returned.

Chapter Three

SOPHIE AND BRETT walked in the direction of her apartment. The city was so alive at every hour, it never failed to excite her. It had been a big adjustment when she'd first come to the city to attend college, going from a small town where almost everyone knew her name and where being stuck in traffic meant she passed ten cars instead of three on the way to the grocery store to a place where cabs weaved through the streets, stopping abruptly and honking their horns at all hours. But she'd craved the change for so long, she saw it as an adventure.

"Is this what we've become?" She patted his hand on her shoulder.

He shrugged. "It feels good. Go with it."

"That sounds like a sexy line to me. Does it work often?" She said it jokingly, but her stomach knotted up with the distressed look in Brett's eyes.

"You tell me. It's the first time I've used it."

That surprised her, but she believed him, and it did feel good to have his arm around her, especially after the way he'd held her at the bookstore. She reached up and held his hand, which was draped over her shoulder. "Yeah, I think it does."

She expected a sexy retort, and when he didn't give her one, she chalked it up to another surprise for the night.

"Tell me something I don't know about you," Brett said.

"Something maybe no one else knows."

She wasn't sure if he was fishing for a naughty response, or really curious about her, so she erred on the safe side. "When I was a little girl, I'd dream about coming here. It felt bigger than life and unattainable."

"Why unattainable?"

"I was a small-town girl. My parents met when they were young, and they've been together forever, living in their own hometown, Oak Falls, where I grew up. My grandfather has a farm he inherited from his parents. It just seemed unreal to think that one day I could live a whole different type of life far away from everything I knew."

He gazed thoughtfully at her. "I'm still surprised you'd think it was unattainable. You don't strike me as the type of person who would let anything stand in the way of her dreams. It doesn't surprise me that you made it. Is it all that you hoped it would be?"

"I don't think anyone's ever asked me that." And she loved that he had. "People usually ask if I like it here, or how it's different from back home. I'm not sure I had hoped for anything in particular. I just knew that I wanted more than what Oak Falls had to offer."

They stopped to wait for a traffic light to change, and Brett's arm drifted down to her waist. "More opportunities?" he asked.

"Yes, but also…This is going to sound bad, and I don't mean it to because I love my friends and family. But being around people with bigger ideas, more complex thinking, I guess, was something else I was looking for. That's why I love working in the legal field. No two cases are the same. The foundation, or processes are similar, which I enjoy, because I do like to know what's coming. But when you bring in the human elements, there's a certain amount of critical thinking necessary to be successful. Mick is brilliant, and I love working with him because of that."

"The feeling is mutual, because he raves about you," Brett said as they crossed the street.

"That's good to know. But there's more about living here that I enjoy, like the masses of people, the noise, and even the exhaust and the smell of *life* that permeates the air. But one of my favorite things is the lights in the windows of tall buildings. It's like they're watching over us, and it makes me feel safe."

"That's a false sense of security. It's the *watching over you* part that worries me," Brett said.

"I have to remind myself that you work in the security industry."

"It's more about being an ex-cop than working in the security industry. It's not like I'm working with the dregs of society anymore."

"I know." Brett handled all aspects of security, from corporate security systems to cyber security and bodyguards for the rich and famous. "You work for most of Mick's clients, remember? I've got the inside scoop on you."

"Babe, the work I do is hardly my *inside scoop*." He nodded toward a skyscraper. "I know all about what goes on behind closed doors in this city. Trust me, you don't want the attention of some of those people."

"You sound like my father when he tried to talk me out of moving here. But I've lived here for years, and I've never had any trouble."

"Let's hope it stays that way."

As they followed a group of people across another street, she said, "Can I ask you something? Do you really not like to read thrillers? I thought all guys liked thrillers and war books."

"I spend my time protecting people from harm, whether it's online or bodily doesn't make much difference. The last thing I want to do is read about it."

"So, what do you read?"

He shrugged. "I'm not a huge reader other than the *New York Times*, *Wall Street Journal*, and the *Washington Post*. Business news, mostly."

They walked around a couple who had stopped in the middle of the sidewalk, and Sophie asked, "What do you do for fun?"

His eyes went volcanic.

She laughed and said, "Let me rephrase that. What are your hobbies?"

"Besides *you*?"

"God, you've got all the lines, don't you?"

"Don't ask if you don't want to know the answers, because I won't lie. It's not my thing."

That was the second time he'd mentioned not lying, and it slowed her down for a beat. There were definitely disadvantages to a man who wouldn't lie, like hearing answers she may not really want. But did they outweigh the advantages? She held honesty in such high regard, she doubted it. "You really have no hobbies?"

"Sure I do. I work out, run. I'm into old movies, plays, musicals, but I don't have much downtime, and I don't watch them much anymore."

"You like plays? Grace and I were in theater throughout high school. We had so much fun. We used to dream about seeing our names in lights. She was going to write and produce plays, which she does, of course, and I thought I wanted to act. But once I got into college, I realized I didn't really want to be in the arts. I had outgrown it, I guess, and I went into prelaw." She realized she'd gotten off track and said, "Sorry. I'm rambling. What were we discussing? Oh, movies and plays. That's the other thing that brought me here. When I was a little girl we watched *Miracle on 34ᵗʰ Street* every winter, and that spurred my love of New York. But I can't see you sitting still long enough to watch a television show, much less a musical."

He gazed out at the road with a faraway look in his eyes and said, "I'm not much for sitting still, but I do have an affinity for the theater…"

They walked for a while, making small talk and going for long stretches without saying a word, sharing heated glances, the brush of their bodies bringing a rush of anticipation. Sophie found herself drawn deeper into him, waiting for the next touch of his hand or a secret smile.

"Hungry?" Brett asked as he took her hand and dragged her into a café. "They have the best slutty pumpkin bars you've ever had." He moved behind her and put one arm around her middle, leaning over her shoulder as he pointed to a layered dessert that looked delicious. "We'll take one of those please," he said to the guy behind the counter.

"Only you could find a dessert with the word 'slutty' in it," she said as the guy bagged their treat.

Brett waggled his brows. When they left the café, he took the bar from the bag and held it up. It looked like a colorful brownie with pieces of Oreos and dribbles of caramel over the top. "You haven't lived until you've had one of these. See the layers of pumpkin cheesecake and brownie, the creamy middle? Tell me that doesn't look delicious."

Her gaze raked down his body. "You look like you snub carbs and sugar, and anything other than muscle-building protein. Do you actually *eat* sweets?"

His eyes darkened again.

"Oh my God, Brett. Do you *ever* not think of sex?"

"Do you ever *not* think about me thinking about sex?" He drew her closer and moved to the side, letting a couple walk past. Then he pulled her even closer, so she was pressed against him, and said, "I like knowing you think about me, Sophie, and the answer is *yes*, I think about other things. But I can't stop thinking about you—with and without sex involved."

She was captivated by the honesty in his voice. Her insides whirled, and she finally managed, "You're confusing me."

"I could say the same to you." His expression grew serious again. "I like you, Sophie, and I think it's time you open up and let me in."

She felt like she was teetering on the edge of reason, wanting to say yes but a little afraid of the emptiness tomorrow would bring.

He lifted the brownie between them and grinned. "*Open up,* sexy girl."

"*Geez,*" she said, realizing she'd taken his words far too seriously. "You are *such* a pain." She took a bite, and the decadent sweetness exploded on her tongue. "Mm. That's *amazing.*"

"See? I'll never lead you astray." He took a bite, and then she went up on her toes and snagged another bite. "I love a woman who's not afraid to take what she wants."

"You just love women in general," she said as they contin-ued walking down the street, sharing the sugary goodness.

"There you go, thinking you know me."

"Don't I? You said you don't lie, and you don't hesitate to say exactly what's on your mind."

"That depends how much you want to know about me." He lifted the last piece of brownie to her lips, and when she opened her mouth, he set it on her tongue. "I think you want to know me *better*."

She was glad her mouth was full, because she just might agree with him.

He kept one hand on her back as they crossed the streets and weaved through the crowds. When his hand slid to the top of her butt, she let it stay there, knowing she was sending a message and not wanting to fight it. A group of teenagers rushed past, and Brett pulled her against him to clear the way for them. He gave them a dark look, and in the next breath, those eyes were on her, possessive and hungry, turning her into a hot and bothered mess. The urge to kiss him was so strong, she felt herself leaning forward.

He lowered his lips toward hers and slicked his tongue along the swell of her lower lip. "Brownie," he said, leaving her breathless.

And kissless.

He lifted his chin and cocked his head, his brow furrowed. "Do you hear that?"

She made a conscious effort to separate the sounds of the city from the rush of desire throbbing through her, but it was impossible. "The traffic sounds?" she guessed.

"Not even close. Come on." He took her hand and turned down the street instead of crossing, heading toward a crowd that was gathered in front of a theater. The sound of men singing the song "Sherry" came into focus. Brett swept her into his arms and began dancing.

"Brett," she said with a laugh, falling into step with him.

He sang every word, changing *Sherry* to *Sophie*. They laughed and danced, and when the group started singing "Can't Take My Eyes off You," she took a step back, assuming they were done dancing. Brett had other ideas. He gathered her in his arms, pressing their bodies together as he gazed into her eyes, singing every word, though he changed the three he was allergic to, to *I need you*. The man was addictive, and surprising, and the feel of his strong arms and warm body made her heart race.

"Who are you?" she asked, only half teasing. She didn't recognize this fun-loving, easygoing guy.

His gaze turned serious. "I'm the guy who's going to ruin you for all other men."

Holy. Cow.

When the song ended, Brett kept her close, swaying to a sensual beat all their own, lulling her deeper into him. She'd never met a man who didn't need to fill the silence, but Brett filled it with a hundred unsaid words. He had a way of moving, of looking at her, that awakened something deep inside her, darker than desire and bigger than lust. It was unlike anything she'd ever felt, and the longer he held her, the more alive it became, until she was sure the people around them could feel it billowing out around them.

Brett's gaze never wavered from hers, and soon he was all she saw.

"What have you done to me, Sophie?" he whispered.

She swallowed hard, completely lost in him. "Nothing."

"If by nothing you mean everything, then yeah. You're right." He threaded his fingers into her hair, his other hand pressed against her lower back the way he'd held her last night at the bar, igniting the flames that had been simmering inside her ever since. He brushed his lips over hers, then lifted his face, gazing into her eyes as if he were seeking her approval. A needy sound escaped before she could stop it.

His eyes smoldered as he said, "I want to kiss you."

Yes. Her lips parted, but no words came.

"But once I get my mouth on you, I'm not going to want to stop."

She went up on her toes, her heart hammering against her ribs, her courage hanging on by a thread, but the words fell freely. "Then you better not kiss me here."

SOPHIE HAD NEVER run so fast in heels as she did on their way to her apartment. She arrived breathless and giddy, but as they waited for the elevator, a knot formed in her stomach. She'd expected a few stolen kisses on the way, but Brett hadn't even tried. The man was a master at turning her on without words. Every seductive look seared through her, bringing his promise with it, *Once I get my mouth on you, I'm not going to want to stop.* She could hardly believe she was really going through with this, and no part of her wanted to put on the brakes, but that didn't stop warning bells from sounding in her head. Including the one that reminded her that Brett had far more experience than she did. She'd never been particularly creative when it came to sex, although she wasn't opposed to the idea of it. She just hadn't been with men she wanted to be creative for.

When the elevator arrived, Brett's hand on her back urged

her inside. As the doors closed, he gently cupped her cheek, putting the tip of his thumb on her lower lip, tugging it down slightly, and holding it there. Good Lord, her entire body pushed forward, wanting more of him. His thumb slid to her chin, moving painfully slowly, *erotically*, down the center of her neck. She swallowed hard, earning a dark smile, as his thick thumb continued its descent down her breastbone, between her breasts, stopping at the edge of her plunging neckline. She was breathing so hard her body touched his with each inhalation.

"I can promise you one perfect night, Soph, nothing more. If you have any hesitation, tell me now." His voice was dead calm and full of desire.

She wanted to tell him she didn't have second thoughts, but she couldn't get the words out, so she shook her head, earning a wicked smile that filled his gorgeous eyes with even more passionate promises.

He touched his thumb to her lower lip again and said, "The next time that'll be my mouth." He lowered his face closer to hers. His hips ground into her so enticingly she could barely focus as he said, "And I'm not stopping there."

The elevator doors opened on her floor, but neither one of them moved. She was rooted in place, riveted by the way he was looking at her and the things he'd said. The doors began closing, startling her out of her trance. Brett reached behind him with one hand to stop them and took hold of her hand with his other.

The hallway felt smaller with him in it. Every step toward her door made her heart pound harder. Somewhere in her head her rational side warned her to take a step back, but she'd wanted him for too long, had seen too much of the man he was hiding—or didn't know existed. Whatever it was, even if she was wrong, she didn't want to back out.

She withdrew her keys from her purse, and as she unlocked the door, that knot in her stomach pulsed harder. She pushed the door open, and he waited for her to walk in, watching her, his jaw tight, as if he was having as much trouble keeping his emotions in check as she was. She knew he was giving her every chance to back out, and as much as she appreciated that, it made her even more nervous. She stepped inside, and when the door clicked shut behind them, she knew there was only one way to get past her nerves.

She set her keys and purse on the table by the door and grabbed him by the collar, tugging him closer. "You need to kiss me now, and you don't need to stop, or check in, or whatever it is you're doing, because I want you, Brett. I want everything you have to give, with one condition."

SOPHIE WANTED EVERYTHING Brett had to give? Clearly she had no idea how much that was. His sexual appetite for her was endless, and giving her *everything* could take a lifetime. As the thought crossed his mind, he realized with shock that she was his one exception to his once-and-done rule, and *that* momentarily stunned him as much as her confession had.

He ran his hands along her hips, seeking relief from the shock of his thoughts, and felt her body sway into him. He was anxious to kiss her, to pleasure her, to satisfy the primal urges he felt every time he was near her. He spread his fingers over her ass and wedged one leg between her thighs. Her slinky dress bunched up at the top of her legs. Oh yeah, this dress was quickly becoming his favorite. He couldn't wait to drop it to the floor.

She pressed her hands to his chest, putting space between them, and said, "One condition, Brett."

Damn, he was so into her, he'd forgotten she had a condition to their coming together. Her eyes were as dark and wild as a summer storm. "Anything."

"None of this gets back to Mick." She was breathing even harder than she had been a minute ago. "Do you agree? You won't tell him? Because he's my boss and that wouldn't be cool."

Being with Sophie was like a dream come true. He felt like he'd won the lottery, and he wasn't about to do anything to fuck it up. "I will not speak a word of this night to Mick or anyone else."

A small smile lifted the edges of her lips. "Then what are you waiting for?"

He lowered his mouth to hers, reveling in its softness and the eagerness of her tongue as it danced with his. Her fingers dug into his shoulders as he took the kiss deeper, exploring the recesses of her mouth and earning a series of sexy sounds. His hands moved over her ass, to the back of her bare thighs. He lifted his leg, which was wedged between her thighs, pressing against her center. His fingers moved beneath her dress, slipping under her silk panties, and he filled his palms with her perfect ass. *Fuck*, he was so hard and wanted her so bad, he didn't know where to begin. He wanted all of her at once, and he wasn't going to stop until she was too satisfied to move.

"Bedroom," he ground out, and lifted her into his arms, unwilling to wait a second longer than he had to. He strode through the living room, taking in the cream couches, brown throw pillows, and pale pink curtains. He passed a reading nook with a tufted pink chair beside built-in bookshelves, which were filled to the gills. It was easy to picture Sophie curled up reading a Kurt Remington thriller.

Holy fuck.

Why was he picturing her anywhere other than on her knees sucking his cock?

He pushed the image of her reading away, then gave it an extra shove to make sure it stayed there as he entered her bedroom. *Christ*, the entire room was decorated in creams and pinks, with frills and a country flair. She was so different from the women he usually hooked up with, he got a pang of something in his chest, like he had the other night. He tried to escape that feeling with another kiss, but the more they kissed, the fuller his chest became. As their lips parted, he noticed a mirrored headboard.

Things just got more interesting.

He claimed her mouth again, more demanding this time. God, he loved kissing her. She gave each kiss everything she had, and it was hot as sin. She was still in his arms, and he followed the line of her legs down to her sexy high heels, carefully slipping them off. They dropped to the floor, earning a sultry smile as he toed off his shoes.

She clung to him as he stripped the blanket to the foot of the bed, and she kissed him hungrily as he lowered them both down to the mattress. When he touched his mouth to her neck, giving her warm, sweet flesh a good, hard *suck*, she made a greedy sound that shot straight to his groin.

"Kiss me again," she pleaded. "I've wanted to kiss you for so long. I don't want to rush through it."

Holy fuck did he like knowing that. As their mouths came

together, he forced himself to slow down. Women asked him to fuck them, to take them, but never to kiss them. Hearing those words from Sophie made his chest constrict. She moaned into his mouth, and he inhaled that sexy sound, wanting to fill himself up with her. He'd never been a big kisser, not when there were more pleasurable ways to spend his time, but he could kiss Sophie all night long and never tire of it. Her hands moved from his arms to his face. Her fingers were soft and warm, and when he drew back with the need to see her eyes, to see what she felt—another new desire—she grabbed him harder, refusing to let him break their connection, sending bolts of heat darting through him.

His hands skimmed down her sides as he rocked his hips, pressing his hard length against her center and earning another heady sound. He wanted to strip her bare and drive himself into her, but the longer they kissed, the softer her body became. All her lush curves molded to his hard frame, and it was heavenly. Her heart thundered against his chest, and the deeper he took the kiss, the more sensual her sounds became, until she was writhing and whimpering, her hands still on his face. Hearing those sinful sounds, feeling her intimate touch, took him higher, made him want to kiss her longer. He felt himself unraveling, disappearing into her very being.

When they finally came up for air, he buried his hands in her hair and kissed her again. Her eyes fluttered open, making her even more breathtakingly beautiful.

"Fuck, Soph. Your mouth is heaven and hell at once."

A smile lifted her lips, and with a hand on the back of his neck, she pulled him down. "Kiss me again."

The ache in her voice pierced his heart, and he took her in a *long*, slow kiss that wound through him, calming all the restless parts of him.

He traced the swell of her lower lip with his tongue.

"Oh God," she said in a heated whisper. "Do that again."

He slid his tongue along the bow of her upper lip, earning a dreamy sigh that was as erotic as it was sweet. He kissed the corner of her mouth, then slicked his tongue across her lower lip, fulfilling her wish. When he nipped at her jaw, she whimpered and trapped her lower lip between her teeth.

He lifted his gaze to hers, and she said, "I want to kiss you more, but I also don't want you to stop what you're doing."

He lowered his forehead to her shoulder and chuckled. "How can you be the sexiest woman I know *and* the cutest?" He lifted his face, meeting her smiling eyes, unable to remember the last time he'd laughed when he'd been with a woman, or for that matter, the last time he'd said more than a few choice words during a sexual interlude.

Her cheeks pinked up, and she put her finger over his lips, her eyes morphing to pure seductress. "Less talky, more kissy."

"Oh, I'll give you more *kissy*, you little minx."

He lavished her neck with openmouthed kisses and sank his teeth into her neck, sucking until she was writhing and clawing at his shoulders. He blazed a path across her breastbone, traveling south along the center of her chest. When he reached the fabric of her dress, he sealed his mouth over the exposed swell of her breast.

"Oh *God*. So good," she panted out.

Her hips rose off the mattress, and he pressed his cock firmly between her legs, pinning her beneath him as he continued his oral exploration.

"You look gorgeous, baby, but this dress has to go before I tear it off with my teeth."

He grabbed the neckline between his teeth and her eyes flamed.

"No. Don't," she said quickly.

He rose onto his knees as he lifted her dress over her head and tossed it onto a chair by the window, leaving her naked save for her black silk lingerie. He sat back on his heels, drinking in the sight of her. Her long brown hair hung sexily tousled over her shoulder on one side and over her breast on the other. He unbuttoned his shirt, holding her gaze as he took it off and dropped it to the floor. Her eyes moved heatedly down his chest and abs. Being fit was an added benefit of working out the rage that had consumed him after he'd lost his sister. He was solid muscle, and he was used to the appreciative looks it earned him, but seeing that look from Sophie made his chest feel full again.

She ran her fingers over the tattoos on his right upper arm and ribs. Her hand trailed across his chest, down his sternum, and traced the lines defining his abs. Her gaze was sultry and intent as she lifted her eyes to him and went up on her knees. She placed both hands on his cheeks and said, "I bet women go crazy over your body, but as much as I like it, it's your face that holds me captive. The look in your eyes right now is so much sexier than all those muscles."

Brett had thought himself impenetrable, but in the space of a few short seconds, Sophie blew through those defenses. His brain told him to annihilate her romantic thoughts by being a prick, but his heart stood in the way. His goddamn heart was taking her words and tucking them away. *Fucking heart.*

He didn't know what to do with those new emotions, so he tried to avoid them. "Soph. Less talk, less clothes." He unhooked her bra and slid it off her shoulders, freeing her gorgeous breasts.

Her cheeks flushed, and he cradled her face in his hands, smiling for the hundredth time since they'd come together. "By the time tonight's over, you won't have the energy to be embarrassed."

He stepped from the bed, withdrew his wallet from his back pocket, and tossed it on the mattress. Sophie's eyes remained trained on him as he stripped off his pants and socks. Her gaze dropped to his throbbing erection straining against his briefs. He stood proudly, taking pleasure in the widening of her eyes and her ragged inhalation.

As he lowered her to her back, she blinked nervously up at him. His heart took notice again, and he kissed her tenderly. "Don't be nervous. We don't have to do anything you don't want to."

"Oh, I want to," she said heatedly. Then her gaze turned tentative. "But what will you do now that you've conquered me?" she asked innocently, and his heart took another unexpected hit.

"There is no *conquering*, Soph. Just two people enjoying each other."

She touched his arm with a shaky hand. He felt like he'd waited a lifetime to be with her, and he knew he'd wait as long as she needed. Those new feelings scared the living hell out of him. He didn't like feeling vulnerable, and while he'd thought he was just going to be scratching an itch with Sophie, he already knew she had the power to break him.

He lowered his mouth to hers, kissing her deeply, and within moments she was melting into him again, her hands traveling up his back.

"That's it, baby. Be with me," he said between kisses. Jesus, when did he become such a verbal lover? It was Sophie. He was unable to hold back a damn thing.

She kissed him harder, made more of those addicting sounds, and when he kissed a path to her ear and whispered, "I want to feast on you," she dug her fingernails into his skin and rocked against his cock. *Ah, Sexy Sophie likes dirty talk.*

He tasted his way down her body, teasing over the swell of her breasts as he fondled them, earning more sinful moans. "Tell me what you like, Soph. Do you like my teeth?" He grazed his teeth along her tender breast, and she arched beneath him. "Or my tongue?" He dragged his tongue over her nipple, earning another whimper. "Or maybe you like both." He cupped both hands around one breast and sealed his mouth over her nipple, sucking the tight bud against the roof of his mouth, then nipped at her skin.

"Oh God," she panted out. "I like it all. I want it all."

"That's my girl."

He licked and sucked and used his teeth, biting and nipping every inch of her flesh from her neck to her ribs, giving extra attention to the areas that caused her to cry out with pleasure, like the undersides of her breasts and the tender skin below her ribs. He palmed her breasts as he devoured her belly, thrusting his tongue into her belly button as he wanted to plunge it into her sweet center. She thrashed wildly as he kissed a path along each hip. Every taste made him ache for more. Every sexy sound she made sent his pulse skyrocketing. He knew she told him not to check in, but he couldn't help himself. He was too caught up in her to trust his judgment and didn't want to risk taking them anywhere she wasn't ready to go.

He moved up her body and pressed his lips to hers. Her eyes fluttered open and she smiled up at him.

"Kiss me," she whispered dreamily.

Hypnotized by her sweetness, he kissed her slowly and tenderly, passion escalating with every sweep of their tongues, unleashing years of pent-up desire. Their kisses turned messy and rough, and he forced himself to slow down again, kissing her deeper, longer than he'd ever kissed a woman. And then he continued kissing her, because he'd be a fool to move away from the most alluring mouth on the planet.

But there was only so much a man could take before he came undone, and if Brett didn't have more of Sophie soon, he was going to lose his mind. He loved his way down her body again, cherishing each and every erogenous zone he'd already discovered, all the way to her promised land. He slid off her panties and kissed his way up her leg, caressing her and learning the curves of her body as he went. He loved her inner thighs and pressed a kiss to the neatly trimmed tuft of hair at the juncture of them, inhaling the sweet scent of her arousal. He was struck by the notion that he'd slowed down to kiss her, to *smell* her. Was it because he'd waited so long to have her? Because he actually felt like he'd been given a gift to be with her right now? Or was it something more? As those thoughts peppered him, he tried to push them away, to fit them into some recognizable form that made sense. But nothing about the way he felt with Sophie made sense, and as he brought his tongue to her glistening sex, taking his first taste of her, those thoughts fell away. There was only this moment. The sultry sounds slipping from her luscious lips, the rock of her hips as he pushed his fingers inside her and feasted on her at the same time.

"Brett," she panted out, fisting her hands in the sheets. "Don't stop, *please*—"

Like stopping was even an option until she came? Even then

he wasn't going to stop. He was only going to change positions to give her more of what they both wanted.

He intensified his efforts, seeking the spot that would make her lose control, and brought his mouth to her swollen cleft. He reached for her hand, surprising himself again with his need to feel closer to her as they crossed this magnificent bridge. She clung to him, her fingernails digging into his skin as he devoured her. She held her breath, and he worked over the magical spot quicker, sucked harder, until his name flew from her lips and she bucked against his mouth. He stayed with her, soaking in every pulse of her climax until she collapsed, spent, to the mattress. As she lay panting, he showered her inner thighs with kisses, earning several tiny gasps. He splayed his palms across her legs, spreading her wider, and kissed the sensitive area beside her sex before pleasuring her once again. When he felt her body trembling, her climax building, he slowed his efforts, teasing her until she whimpered and begged. Only then did he push his fingers inside her slick heat and send her soaring again. She cried out, buried her fingers in his hair. Seeing and feeling her in the throes of passion, panting out his name, was all too much. He needed more, and he needed it *now*. He stripped off his briefs and reached for his wallet.

Sophie's eyes fluttered open, and she rolled onto her side, watching him tear the condom packet open with his teeth. Without a word, she wrapped her fingers around his cock, pulled him toward her, and took him in her mouth. Fireworks exploded in his chest as she sucked and stroked him with masterful precision. She cupped his balls, her gaze locked intently on his as she licked his shaft. She slicked her tongue around the broad head, fisted his cock tighter, and drove him out of his frigging mind. When she pulled him closer and used that talented tongue of hers on his balls, he almost lost it. She sucked one into her mouth, still stroking him with her hand, and his chin fell to his chest with an unstoppable groan.

A satisfied smile lifted her lips as she repositioned herself, sitting on the edge of the bed. She guided his cock into her mouth again, and he fisted his hands in her hair but allowed her to set the pace. She grabbed his ass, using it to direct him and take him deeper. Her mouth was wicked and hot, but it was her baby blues locked on him that did him in.

He grabbed the base of his cock, squeezing tight to stave off his orgasm as he pulled out of her mouth. Her brow furrowed.

"I want to come in your mouth, but not before I bury myself so deep inside you you'll never forget what we feel like."

Her eyes narrowed and she said, "Promise? Because if I only get one night with you, I want it *all*. I don't want to be left wondering what anything might have been like."

Damn, he liked hearing that. "You have my word," he promised, and sheathed his cock.

She rose onto her knees looking sweet and sexy, and his heart stumbled again.

"Kiss on it?" she asked just above a whisper.

"I'll kiss on it, fuck on it, do whatever you want on it."

"*Kiss.*"

She pulled his mouth to hers, and they tumbled to the bed in a tangle of limbs and frantic kisses. Any hopes of taking it slow went out the window with her desperate sounds and that sinful mouth of hers driving him mad. He touched her everywhere at once, her breasts, her ass, her *hair*, as their bodies aligned. She was right there with him, clawing at his shoulders, his arms, and when the head of his cock pressed against her center, she grabbed his ass and broke the kiss. Her eyes flamed as he thrust his hips, burying himself to the hilt in one swift push.

She pressed her hands to the back of his hips. "Don't move," she pleaded. "Just let me feel you."

Holy fuck. The way she said it, greedy and needful, like she'd waited her whole life for this moment, rattled him to his core. And hell if he didn't feel exactly the same way. He only wished he could rid himself of the condom and feel all her warmth engulfing him. Remaining still was blissful torture. Her inner muscles squeezed his shaft, and the pressure became so exquisite, he was afraid he'd lose control.

"Gotta move," he ground out.

His mouth came hungrily down over hers as they found their rhythm. Her legs hooked over his thighs, and he shifted them higher, taking her deeper. He groaned into their kiss with the pleasures of her tight heat and her needy sounds. Gone was the need to find his release, replaced with the desire to experience her for as long as he could. He slowed them down, running his hands along her hips and ribs, brushing the sides of her breasts. He wanted to know every curve, every erogenous area and tender spot by heart. He pushed his hands beneath her hips and lifted them up, pulsing his hips slowly, and broke their kiss so he could hear every sweet sound and see the pleasure simmering in her eyes.

"Don't stop," she begged, pulling his mouth toward hers again.

"I want to look at you," he said, shocking himself for the hundredth time and earning a sheepish smile from her. "You are truly beautiful, Soph." *Stop-my-heart beautiful.*

"You're not so bad yourself," she said saucily, and smacked his butt.

He laughed at how quickly she went from bashful to sinful. "Damn, girl, you are an evil combination of sweet and so-fucking-hot-you-blow-me-away."

"You stopped me from blowing yo—"

Her words were smothered by the urgent press of his lips. Electricity arced through him with the memory of her luscious lips around his cock and her tongue wreaking havoc with his balls. He pounded into her harder and lifted her hips higher as they ate at each other's mouths. She dug her nails into his shoulders, crying out into their kiss as she shattered around him. Her sex pulsed so tight, so perfect, he grunted out her name as she coaxed the come right out of him in an earth-shattering release.

Her legs dropped to the mattress, and he cradled her beneath him, both of them panting. Their bodies were covered in a sheen of sweat, and he was still buried deep inside her, experiencing every aftershock as it rattled through her.

He didn't want to move. Didn't want to break their connection.

Her eyes fluttered open, soft and sated, with so much emotion swimming in them, the pit of his stomach dipped.

"*More kisses*," she whispered, her eyes fluttering closed again.

Their mouths came together slowly and sweetly, and all those noises she'd made turned into sleepy, spent sighs that made his insides melt. She was warm and soft as she nestled into the lines of his body. He didn't know how long he lay there soaking in her sleepy kisses and enjoying the feel of her safely cocooned in his arms, but it was long enough for him to note those things, which was *too* long.

He got up to take care of the condom, and when he came out of the bathroom he picked up his briefs, catching a glimpse of himself in the mirrored headboard. He'd thought those mirrors would come into play during their interlude, but he'd been so entranced by Sophie, he'd forgotten all about them. *Until now*, as he put on his briefs and mentally prepared his exit speech.

He wasn't sure he liked what he saw, and he definitely didn't like the idea of an exit *anything* with Sophie. He swallowed against the truth of the man he'd become, or the man he always had been, feeling remorse about it for the first time in his life.

Sophie rolled onto her back, resting her arm across her forehead. She looked beautiful, with her eyes at half-mast and her hair a tousled mess from his hands. She made no move to cover herself up, and somewhere in his mind he cataloged that with satisfaction.

"Stay?" she asked sleepily.

"That's not a good idea," he answered tightly. Like his father, Brett had turned into a bitter, angry guy after Lorelei died. It wasn't until he was older and poured that rage into working out that he learned to rein in his temper. Even still, unresolved anger lingered just below the surface, making him agitated and restless. That agitation hit him hardest in the mornings, and the only way for him to get through the day was to run or work out hard enough to settle his ghosts. As a rule, he never spent the night with women, but even if he did, he wanted to keep those morning hauntings away from Sophie.

The slightest frown curved her lips. "Then just hold me until I fall asleep?"

She lifted her hand in the sweetest invitation he'd ever been offered. He knew it was a bad idea, but as he stood beside the bed watching the woman he'd pursued for longer than he'd wanted anything in his life, how could he not accept it? He climbed into bed and gathered her in his arms.

As he drew the covers over them, he told himself the ache he felt at the thought of leaving meant nothing, that the warmth spreading through him was meaningless. But Brett had told Sophie the truth when he said he didn't lie, and he couldn't pull it off, even to himself.

She rested her fingers on his cheek and murmured, "You lied to me."

He froze, wondering what she could possibly mean. He couldn't remember ever lying to her. "I'd never lie to you." He respected Sophie and genuinely liked who she was and how she treated people. He'd never risk hurting her.

She sighed again and snuggled in closer. "You said you'd give me *everything,* and then you wore me out so you didn't have to."

"So I didn't *have* to?" He tipped up her chin and pressed his lips to hers. "You can't really believe that. I'm ready to go again if you are."

"Too tired," she said with a yawn. "You owe me another night."

In his heart he knew one night with Sophie would never be enough, but he also knew he wasn't the white-picket-fence kind of guy Sophie wanted and deserved.

As he lay battling emotions he didn't want to feel, Sophie dozed off.

A short while later he made his silent escape.

Chapter Four

SUNDAY MORNING SOPHIE ran on the treadmill like her life depended on it, and it sort of did. If she couldn't outrun thoughts of Brett, which came with equally hefty doses of regret and desire, how could she possibly act normal when she saw him at the office tomorrow? She stared at her reflection in the mirror. The determined woman looking back at her didn't appear any different from the one she'd seen in the mirror yesterday morning, but she felt nothing like that person. She felt raw and emotional. She'd known being intimate with Brett would be amazing, but she hadn't expected to feel so much or that he'd leave with a piece of her heart in his hands. She saw Grace approaching and tried to convince herself not to share any more details about her and Brett's tryst than she already had.

But *come on*.

How could she keep something so new, exciting, and *terrifying* to herself?

"Are you almost done chasing away your one-night stand?" Grace wiped the sweat from her face with a towel. They'd been working out together forever, and although they weren't always able to connect in the mornings because Grace often had to work late in the evenings, they usually made it at least once on the weekends.

"I'm not sure that's possible." She slowed the treadmill to a walk. "I ran four miles instead of two. If this is what one-night stands do to a person, maybe I need more of them."

"You do realize that in order to do that you'd need to have more than one horse in your stable. Otherwise you're breaking in the stallion, not taking a single trail ride." Grace pulled the ponytail holder from her hair. Dark waves tumbled around her face, making her eyes look even greener.

"Then line 'em up." Sophie took a swig from her water bottle.

Grace laughed. "I've known you since we were playing pat-ty-cake in the schoolyard. You could no sooner 'line 'em up' than I could."

"Yeah, that is a problem." She turned off the treadmill and followed Grace toward the locker room. "Why is it that our younger sisters have all the fun and none of the regret, and we're wired for long-term relationships?"

"Because we're the oldest, and that's the way it works. We take care of them; they get in trouble. It's sibling law or something." She pulled open the locker room door. "After you, sexpot."

"That's *Sexy Sophie*, thank you very much." As she said the words, it was Brett's deep voice she heard saying it, and a wave of longing pushed through her. She dipped her head so Grace wouldn't notice as she unlocked her locker and withdrew her sweatpants and sweatshirt.

Grace pulled on a sweatshirt and hoisted her gym bag over her shoulder. Leaning against the lockers, she watched Sophie intently. "It's okay that one night didn't break you of wanting him, Soph. It's been forever since you've been with a man, so I'm sure you want seconds."

Seconds? What if she wanted thirds, fourths, the whole darn meal? *Ugh.* She didn't know what she wanted. Maybe a ticket out of town so she could escape before her heart got broken.

"No, it's not okay," Sophie said as she put on her sweatshirt. She pulled her sweatpants over her running shorts and stowed her water bottle in her gym bag. "I opened a door that I thought I could handle, but you weren't there last night. You didn't see the look in his eyes or feel the way he touched me, and his kisses. *God*, Grace. His kisses were…" She turned away, unable to put into words the way his kisses transported her to some wonderful, unearthly place and how he was right there with her, in the moment. And then he was gone…

"*Forever kisses?*" Grace moved into Sophie's line of sight.

Sophie closed her eyes briefly. When she was a teenager and had her heart broken for the very first time, her mother had told her that the guy she was crying over wasn't her forever love. When she'd asked how she would know who was, her mother had said, *The man whose kisses last forever. Forever kisses remain long after he's left the room.*

"That's it. You think he's your forever-kiss guy." Grace's gaze softened. "Oh, Soph." She hugged her with an empathetic expression. "Then maybe it's *not* just a one-night thing."

Sophie rolled her eyes and headed for the door feeling empty and confused. She didn't want to feel this way about him, *but those kisses…* She could still feel the press of his lips, feel his tongue moving over hers, and what was worse, she could still feel the way he sank into those kisses like he felt it, too.

"Come on, Soph. Why not?"

"Because it's Brett. He never goes out with a woman twice, and he makes no bones about it. We both knew what we were getting into." She pushed through the door and walked into the gym. "And he's working in our office tomorrow. How am I going to face him? What was I thinking?"

"That the guy you fantasize about swept you off your feet, introduced you to your idol, and then turned your world inside out." As they passed the reception desk, Grace whispered, "Wave to Hot Guy."

They both smiled and waved to the tall, blond, *built* new personal trainer.

"Nice workouts today, ladies." He flashed a boyish smile that usually made Sophie melt.

She felt nothing. Not even a flutter.

"Brett broke me," she said as they left the gym and blended into the crowd on the sidewalk.

"No, that's just what he wants you to *believe*."

"I didn't even *sigh* when I saw Hot Guy. I felt nothing, Grace. Brett told me he would ruin me for all other men, and he was right."

"Boy, Mr. Bad sure did a number on you. I still think you're wrong about him and last night being a one-night stand. You're an amazing woman, and no man can have you for just *one* spectacular night."

"*He* can. Trust me. This is what he does. And it's cool," she said as nonchalantly as she could. "Whatever. I'll get over him."

Grace gave her a doubtful look. "Well, I don't believe *he'll* get over *you*. I think you're too incredible to be forgotten." She looped her arm through Sophie's, guiding her toward the coffee vendor at the corner. "But I also don't want to see you get hurt. You lived out your fantasy, which is more than most people get."

A sad expression washed over Grace's face, and Sophie wondered if it was empathy or if she was thinking about the guy she'd fallen for all those years ago before leaving him in search of a bigger life.

"Maybe it is time to move on," Grace said, pulling her from her thoughts. "Just act normal at work tomorrow. You were used to blowing him off, so just do that."

"Act normal? Blow him off?" She lowered her voice and said, "Did you forget I've actually *blown* the man? How can I pretend I haven't seen him naked or had him *inside* me?" She leaned closer and said, "Not to mention, spending years dreaming about what it would be like to finally be in his arms and having those dreams obliterated by pure, sexual *perfection*."

"Then we have to make it our mission to find some other hot guy to wine and dine you and make you forget him. Maybe we can change your search for forever kisses to a guy who dips his fruit in yogurt. Food compatibility is important."

"Mm-hm. Sounds promising." Even if she doubted it would ever happen, she could try. "Now what?"

"Coffee, of course. Isn't that what we always do?" Grace ordered two lattes, and when Sophie took out her wallet, Grace covered it with her hand. "My treat. You're in turmoil."

After they got their coffee, they walked two blocks to the corner where they'd go their separate ways and Sophie would be left alone to deal with her thoughts.

Grace hugged her again and said, "Here's the thing. I totally know where you're coming from. You put your heart into last night, whether he knew it or not, even though you didn't want to. You fell asleep in his arms and woke up alone, which feels awful regardless of whether you knew you would."

"Like you would know about falling asleep in a guy's arms and waking up alone?" Sophie teased. Grace was so busy with work, she rarely had time to relax, much less have overnight playdates.

"Remember that one time? The left-handed guy?" Grace shrugged. "Even we good girls go bad sometimes."

Sophie was glad for the smile that brought, although Grace's "bad" began with a lowercase *B* and hers didn't.

"Give it a day or two," Grace suggested. "See what happens and how you feel. It might be easier to handle him tomorrow than you think. And most importantly, don't forget who you are, Sophie. The hottest legal assistant in the city. He's a fool to stick to his one-night rule and let you slip through his fingers."

"Thank you, Grace. I needed to be reminded of that."

"Don't forget, you've got your grandparents' fiftieth wedding anniversary next weekend. I'm sure Nana and Poppi will have a nice single guy on hand to help you forget Mr. Everything."

Sophie groaned. She adored visiting her family, but the last few times she'd gone home to Oak Falls, her grandparents tried to set her up with 'nice, down-home fellas,' and she'd had to wrangle Lindsay into playing interference so she could slip away. Her grandmother celebrated every holiday and event as if it were her last chance to do so, and their anniversary parties were big, all-day community events. Like Sophie, Grace usually went home to attend the parties, but she was mid-production on her play and wouldn't be able to make it.

"Do *not* remind me," Sophie said. "If you were going, I'd pawn him off on you this year instead of Lindsay."

They talked about the party, and after another quick hug, Sophie headed home. She tipped her face up to the sun, enjoying the warmth as a breeze swept over her cheeks. It was a beautiful morning, and she'd kicked butt with her workout. Maybe Grace was right. She'd had her fantasy. It was time to move on before Brett Bad took up any more of her thoughts.

It's his loss. The thought felt wrong when she was so full of hope.

As she waited at the crosswalk for the light to change, she remembered the way he'd sung to her and danced with her like they were the only people on the sidewalk. He hadn't cared that people were watching them.

Is it your loss? Or is it mine?

She knew she was letting him cloud her thoughts again. He hadn't minced words when he'd told her he couldn't promise anything past last night. Why was she even bothering to hope for more? She crossed the street and made her way to her apartment building, deciding once and for all that she wasn't going to do this to herself. It was the perfect day to take a book down to the park and disappear into a world of victims and villains.

An afternoon at the park was just what she needed before watching the football game. She loved football, and four o'clock couldn't come fast enough. She entered the elevator feeling good about her decision, but as the doors closed, she was thrown right back to last night. She could feel Brett's thumb on her lower lip and the heat of his gaze boring into her. Her pulse quickened, and she closed her eyes, but that only made the images of him more vibrant. She could *smell* him all around her.

She was losing her mind.

The elevator stopped on her floor and she bolted out of it, digging her keys from her bag. She looked down the hall, and her heart leapt into her throat at the sight of Brett leaning against the wall beside her door. His arms were crossed, and as their eyes connected, electricity blazed a path between them. Sophie swallowed hard, too confused to think. Her legs turned to noodles, but she forced herself to straighten her spine as he pushed from the wall, looking unfairly *hot* in a pair of running shorts and a sweaty shirt. His lips curved up in the same smile she'd seen at the bookstore, and she felt her resolve chip away.

She was *not* going to end up in bed with him again. *Nope.*

What if he was there to say last night was a mistake? That would be mortifying. *Shit, shit, shit.* Maybe she could get back into the elevator. *Oh Lord,* he was a few steps away, and his eyes smoldered.

No! Don't smolder.

Smoldering made her knees weaker. She looked away, but it was too late. Lust simmered low in her belly, filling her up, streaming through her veins until it pulsed inside her like an animal needing release. She focused on unlocking the door and refused to look into his eyes.

"Hi," she said, hoping she didn't sound as nervous as she felt. "What are you doing here?" *Please don't say it was a mistake.*

He followed her inside, swept her in his arms before the door even closed, and captured her lips in an intoxicatingly sweet kiss. Her bag and keys *clunk*ed to the floor as he backed her up against the door, forcing it closed. She told herself not to enjoy it, not to kiss him back. But he took the kiss deeper, held her tighter, and her thoughts spun away. She couldn't remember *why* she shouldn't enjoy him, and as a needy noise slipped from her lungs and he smiled against her lips, she stopped trying and surrendered to their passion.

Her arms circled his neck, and he eased his efforts, placing a series of feathery kisses on her lips, her cheek, her jaw, and a single tantalizing kiss on the hollow of her throat. There was a dreamy intimacy in every touch of his lips, but it was the intensity of his gaze that had her holding him tighter, hoping for more.

"You wanted *everything*," he said heatedly.

"*Yes.*" She was unsure if he meant between them, or sexually, and right then she didn't care which.

"I can't promise you tomorrow, but I couldn't leave you wondering what *our* everything would feel like."

"Me?" she asked hastily. "Or *you* couldn't be left wondering?"

His gaze moved over her face for so long, she thought he might not answer. And when he touched his forehead to hers and said, "Both," a laugh of shock and disbelief fell from her lips.

"Both?" she repeated. Elation danced inside her.

"I can't promise more." Pained honesty brimmed his eyes. "I'm not a *more* guy. You know that, right?"

She nodded. As much as it hurt to hear it, she knew it was a huge step that he was standing there with her, wanting seconds as much as she did. "I know. I don't need more." She *wanted* more, but she knew *want* and *need* were two very different things.

"You do, and you deserve it, but I've never lied to you, and I'm not going to start now. Be sure you want this, Sophie. If you don't, I'll walk out that door and never bother you again." A glimmer of heat rose in his eyes and he said, "Or at least I'll try not to. No promises."

She laughed again, feeling overwhelmed, excited, and frightened by the renewed hope swelling inside her. She'd always followed her heart, even when it hurt. Leaving home for the city was the hardest thing she'd ever done, but it was the right thing. She had a feeling this was the right thing, too. "I'm sure I want this. I want you."

THERE HAD TO be sins wrapped up in offering a woman like Sophie another commitmentless tryst, but even if it landed him in hell, it would be worth it. He'd spent half the night hating himself for leaving her and the other half berating himself for being such a pussy. The whirlwind of emotions she'd unearthed in him were new and overwhelming. He'd hit the industrial gym in his home at three in the morning, hoping to work off his confusion, and then he'd crashed for a couple hours before meeting Dylan and Carson for a run. But every mile they'd covered was just another handful of minutes when his mind wandered back to Sophie. He had no idea how he'd ended up at her apartment, as his morning had blurred together. It was as if they were tethered by an unseen cord and he had no chance at staying away. As he claimed her luscious mouth in another steamy kiss, he couldn't care less about the *hows* or *whys*. He was there, and she wanted him.

Nothing else mattered.

Except the fact that he hadn't thought this through well enough. He was sweaty from running and he probably stunk. *Christ*, she'd really gotten to him.

As their lips parted, he snickered at himself for being such an idiot and glanced down at his sweaty shirt, earning one of her gorgeous smiles. "I was out for a run when I decided to come over. I should probably shower before we…"

"Lucky me," she said with a sultry expression.

She toed off her shoes and pulled off her socks, and he did the same. Then, without a word, she led him through her bedroom, bringing another wave of unfamiliar emotions as sinful memories consumed him. He'd thought of her sucking him off last night so many times, he'd taken things into his own hands to find relief. But there was no escaping his desire for Sophie, and jerking off had only made him crave her even more.

"I was at the gym," she said, pulling him from his reverie as they entered her too-small bathroom. "I need a shower, too."

He drew her into his arms, his body already on fire from their insatiable kisses. "Babe, you have no idea what the idea of you working out does to a gym rat like me."

"Really? Why?" She tilted her head curiously.

"I don't know. It's such a big part of my life. I just like the idea that it's something we have in common." There he went again, saying shit that was so far out of the norm he had no idea where it came from. Those feelings he'd gotten the other night in his chest and in his head were happening again. The smile his response earned was worth every confusing second.

"I love running and working out with weights. It helps get rid of stress." Her eyes darkened, and she said, "Maybe you'd like to see my running shorts?"

Jesus, she ran, too? He'd never had a list of what he might enjoy in a woman beyond sex, but if he had, she'd just nailed the two things that would come right after being close to her family and honesty. That made her four for four.

What the fuck am I thinking? Four for four? He was starting to sound like Dylan, the brother who was most in tune with his emotions, while Brett spent a lifetime trying to avoid them.

Sophie stripped from her sweats and made a dramatic show of tossing them into a hamper in the corner of the bathroom, leaving her in the tiniest pair of black and pink shorts he'd ever seen and a pink workout bra. He couldn't have held on to a thought if he'd wanted to.

He hauled her into his arms. "You go out in *public* in this?"

"You like?" she asked with feigned innocence.

"Yes, I fucking *like*, but I'm sure every other man who sees you does, too." He clenched his jaw against the jealousy spiking through him. Her shorts barely covered her ass, and they rode so low on her hips, they were only slightly bigger than a bikini bottom.

She pushed up at the hem of his shirt. "I really don't like to wear clothes while I work out. They're too confining."

He tore his shirt over his head, trying not to let the growl in his throat escape. "You should work out at my place."

She turned on the shower. With her back facing him, she peeled off her bra. "I'm pretty sure sex doesn't count as a workout."

"Not for sex," he snapped as he stripped off his clothes. The thought of any other man seeing her in that outfit sent fire through his veins. "I've got a full gym at my house. You can work out there."

"According to some very wise women I know, the Bad men never take women back to their place. Better be careful or I could get the wrong idea." Giggling with her tease, she bent at the waist, slid her shorts and panties down, and stepped from them. Then she put one hand in the shower, wiggling her fingers under the water, and glanced over her shoulder with a come-hither look in her eyes. "Nice and *hot*."

Christ, she was every wicked fantasy he'd ever had come true. He followed her under the warm shower spray, wrapping his arms around her from behind as she poured soap into her hands. His cock rocked against the seam of her ass. She ran her hands along his arms, down his thighs, and reached behind her, soaping up his erection.

"You're a little tease," he growled as he fondled one breast and slid his hand down her stomach to the juncture of her thighs. She was already aroused. "Aw, baby."

She ground her ass against him, leaning back so he could kiss her neck. "I've been thinking about you all morning, and then you showed up and—"

He pushed his fingers inside her, earning one of those cock-hardening sounds that had ricocheted in his dreams last night.

"Kiss me," she pleaded.

Another sound that had haunted him all night, her plea for his kisses.

She craned her neck, and their mouths came frantically together. She put her hand over his, holding it between her legs as she rode his fingers. He cupped her breast with his other hand and felt tremors climbing up her body as warm water rained down on them. She grabbed his head, keeping his mouth against hers as she went up on her toes, grinding against his cock as her climax claimed her.

"*Brett!*" she panted out.

He knew how much she loved kissing and reclaimed her mouth, refusing to relent, even as she sank down on her heels and turned toward him. He kissed her deeper, backed her up against the tiles and devoured her mouth. Her fingernails dug into his chest, and when their lips parted, he went back for more. She was deliciously addicting.

"Want you," she said against their kisses, and slid lower, taking his hard length in her hand and gazing up at him. "I should have asked yesterday. Anything I should worry about? Diseases?"

Jesus, why did that make him feel guilty? She shouldn't have to ask. He reached down and caressed her cheek. "No, baby.

I'm clean."

"Good, because I told you I wanted everything, and I have a really *long* list." She lowered her mouth and took him to the back of her throat.

Sparks lit beneath his skin. He leaned one palm against the tile, watching as his shaft slid in and out of her lips. She bent lower, licking his balls as she stroked his cock, oblivious to the water raining down on her. It felt so fucking good, and she looked so sexy, he couldn't stifle a groan.

"Careful, babe. You'll make me come," he said between gritted teeth.

Her eyes turned fierce as she dragged her tongue along his full length. "Take my mouth the way you took me last night."

She watched him as she took every inch of him into her mouth. He grabbed her head, pulsing his hips slowly, so as not to hurt her. Her brows knitted, her eyes pleaded, and she bobbed her head faster, snapping his last shred of control. He pumped his hips, earning a smile around his cock that made him move even faster, rougher. Good God Almighty, nothing came close to this incredible woman. He reached down with one hand and took her nipple between his finger and thumb as he fucked her mouth. And then her hand dropped between her legs, and holy fucking hell, she worked herself over. Her eyes closed, and her moans vibrated around his shaft. Heat streaked down his spine at the sight of her sucking him while she fingered herself, spurring him on. He pinched her nipple and she grabbed his ass, holding him in her mouth as his orgasm crashed over him. He felt the head of his cock rubbing against the back of her throat. Sophie's sweet sounds of pleasure made him come even harder.

He leaned against the tile as the last of the aftershocks rumbled through him. Sophie rose to her feet and said, "Kiss me."

He lowered his mouth to hers. The first taste of her mixed with the taste of his arousal, bringing a shock, as he'd never kissed a woman after she'd blown him. But as quickly as the shock came, it subsided, and he lost himself in Sophie's delectable kisses and the feel of her wet body against him. He pushed his fingers inside her, determined to make her come. When she moaned into the kiss, fondling his balls, his shaft greedily rose to the occasion. She reached between them and went up on her toes, trying to guide him inside her. He lifted her into his arms and her legs wound around his middle.

When the head of his cock slipped into her tight heat, he tore his mouth away and said, "No condom."

"I don't have any." She pressed her hands to his cheeks and ran her tongue along his lips, making his entire body throb. "You can pull out, can't you? I need to feel you inside me."

Fuck. Tack another *first* onto the Sophie chart. Their mouths came together as he lowered her onto his shaft slowly, reveling in the feel of her tight heat engulfing him. The pleasure was pure and explosive as they moved in perfect harmony.

"Christ, Sophie."

Her hands moved over his cheeks and into his hair as she met each of his thrusts with a pump and grind of her own.

"I want to disappear into you," he said as he backed her up against the tile so he could thrust harder, take her deeper.

She grabbed hold of his shoulders. "Don't come yet," she begged. "I love feeling *all* of you."

Her words, her voice, her sweetness slayed him. He crashed his mouth over hers, struggling against the pressure building up inside him. He kissed her harder, thrust in deeper, and she cried out into his mouth. Her sex squeezed him like a vise, pulsing around him. He tore his mouth away gritting his teeth against the urge to come as her orgasm went on and on. He didn't want to stop, didn't want to miss a second of being close to her. She moaned and mewled, clinging to him until she collapsed in his arms. He pulled out, still holding her against him with one arm, and stroked himself through his powerful release.

They were both panting for air as she slid down his body. The evidence of their passion spread over her thighs and that sweet tuft of hair between them.

"Damn, baby. That was too close. I pulled out in time, but the last thing either of us needs is a kid."

"Sorry. I've never wanted anything in my life as much as I wanted you. I wasn't thinking."

Her words pierced his chest, bedding down beside his heart, and guilt set in. "I should have done the thinking for both of us." He lowered his mouth to hers, kissing her slowly and tenderly, and vowed to be more careful with her in the future.

Holy fuck, another first. He wasn't ready to give her up.

Chapter Five

BY MIDMORNING, SOPHIE was relaxing in Central Park, enjoying the peaceful sounds of leaves swishing in the gentle breeze, people milling around the lawn, and the warm sun on her face. Hanging out in the park reminded her of home, and when the world, *or thoughts of Brett*, overwhelmed her, it was her go-to relaxation spot. She set her new Kurt Remington novel on the blanket and lay on her back, thinking about her morning with Brett. He'd sought her out again, which she wanted to believe meant something special. But how could she know? The gravity between them had pulled her right out of careful-Sophie mode and into some sort of sexual-wild-woman persona. She couldn't have held back if Brett had been wearing a neon warning sign that read DANGER! AFRAID OF COMMITMENT! The way he'd kissed her with so much passion, she'd felt it soaring through her, and the things he'd said had made her believe he'd been right there with her, thinking they might have something more. But after their shower, things had gotten a little awkward, and she was still trying to come to grips with that.

She thought about calling Grace and getting her two cents, but she didn't want to share their morning with anyone else yet. She was still reveling in it like a cozy blanket. She knew it wasn't smart, especially since after their shower he'd put on his running clothes, given her one last incredible kiss, and then left without saying anything about seeing her again. In those wordless last seconds, she swore she saw her own emotions mirrored in his eyes, but she knew that was wishful thinking, too.

She watched the afternoon clouds move in front of the sun and wondered if that was a sign that she should stop seeing things that weren't really there. They both knew he'd come over just for sex, regardless of her hopes. But how could she not romanticize after he'd shown up like that for a second time? Had she read too much into his taking her to meet Kurt, too?

Regardless of whether it was stupid or not, she treasured this morning's encounter even more than last night's. Last night she could have been his *challenge*, but he'd already conquered her before showing up at her apartment this morning.

The sun broke through the clouds, and she closed her eyes, letting the warmth on her face bring back the sting of his whiskers on her cheeks and the heady taste of his arousal. She rolled onto her stomach and opened her book, needing an escape from her rising emotions. Overromanticizing or not, being with Brett felt more real than anything ever had.

She tried to focus on the story, and eventually the horrific killer in the book overtook the hot man in her morning shower. As the afternoon passed, she was vaguely aware of people walking by and the sun appearing and disappearing like waves of the sea. Her heart raced as the villain snuck up on his unsuspecting prey.

She was a million miles away when the hard press of a body came down over her, sending fear surging inside her. Instinct brought her fist back, smacking into a man's face as she rolled out from under him.

"Shit, Soph!" Brett said, one hand covering his eye.

"Oh my gosh! I didn't know it was you. I'm so sorry!" She crouched in front of him, shocked he was there and feeling horrible about hitting him. "I thought you were a pervert."

He smirked, and she swatted his arm.

"Man," he said with a playful smile as he lowered his hand. "You're vicious."

She winced at the redness beneath his eye. "What would you do if you were me and a guy just lay on top of you in a park?"

"Fair enough. How does it look?"

She studied the tender spot and met his honey-brown eyes. "Like you got hit by a girl. It's a little red."

"Good thing I like you fierce." He flashed a cocky grin.

She clung to that statement tighter than she probably should have and tried to push back the urge to wrap that compliment up and tuck it away. "What are you doing here, anyway?"

"I was…um…" His gaze darted away, then back again, with a hint of *aha* in his eyes. "I was out running errands and felt like going for a row in the lake. I remembered you were headed here and figured *what the hell*. I thought we could hang out for a few minutes. I know how you forget to eat sometimes, so I brought you a few things in case you need to power up after this morning's *workout*."

He reached for a bag she hadn't noticed, and she didn't even try to calm the happy dance taking place inside her. She sat down as he placed a sandwich, apple slices, a container of yogurt, and a bottle of her favorite drink, unsweetened mint honeysuckle Runa, beside her.

Overromanticized, my butt. He'd definitely thought of her. "How did you know I sometimes forget to eat?"

He focused on unwrapping the paper from around her sandwich and said, "I've been in your office often enough to know you work through lunch a lot."

She didn't think anyone other than Amanda and Mick had noticed.

His gaze flicked up to her as he handed her the sandwich with a slightly uncomfortable smile. "Turkey, lettuce, light mayo."

"Thanks," she said, a little awestruck. She didn't want to be one of those girls who thought they knew what was going on in a guy's head, especially Brett's head. He hadn't pretended to want more with her, despite the fact that he kept showing up. As he unwrapped his own sandwich, she knew she needed to get some answers before she drove herself crazy wondering where they stood.

"Brett, why are you *really* doing this?"

"I told you." He bit into his sandwich. He must have seen something in her expression, because he added, "Look, if you hadn't punched me in the eye, we'd probably be making out right now, so don't overthink this, Soph."

"I'm not," she lied, trying to dodge the sting of his hurtful words pinging through her. She picked up her sandwich, but she wasn't hungry anymore and set it back down. Brett was watching her with a serious look in his eyes, making it even harder for her to avoid the pain of his words. Needing another distraction from her conflicting feelings, she opened the yogurt.

"Not hungry?" He handed her a plastic spoon from the bag.

"Not very, but I appreciate you bringing lunch." She noticed the redness under his eye was still there. *Good.*

Ugh. She didn't *want* to hurt him. She just wished he didn't want to hurt her, either. The trouble was, he probably didn't even realize he had. Why should he? He wasn't leading her on. He'd been nothing but honest with her. She was the one with the runaway dreams.

"So, you're going rowing?" she asked to keep from picking apart her thoughts.

"Beautiful day. Why not?" His lips curled up, and he waggled his brows. "Gotta keep the old bod in shape for my *extracurricular* activities."

She didn't enjoy how that comment made her feel like one in a long line of *activities*.

"How's the book?" He reached for it, and his arm brushed against her chest, sending a different sensation skittering through her despite her heartache. He flipped open the pages and read what Kurt had written.

Having read too much hope into Kurt's words, she'd memorized the inscription. *Sophie, you must be a very special person to have gotten my buddy Brett in for a reading. Maybe you can bring him over to the literary dark side. I hope you enjoy the book. Kurt*

"Yeah," she answered absently. "I was totally into the story until you scared the shit out of me."

"Sorry about that. Like I said"—a twinkle of heat rose in his eyes—"we could have been having even more fun right now." He finished his sandwich and shoved the trash into the bag, promptly diving into the fruit and dipping it in his container of yogurt.

Are you frigging kidding me? You're a fruit dipper?

He popped the dipped fruit into his mouth. "Hey, I've got an idea. Why don't you come rowing with me? It'll be fun."

Even though she knew he was truly in their relationship only for sex, the urge to say yes was so strong, Sophie worried that when she opened her mouth that's what would fall out. She shoved her empty yogurt container into the bag, determined not to be his *afterthought,* even if she'd seemed to be his first thought that morning. And when he'd decided to stop and bring her lunch.

This was so hard and confusing. She couldn't make heads or tails of her thoughts. On the one hand, he was spontaneous and she loved being with him, but on the other hand, he couldn't commit, which left her wondering why she was even bothering. She needed to protect her sanity and her heart.

"I can't. I'm meeting a friend soon. But thanks anyway." She began gathering her things, more to secure that excuse in her head than for his benefit.

"Oh." His brows knitted. "Meeting Grace?"

"No," she answered, shoving her book into her purse. She had no idea *why* she said no. Grace would have been the perfect excuse because Brett knew her other girlfriends, as they were attached to his brothers and friends.

"Amanda and the girls?" he asked as he pushed to his feet and picked up the blanket.

"No. Just a friend from work." *Shit. Seriously? From work?*

"What about the game? Are you watching it later?"

"I don't know, maybe. I'd better run so I'm not late."

"Right, okay." He handed her the blanket and stepped closer. "Thanks for hanging with me. It was great to see you."

"Yeah, you too. Sorry about your eye." A little voice in her head wished he'd say something about seeing her again.

His gaze darkened as he leaned in for a kiss, and her traitorous eyes closed. *Just one more...*His lips were soft and insistent, and when his arms came around her, she felt herself melting against him, the hurt of his words washing away. A greedy sound slipped from her lungs, and she had the strange thought that Brett's mouth was the frosting on that dark chocolate cake she loved. She knew she shouldn't overindulge, but he was too good to turn away. She needed to get a grip, to put distance between them. But when they kissed, it felt so right.

I'm a fool.

She stumbled back, breaking their connection, but his hand swept around her, pulling her closer, and he said, *"Kiss me,"* in a voice full of lust, a mix of too many other emotions to pick apart, and so much heat she couldn't stop herself from fulfilling his request.

LATER THAT AFTERNOON Brett pushed away from his desk and paced his office, unable to concentrate on the security details he was supposed to be reviewing for an upcoming concert. He didn't usually work on Sundays, but it was a last-ditch effort to get his mind off Sophie. He gazed out the window, looking down at the city and instantly searching for her. *As if I could spot you from twenty-five floors up.* He rubbed a knot at the base of his neck, wondering what was going on with him. He'd rowed around the lake for as long as he could, trying to escape the agitation grating on his last nerve ever since Sophie had turned down his offer to spend the day with him and had gone to meet her *friend.* He'd be damn sure to figure out who the friend was tomorrow when he was working in her office.

He heard footsteps approaching and walked into the hall, spotting Carson and his daughter, Adeline. Carson had classic features, tall, dark, and flawless, and was the most reserved of Brett's brothers, prone to thinking before acting, while Brett was rough around every edge, hardly ever clean shaven, and had nicks and scars from years of acting on impulse and starting trouble.

"Uncle Bretty!" Adeline's smile lit up her blue eyes as she ran toward him. Her long dark hair was pinned up in two ponytails secured with bright pink bows, her favorite color.

"Hey, monkey." He swept her into his arms and kissed her cheek, nodding toward Carson, who beamed with pride every time he was near his daughter. Adeline liked to swing from Brett's biceps, hence the endearment *monkey*. She was a pixie of a girl and so full of life she reminded Brett of the sister they'd lost, which made their interactions bittersweet. Leukemia had set in and stolen Lorelei from them so quickly, it was a constant battle for Brett to accept that bad things could happen to children and he couldn't protect them like he could protect his clients.

He touched her leopard-print dress and said, "Did you escape from the zoo?"

She giggled, and her cuteness was so infectious, Brett laughed, too.

"No, silly! Animals don't wear boots." Her French accent made every word she said sound impossibly adorable. She stretched out her little legs. Her white tights ended in bright pink boots, which she'd gotten a few weeks ago for her sixth birthday.

"I think I should call the zookeeper just in case a leopard-skinned monkey escaped."

She shook her head. "No! I feel *orange* today. Do I look orange?" Adeline put colors together the way Tawny did fragrances. When asked how something tasted or how she felt, she always answered with colors rather than taste or feelings.

Before Brett could respond, she said, "But you look green and also kind of yellow. Why do you look so funny, Uncle Bretty? You were *red* at Mommy's perfume party."

Green? Really? Was he that transparent?

Carson arched a brow. "You do look a little green. Something going on? Why are you back at the office? Trouble with the concert detail?"

Brett had forgotten he'd told his brothers he was heading into the office at the end of their run that morning when they'd invited him to Dylan's for breakfast. In reality, he'd run straight to Sophie's apartment.

"No trouble." *At least not with the business.* "I thought I'd put a few extra hours in since we'll be at Mick's office tomorrow."

"You're going to see Uncle Micky tomorrow?" Adeline wiggled out of Brett's arms and turned pleading eyes to Carson. "Can I go, Daddy? I want to see Uncle Micky and Aunt Amanda."

Carson's features softened at the sound of her saying *Daddy*. Adeline had lost her parents and had lived in an orphanage in Paris, where Tawny had lived for two years. The two of them had developed a strong relationship, and there was never any question that Adeline would forever be a part of their family. Before Carson and Tawny had married, Adeline had called him *My Carson*, and once they'd tied the knot and formally adopted her, she'd begun calling them *Mommy* and *Daddy*. He glanced at Brett, who was glad she was asking Carson, because just like he couldn't refuse Sophie a damn thing, Carson's little monkey owned a big piece of him. He'd give her anything she wanted, which was why he shifted his eyes away from his brother rather than letting him see his struggle.

"You know what, Addy girl?" Carson touched the tip of her nose. "You have school tomorrow and Daddy has to work, but how about if I ask Uncle Micky and Aunt Amanda to have dinner with us tomorrow night?"

She nodded with wide, happy eyes. "Okay! I can play 'Twinkle, Twinkle' for them!" Adeline had no interest in books, computers, science, or anything else academic. She loved socializing, music, and arts. She and Carson had been taking piano lessons for months, and she was getting pretty good at it. She loved playing "Twinkle, Twinkle Little Star." Mick and the rest of their family had heard her play it about a thousand times, and not one of them would complain about hearing it a thousand more.

She grabbed Carson's hand and tugged him toward his office. "Let's get our work done, Daddy, so we can surprise Mommy and get home early."

"Go ahead, sweetheart. You know where your toys are. I'll be right there." Carson kept a stash of toys in a basket in his office. Adeline loved coming to work with him, and everyone in the office fawned over her. She'd gone from being an orphan to having the biggest extended family a girl could ever want.

As she skipped toward his office, Carson turned a serious expression on Brett. "Are you sure you're okay? You have that look in your eyes."

"What look?" Brett crossed his arms, feeling exposed.

"Like you want to kill someone."

He scoffed. "I'm fine. Just got a lot of shit to get through this week."

"You can delegate the oversight. I've told you a hundred times, you don't have to micromanage the team like you do."

Carson was great at delegating and trusting people to get

things done. Brett hated leaving things in other people's hands, and if that made him a control freak, then so be it. But that wasn't what was eating at him now.

"I've got it under control, bro. No worries."

"I know it's a tough time of year for all of us. You want to talk about it?" Carson knew his daughter had touched Brett so deeply from the very first time he'd met her. She'd stirred his toughest memories of their sister.

Brett ground his teeth together. It was no secret that he had a hard time around Lorelei's birthday. He had been the closest in age to her, and she used to pretend he was her bodyguard. *Some fucking bodyguard I turned out to be.* He struggled to push those thoughts aside. He had enough turmoil trying to figure out what was going on with him and Sophie. He didn't need to be buried under grief, too.

"No, man. I'm good, really. I just wanted to get some stuff done." He put a hand on Carson's shoulder and said, "Go watch your little monkey before she colors on your walls or something."

A wide smile spread across Carson's face. "I'd welcome it."

"Yeah, I get it," Brett said. "I'll see you later."

He headed home on foot, thinking he'd stop at NightCaps, but when he reached the bar, his gut roiled. That wasn't where he wanted to be, chasing skirts for a meaningless fuck he didn't want to have. He ate up the pavement as he passed the entrance. His phone vibrated with a text, and he whipped it out of his pocket hoping it was Sophie. As quickly as he'd filled with hope, he deflated. It was a text from a comedy club, a client of theirs, about their show later that evening. The theater was founded by four well-known comics who often showed up out of the blue to perform. The place was a total dive, but the shows were funny as hell. Brett had been to the theater a few times with his brothers. The comedy had been raw and dirty, and though most of the women he knew would probably find the show revolting, he had a feeling Sophie would love it as much as he did.

After a quick call to make arrangements at the club, he typed a text to Sophie. *Are you home or still out?* He didn't want to acknowledge that she might still be with another guy. He deleted the text and thumbed out, *Are you home?*

Carrying his phone, he headed for her place instead of his. Her response rolled in a minute later. *Yes. Why?*

Game on. He sent another text. *I'll be there in fifteen minutes. Be ready.*

Her response came instantly. *For???*

He felt a grin spreading across his lips as he ducked into a convenience store to pick up a few things and sent his reply. *Anything.*

Chapter Six

SOPHIE DIDN'T CHANGE out of her ratty jeans and sweatshirt to get ready for Brett's spur-of-the-moment *anything*. She refused to even look in the mirror or do anything else that proved how much she liked him. After she'd left the park, she realized she had a problem. A *big* one. Her idea of getting over Brett by finally being intimate with him had failed epically. Those glimpses into his softer side, his sense of humor, and seeing all his heat radiating only for her made her fall even harder for him. But she wasn't sure he'd be there to catch her, and the last thing she needed was a broken heart—especially from her boss's brother.

She paced, trying to figure out what she'd say when he showed up. Her pulse kicked up with each passing minute as she rifled through excuses. A short while later, when his knock sounded, she stilled, staring at the door as if it might have the answers. He knocked again, and his impatience made her smile. It was so *Brett*.

And she was a fool for letting herself get swept up in even the thought of him.

She huffed out a breath and pulled open the door. Brett stood before her with an easy smile, wearing a faded black T-shirt and a pair of jeans, worn in the thighs and frayed at the hems, looking so delicious, desire pinged through her despite her best efforts to keep it at bay.

"Eyes up here, Sexy Sophie."

She met his gaze, and that easy smile morphed to cocky heat. She tried to hide the way he affected her and set her hand on her hip, giving him her most serious stare. "What are you doing here?"

He stepped in so close she could barely think. "Taking you out."

"Brett…" She shook her head, struggling against the war waging inside her.

"Oh, shit. I forgot." His brows drew together as he set a bag on the table beside the door and took both of her hands in his. He gazed deeply into her eyes with all the emotions of a man who saw beyond sex with her. "Sweet Sophie, there's a comedy show tonight, and I'd really like to take you to see it."

Her silly heart did another happy dance. "Don't you ever plan *anything*?"

He gritted his teeth, and as quickly as that scowl formed, it morphed into another dark grin. "Sure I do." He handed her the bag he'd set on the table.

She peeked inside, and her stomach sank. "Condoms? Seriously?"

"What? After what happened this morning, I thought that was a thoughtful gift. I don't want you to get pregnant. I'm trying to be prepared."

"Yeah, for a *hookup*," she seethed. "I'm done hooking up, Brett. I can't do it. I thought I could, and I know that's not what you want to hear, but…"

"Soph." He took the bag from her and set it on the table. "That's not what I meant."

"No? Because it sure seems that way. Look, I'm not blaming

you. This is all on *me*. I went into this with my eyes wide open and knew exactly what I was getting into. I just hadn't realized I'd feel so much. It's too hard, Brett. I like you way more than I should, and I work for your brother. I need to put on the brakes before we skid out of control and end up hating each other."

"Hating each other?" Confusion and irritation rose in his eyes. "Sophie, I could never hate you. Jesus, is that what you think of me?"

"I don't know what to think," she admitted softly. "You look at me like I'm so much more than a quick fuck, and you showed up this morning and then at the park, but you said yourself we'd have been making out if I hadn't hit you." She glanced at his eye and noticed a slight bruise near the corner.

He raked his hand through his hair and paced. His chest expanded with his quick inhalations, and she knew she'd affected him, but *how* she wasn't sure. Was he upset that she wouldn't be his booty call, or…?

He planted his feet on the floor and crossed his arms. The anguish simmering in his eyes made her heart hurt.

"Soph, I don't know what to say."

"You don't have to say anything. I mean, it's not like you led me on, or planned any of this."

"I don't plan. *Ever*," he said almost angrily. "I didn't plan to see you every day, or to follow you to the park, or come over this morning. Fuck, Soph. I didn't plan on showing up here tonight. But I can't stop. It's like I've got an insatiable appetite for you."

"For *sex*," she said flatly.

"No." He stepped closer, shaking his head. "*Yes*, for sex with *you*. Being close to you is beyond amazing, and your incredible kisses completely wreck me. But it's more than that, Sophie. I want to be with you for so many reasons. For your smile, your laugh." He slid a hand to the nape of her neck, drawing her closer. "For the way you do that thing with your tongue that drives me out of my mind when you've got your mouth on me."

She felt herself blush. "Brett, don't lead me on."

"And for *that*. Definitely for that. You take what you want, but you *demand* what you need." His gaze moved slowly over her face, and pain shone in his eyes as he disarmed her one word at a time. "I can't be your great love story, Soph. I'm not wired for that, and I wouldn't know how to be that guy. I've got too many demons. I'm too restless, and I'm not a call-and-check-in type of guy. But I won't walk away from you. It feels too right when we're together, and not just when we're having sex." He paused, his chin dipping for a beat before he met her gaze again. "I'm too selfish to let you go. That's a shitty thing to say, but I promised I'd never lie to you. The real question is, can you walk away from me?"

"You...I..." Her thoughts spun with his confusing confession. "I just promised myself I wouldn't be your booty call."

"Then don't," he demanded. "You're not. I don't see you as that."

"I love being with you," she said honestly. "We have fun. You make me laugh and feel so good."

"Me too."

"But I hate feeling like an afterthought. It wipes all that goodness away and makes me feel awful."

"You're not an afterthought. You're on my mind every second. I just don't know what to do with that."

He said it with such vehemence, she wanted to shake him and rattle his insides until the pieces fell back together in a way that made sense, or made things easier.

"I don't know what you're asking of me," she said honestly.

"I'm asking you not to end this, whatever it is." He brushed his lips over hers and said, "Don't tell me to leave, Sophie."

She pressed her hands to his chest, keeping space between them, and at the same time, she curled her fingers into his shirt so he couldn't retreat. "You'll hurt me."

"No. Never on purpose. I'll make every effort not to."

She stared at his chest to keep from getting lost in his eyes. "You're asking me to be okay with sharing you? To be okay with no commitment?"

"Not sharing. I can't even look at another woman without comparing them to you. You've gotten so far under my skin, I feel your kisses when we're miles apart."

She tried to blink away her confusion, but it clung to her like a disease. "Then why can't you commit?"

"Because then I'll be sure to fuck us up. It's how I am Sophie. If I feel trapped, I run. I fight. I don't want to do that to you."

"But…" She looked into his eyes and saw that he was just as confused as she was. "You're asking for a commitment *without* the commitment?"

He lifted one shoulder in a half-hearted shrug, a small smile curving his lips. "I guess so. I like you, Sophie. I more than like you. But I'm not like my brothers. I can't just switch off the shit that goes on in my head. And I can't switch off my feelings for you, either. You don't have to answer now. Come with me tonight. Let's go see the show, have a few laughs. No expectations of sex later. I just want to be with you and to stop feeling so fucking lost when I'm not."

She pressed her forehead to his chest. His scent had already taken on an aura of familiarity and safety even though he was the least safe person for her heart. He pressed a kiss to the top of her head, and she lifted her eyes to his.

"Please?" he said softly.

"*God*, I can't say no to you," she whispered. "That makes me weak and pathetic, and I'm not either of those things."

"It makes you right there with me, Sophie, not weak or pathetic. Just too strong to walk away from whatever this is, because you feel the power of it, too."

Her heart was racing, but for his honesty, not because he was jerking her around. He was right. She didn't want to walk away, despite knowing she might get hurt. "This is the weirdest thing I've ever agreed to. It feels like I'm setting myself up to be let down."

"I don't want to let you down. These feelings are all new to me, and I'm trying to figure out how to handle them. The one thing I'm certain of is that I'll never purposely hurt you."

"Hurt happens accidentally. You hurt me when you handed me that bag."

He winced. "I told you I'm not wired for love stories, Soph. But I didn't mean that I only wanted you for sex. I was trying to think ahead, just in case. To protect you."

"*Just in case*," she said with a laugh, because she believed him. She understood that part of him. That was the easiest part to understand. "What *are* you wired for?"

"I don't know. I've never known." Something harsh flashed in his eyes—*longing, regret, sadness?*—she didn't know which.

"Maybe together we can figure it out," she suggested.

"I've gone thirty-plus years not knowing. Don't take this wrong, but don't hold your breath."

"I'm done holding my breath," she said. "I have to jump in with two feet and accept that this is what you can give me, but I don't have to give up on making this the year you figure things out."

He exhaled as if he'd been the one holding his breath. "Thank you."

"Now kiss me and make all my thoughts go away before the legal girl in me reads us the riot act."

Heat rose in his eyes again. "Does this legal girl wear tight black skirts and fuck-me heels?"

Smiling, she said, "Shut up and kiss me before I change my mind."

He lowered his lips to hers, and despite all the unknowns, the power of their kisses worked their magic, easing the tension that had been running so high between them and turning into something much bigger, hotter. Something *inescapable*.

BRETT HAD BEEN gutted when Sophie had said she couldn't be with him, and for the first time in his life, he hadn't hauled ass to the gym or taken off for a head-clearing run. He hadn't been able to walk out the fucking door—and he hadn't wanted to. Now, as they hurried to catch the comedy show and he helped Sophie from the cab and pulled her into his arms, he thanked his lucky stars that she hadn't sent him packing.

"I thought we were already late," she said as he gazed into her sparkling eyes.

"We are, but this'll just take a sec. I've never met anyone like you. Some people hold grudges; others walk away and never look back. Thank you for not doing either. You make me want to be a better man, and I want to try. I might be miswired, but

I'm not an ass on purpose. I'll make up for hurting your feelings. I don't know how, but I'll figure it out."

Her gaze softened. "Thank you." She wound her arms around his neck and said, "You can start by kissing me again."

"I don't know what I did to deserve you. Why are you so forgiving?"

"Because I believe in following my heart, and after listening to all the things you said to me tonight, my heart tells me that you're worth believing in, even if it's hard."

Several passionate kisses later, they made their way to the back of the building.

"Why are we going in the back?" she asked as they approached an unmarked door.

"We don't have tickets, but my company handles security for the theater. We have a standing invitation."

"I wish I had changed my clothes, or at least freshened up my makeup."

"You're gorgeous, and you look hot. If I weren't trying *not* to be an ass, I would have bent you over your foyer table and—"

She covered his mouth. "Stop. Don't get me all revved up before we go in there."

He chuckled as he knocked on the door. Ryan, an Elite Security employee, answered the door and stepped aside to let them in. "The seats are all taken. You'll be on the floor."

There was nothing fancy about the small venue. Chairs formed an arc around the stage area, though there was no actual stage. Once those seats were sold out, people stood in the back or sat on the floor.

"Thanks, man," Brett said as they made their way past him, toward the stage. As they neared the curtains separating the back area from the stage, he whispered, "Do you mind sitting on the floor?"

Sophie shook her head. "It makes it even more fun."

He pressed his lips to hers, smiling against her lips as he said, "I'm so glad you didn't blow me off tonight."

"If you keep kissing me, I'm not going to want to see the show."

Man, he liked hearing that.

They snuck into the theater quietly and sat on the floor by the stage. Brett pulled Sophie tight against his side. He couldn't take his eyes off her as she watched the show. She laughed unabashedly, and she had the most infectious smile. She turned that smile on him, and his heart beat a little harder. Her brows knitted, and only then did he realize the place had gone dead silent—and the twentysomething comedian was standing in the center of the stage looking at them.

"Check out this guy," the comedian said, eyes trained on Brett. "He comes in late, glues the babe to his side as if someone might *abscond* with her, and watches *her* instead of the show. Dude, really? Look at you. You have more muscles than Popeye, a face that could grace a billboard, and still you're hanging on to her like she's the best thing since crunchy peanut butter?"

The crowd laughed.

Brett tightened his grip on Sophie, feeling the eyes of every person in the place on them. He did not need this bullshit after the way their evening had started. He glared at the comedian, which only sparked amusement in the guy's eyes. Sophie's smile returned, but it was guarded, like she wasn't sure if she should be smiling or not. *Goddamn it.*

"If I looked like you," the guy said, "I'd be sleeping with every female within a fifty-mile radius."

The crowd laughed, but the light drained from Sophie's

eyes, bringing fire to Brett's gut.

"No offense to your gorgeous date, but *come on*. Like you have to worry?" The comedian motioned toward his own body. "I'm five nine, one fifty. Girls think of me as a waiter, where you're the *entrée*. One look at you and women probably cream their pants. Hell, dude, *I'd* sleep with you."

Laughter rang out again.

Sophie smiled, a soft laugh slipping from her lips, calming Brett's mounting ire.

"I like sex," the comedian said as he paced, thankfully taking them out of the limelight. "Hot, sweaty sex, quick, dirty sex. Hell, it's all good, right? Who here likes sex?"

The audience cheered. Brett and Sophie exchanged a secret vow of silence, her cheeks pinking up.

The comedian stopped walking, his amused gaze trained on Brett and Sophie again. "I think we have a problem over here." A low laugh rumbled through the crowd. "You can't tell me that two beautiful creatures like you aren't banging the hell out of each other. How hot must that be? If I looked like you, dude, I would want to do it in front of a mirror just to look at myself."

The audience roared with laughter, hanging on his every word. Brett's eyes never left Sophie's. If the guy only knew the truth. The second Sophie was naked, nothing else existed. Hell, the way she was gazing into his eyes right now, like she was trying not to laugh and thinking about *him*, heat pushed the humor from her eyes, and made him want to strip her bare right there.

"Your girl is hot, but do you even need her?" the comedian teased. "I'm straight as an arrow, but you know, I take off my shirt and girls laugh. They're like 'Oh. I thought you were one

of those ripped guys, not just *skinny*.' They must drool on you.
How perfect would that be? Come here, baby. Aim that drool
right here between my legs. Atta girl, lube it up."

Laughter filled his perfectly timed pause.

"Seriously, though. Everyone else in here likes sex, and you
two...*don't*? Oh man, I think I get it now." The comedian
crouched before them and lowered his voice. "Little Johnny's
got problems? He's not always in the game?"

A hushed laugh rolled through the crowed. Sophie's eyes
widened as she pressed her lips together, stifling a laugh.

"Ouch, man. I'm sorry. I hit a sore spot."

Brett's hands fisted. It would not be cool for him to deck
the guy in his clients' venue. He focused on Sophie and the if-
he-only-knew look in her eyes. Her tongue slicked across her
lower lip, heat sparking in her eyes. *Oh, baby, you are so much
smarter than me.* He didn't need to deck the guy to make his
point, and his sexy girl knew it. He slowly threaded his finger
into her hair. Neither one of them blinked, and when he pulled
her mouth to his, everything else faded to black. She met every
greedy stroke of his tongue with one of her own, unleashing all
the emotions of the last couple of days—last couple of *years*. He
took the kiss deeper, wanting to taste all of her, to wash away
the fear that had crashed over him earlier when she'd said she
couldn't be with him. Then her hands were on his face, holding
his mouth to hers, and he hauled her closer. She was soft and
eager. Pleasure radiated through his limbs, and his thoughts
fragmented. He angled her mouth beneath his, intensifying the
kiss, and she made one of her sinful noises, slowing him down
just enough to register the crowd cheering and clapping.

Fuck.

He'd lost track of where they were. He forced himself to

break their connection, but his eyes remained locked on Sophie, captivated by the raw emotions staring back at him. The comedian said something, and all around them laughter erupted, but Brett and Sophie were in a space and time all their own. Their synergy was hotter and darker than anything he'd ever known, and he wasn't about to let it fade.

He took Sophie's hand and drew her to her feet. She was grinning and laughing as the comedian said something about there not being any problem with the goods tonight.

Sophie went up on her toes, placed her free hand on his cheek, and said, "Kiss me," in that pleading voice Brett couldn't resist. As their mouths came together, more cheers rang out. They both laughed into the kiss as they stumbled through the curtains toward the back door.

Twenty minutes and one steamy cab ride later they were still making out, kissing their way out of the elevator in her apartment building. They barely made it into her apartment before their clothing went flying through the air. Brett tore open the bag on the table by the door and quickly sheathed his raging erection, while Sophie fondled his balls with a hungry look in her eyes.

"Fuck, baby," he growled as he lifted her into his arms and she sank down on his shaft, righting every upended thing inside him.

"Kiss me," she pleaded. "Don't stop kissing me."

Christ, her words, her voice, her *mouth* had the most devastating effect on him. His insides softened, while his cock throbbed to painful proportions. Even being buried deep inside her wasn't enough. He needed to feel more of her, *all* of her. He carried her into the bedroom, stripped down the covers, and lowered them both to the mattress. His body sank into hers.

Their legs, their chests, and all their parts in between became one as their kisses turned fierce. When they were close his world felt right, his demons remained at bay, her sweetness filled all the empty spaces inside him, and his ability to think whirled away as she shattered around him. Her sex pulsed and clenched as she moaned into his mouth, and he followed her over the edge, catapulting into a world of explosive sensations.

When their mouths parted, they were both barely breathing, but the pull was too strong, and his lips found hers again in a series of intoxicating kisses. He didn't want. He didn't need. Everything he craved was right there in his arms.

A million kisses later, after he took care of the condom and Sophie lay tucked into the confines of his body, she whispered, "Hold me until I fall asleep."

As she snuggled against him and drifted off to sleep, Brett struggled with the urge to do the same so he could wake up with her in his arms. He'd never understood how his brothers could turn off their desires toward other women, but ever since his and Sophie's first kiss, she'd been the only woman he noticed, much less thought about, and the only one he wanted.

Who am I kidding? He pressed his lips to her cheek, and she murmured something in her sleep. *There's been only you for a hell of a lot longer than that.*

Chapter Seven

SOPHIE WAS PRETTY sure that the world had taken crazy pills while she slept, because Monday at her office was more chaotic than ever. The phone rang off the hook, Mick had an emergency meeting with a client, which meant she had to race through preparing the documents they needed, and she had a stack of contracts to work through and research to do for tomorrow's meeting with a new client. To top it all off, Brett and Carson were there with several of their staff members, checking security on each of the computers. Every time she caught sight of Brett she blushed like a schoolgirl. She'd been trying to keep her nose to the grindstone, but she felt his presence like a shadow, even when he was nowhere in sight.

"Sophie?" Mick's voice came through the speakerphone.

She picked it up. "Yes?"

"I left the Mortinson files on my desk. Can you please bring them into the conference room?"

"Sure." She hung up the phone and headed into Mick's office. He was a considerate, intelligent boss, and she liked working for him. She felt a little guilty for keeping her relationship with Brett a secret from him, but there was no need to rock the boat with their *commitment not to commit.*

As she picked up the file from Mick's desk, a pang of sadness whispered through her. She believed in following her heart, but what if her heart was wrong? She held the folder against her chest and gazed out the window, thinking of how nice it felt to fall asleep in Brett's arms. She wished he'd stay overnight, but she knew it was probably better that he didn't. Waking up with him would make it even harder if he realized he couldn't commit to their noncommitment after all.

If I feel trapped, I run. I fight.

She saw Brett's reflection in the window as he snuck up on her, and her body thrummed with anticipation. He slid his arms around her waist from behind. His eyes were soft and happy, and a sexy smile played at his lips as he placed a sweet kiss on her neck.

"Did you get my note this morning?"

She'd found a note beside her bed and had read it a hundred times. *Hope you slept well, Sexy Sophie. I really don't like you only for sex, even though it probably looks that way. I guess asking you to meet me in the break room today would make that even harder to believe.* He'd added a winking smiley face. The note was pure *Brett*, and even knowing she'd *never* make out in the break room, she'd dressed in a black pencil skirt and a white blouse that was just tight enough to show off her assets, and she'd added a pair of black heels, because if she couldn't be the bad girl, she could at least drive her Bad man crazy.

"Oh, that was you?" she teased. "I was trying to figure out which of my lovers had left it." She turned in his arms, enjoying the jealousy shining in his eyes. "You shouldn't hold me like this at work."

"Why not? Because of the *friend* you met yesterday after-noon?"

Shoot. She'd forgotten about that excuse. She peeled his arms off her and said, "Because I don't need Mick or anyone else finding out about us and making things uncomfortable."

He gathered her close again with fire in his eyes. "What if I want them *all* to know?"

"*All?* Or just that *friend* you mentioned?" She should tell him there was no friend, but she liked knowing he cared enough to be jealous.

His eyes narrowed and he ground out, "*Everyone.*"

"Then you'd better get over your commitment phobia, because I can't chance making my workplace awkward for a guy who might run scared when things get serious." She stepped out of his arms, but he snagged her hand and held tight. "Brett, I have to get these to Mick before he thinks I've gotten lost."

"Soph…?" His eyes filled with a curious, deep longing, and the troubled gaze hit her smack in the center of her heart, making her want to walk right back into his arms.

"Relax. I'm *with* you, regardless of who else knows. I don't want to cause gossip in the office, but I'm *in*, remember? You're the one who's a little slow on the uptake. One day you'll wake up and realize I'm the best there is. Until then, no kissy-touchy in the office, okay?" With a sassy shrug, she left the room, wondering where in the heck that courage had come from.

Sophie brought the documents to Mick, and when she returned to her desk, she found their newest associate, Charlie Hammond, waiting for her. The other girls in the office called him *Charming Charlie*. He exuded Southern charm, with his side-parted blond hair and wise brown eyes. He was an old soul who took the time to ask how everyone was doing and really seemed to care about their answers.

"There you are," Charlie said. "Busy as a bee today?"

"Busier, but I always have time to help. What do you need?" Sophie came around her desk, trying to remember which task she needed to take care of next, but her mind was still playing with Brett's expression. The stubborn stud was totally into her. Why couldn't he just take a leap of faith and go with it?

Charlie sat on the edge of her desk and opened a file. "I need some research done for a new client." He thumbed through the file, explaining what he needed, and when he was done, he glanced at the stack of work on her desk. "Are you sure you can fit this in? I don't mind asking someone else."

"Absolutely. I'm working through lunch today. I'll get it done and have it to you by five."

He thanked her, and when he walked away, she noticed Brett standing down the hall talking with Carson—and watching her. She was surprised the carpet hadn't caught fire with the way he was looking at her.

"Lunch today?"

The voice startled her, and she turned to find Amanda standing behind her. "Hi. Thanks, but I can't. I'm swamped."

Amanda glanced down the hall at Brett and Carson and crossed her arms over her navy dress with a serious expression. "Is Brett behaving himself today?"

"Oh, you know Brett. He doesn't really know how to be-have." *And I like that about him. Most of the time.*

"True, although Mick thinks he's growing up, or going through a rough time about something and doesn't want anyone to know. We had breakfast with the girls and his brothers yesterday, and Brett didn't come. Carson said he went directly into the office after their run instead. And you know Brett. He *never* works on the weekends." She gazed down the hall at him again. "Dylan mentioned that Brett hasn't left NightCaps with a woman in months. Ally and I think he's seeing someone, but the guys think we're crazy."

Sophie and Amanda had been friends since she'd begun working at the firm. Did it make her a bad friend for not telling her about her relationship with Brett? She didn't want to risk Amanda telling Mick. Even though they were all friends, Mick was still Sophie's boss, and the last thing she wanted was for him to think she was Brett's newest plaything.

Her gaze darted down the hall, and Brett's lips tipped up in a secret smile meant only for her. She wondered if he could read her thoughts, too—*I am your plaything and you are mine, but we're so much more than that. I have faith in you. I hope you don't let me down.*

"I don't think you're crazy," Sophie finally answered. "I think your woman's intuition and Mick's male intuition are both probably right. Maybe he's finally met his match and he doesn't know how to deal with it."

Amanda smirked. "Then maybe he should start by not looking at you like he'd like to drag you into an office and inspect your briefs."

BRETT HAD NEVER been driven by jealousy before, at least not the way it was currently fueling him as the workday came to a close and he found Sophie and Charlie chatting by the coffee machine in the break room. She looked hot in her tight skirt and blouse, but she also looked professional, all clean lines and perfect makeup. She belonged in a frigging fashion magazine, and he hated to admit it, but so did Charlie with his tailored suit and expensive shoes. He'd seen them together several times today, their heads close enough to kiss as they looked over documents, and each time grated on his nerves more than the last. The urge to walk over and stake claim to his beautiful Sophie was so strong, he grabbed a bottle of water from the fridge to keep from reaching for her.

"How's it going?" Brett asked too gruffly.

"It's been a long day, but the end is finally here," Sophie said with a smile. "How'd the security inspection go? Did we pass?"

I'll know after I interrogate this guy. "The company is locked down tight. I just need to tie up a few loose ends." He took a drink of water. "Hey, Charlie. Did you catch the game on Sunday?"

Charlie picked up a folder from the counter and said, "No. I'm afraid I'm not much of a sports fan."

"Really?" He lifted his brows to Sophie, knowing she'd read *did you hear that* in the look. She loved football, and he realized she had given up watching the game last night to be with him. But he still wanted to know who her friend from work was that she'd gone out with yesterday. "Were you around here Sunday? Working?"

"No," Charlie answered uneasily.

"Hot date?" Brett ignored Sophie's eye roll.

"Actually, no." Charlie stood up a little straighter. "And you're asking because…?"

"Just trying to get to know the employees. We take security seriously around here and like to know who's in and out of the office, that sort of thing."

"Brett's amazing at security, but his desk-side manner could use a *tweak*." Sophie emphasized the last word, giving Brett a disapproving look. "I think he's trying to make sure there were no unauthorized people in the office this weekend. Right, Brett?

You're not just being nosy."

Brett clenched his teeth. "Right. Exactly. Sorry if I came across any other way. Just doing my job."

"Well, I wasn't here." Charlie smiled at Sophie. "Thanks for taking care of that research today. I appreciate your time."

"My pleasure," she said professionally. As soon as Charlie left the room Sophie turned on Brett, anger and amusement warring in her eyes. "What was *that*?"

"Just checking out my competition." He felt like a prick, and the worst part about it was that he was the one keeping them from going public with their relationship, not Sophie. He hated this part of himself. The part that had always fought being boxed in like a rebellious teenager. He didn't know what drove his need for freedom, or rather, his hatred of feeling restricted, and he had no idea how to get it under control. *Although lately all I've wanted is to be boxed in with Sophie.*

"Your *competition*?" She laughed softly.

"I assume he's your special *friend* from work. And hey, if that's what you're into, a guy who doesn't watch football, with his too-white teeth, perfect hair, and—"

"Ability to commit?" she asked with a playful smile, but he knew it was a loaded tease.

He pulled her into his arms, unable to tease *or* keep his distance a second longer. "Soph, I'm *trying*."

She stole a glance over her shoulder and then whispered, "I know you're trying. Thank you. I'm with you, Brett, and I'm hoping this works for us, but you can't go around scaring off any guy I talk to. There was no *friend* Sunday. I'm sorry for telling you there was. It was the only excuse I could think of at the time."

His heart hurt at that. "You lied to me so you wouldn't have to spend the afternoon with me?"

She nodded. "I was hurt by what you said about if I hadn't slugged you, but we already talked about that. I'm learning to speak the language of Brett Bad, and we're communicating better every day. But if you want me to be yours, you have to trust that even though you can't function in a committed relationship, I can."

"Jesus, Sophie," he said softly. "I've never been jealous, but I can't stand the thought of you with anyone else."

"And you've turned me into one of those ridiculous women who can't walk away when red flags are waving."

He couldn't suppress his smile. "You're anything but ridiculous, and those red flags are for passion, not pain."

"You're impossible." Her eyes darkened, and she glanced over her shoulder again. She put her arms around his neck and whispered, "Kiss me quick."

He lowered his lips to hers, and they both sighed into it. Just like that, all the jealousy went out the window. She righted his world, centering him, making all his edginess subside, and as he deepened the kiss, he knew he was skating on thin ice. She already owned him.

"Oh!"

They jumped at the sound of Amanda's voice. Sophie's cheeks turned bright red, and she fidgeted nervously with her blouse, but there was no hiding her arousal—or his. Brett turned away to adjust himself.

"I um…What was…?" Amanda started to turn away, then spun back around, her finger moving between the two of them, her face as red as Sophie's. "What did I just…? Did I see you two…?"

Brett cleared his throat and grabbed his water bottle. "I'm

tryin' and Sophie's denyin'. Same song, different day." He winked at Sophie, hoping it came across as the overzealous flirtation Amanda was used to seeing. "Maybe next time you'll kiss me back."

Sophie scoffed, gratitude rising in her eyes. "In your dreams."

"I've told you before, I call them fantasies. And you star in every last one of them." He walked past Amanda and said, "One of these days she's going to be mine. You just wait and see."

Chapter Eight

"COME ON, BABY, you've got this," Grace urged. She stood at the head of the bench press, spotting Sophie as she struggled through her last set Wednesday morning. Grace helped guide the bar onto the rack and smiled down at Sophie. "Way to go. Maybe next time you can do it like you mean it."

Sophie rolled her eyes as she sat up and caught the towel Grace tossed to her. She wiped the sweat from her face. "Your turn, *Cruella*."

"I welcome your torture," Grace said as they switched places, and she lay on the bench. "Speaking of torture, what's going on with your midnight leaver?"

"He's amazing. *Every. Single. Night.* I swear, I feel like our friendship and all the propositions, the jokes, every conversation, were leading up to what we both secretly hoped for. I just wish he'd stay overnight."

"So, in addition to giving you multiple orgasms and kissing you until you can't see straight," Grace said as she pushed the bar up, "you want him to be a mind reader?"

"No. *Yes.* Kind of. I mean, at what point does a guy start staying over?"

"You're asking the wrong person," Grace said through gritted teeth as she pushed through the last of her set.

Sophie grinned down at her, blocking the bar from the rack.

"Two more for giving me crap about working out harder."

"Whatever! I'll do *five* if you'll tell Bad boy you want him to stay overnight."

Sophie wrestled with her emotions. "I want to ask him, but he's got this weird thing about feeling boxed in."

"Don't we all?"

"I don't. Good job. That's three. You can stop."

"You haven't said you'll tell him how you feel. I'm going to torture myself until you agree to stop torturing yourself." She pushed the bar up again with shaky arms.

"God, you're a pain, but thank you. I think I need you in my life."

Grace flashed a deadpan expression. "You *think?*"

Sophie laughed. "He told me if he feels confined he does whatever he can to break free and things will go bad. Things are *so* good right now, Gracie. I don't want to mess that up."

"So, he's calling before he comes over? Asking you out on dates?"

"He's not a call-and-make-a-date kind of guy. He's more of text-at-the-last-minute-and-show-up kind of guy."

"And you don't see that as a red flag?" Grace racked the bar. She sat up, and Sophie sat beside her on the bench. "Sophie, talk to me, because it's not like you to overlook things like this."

"Fine, but don't judge me."

"Do I ever?"

"No," she admitted. Sophie looked around the gym. "You know how we have a schedule that we try to maintain, working out, going to the office, picking up groceries?"

"Yes, I call that *life.*"

"Right, for most of us. But look at Lindsay. She could never go into an office every day knowing she had to handle the same tasks over and over." Her sister was an event planner and photographer, and what she loved most about her business was that every day was different. There were different people to photograph, different themes, locations. Even though her specialty was weddings and families, each job was unique.

"And she never wants a real relationship, either," Grace pointed out.

Sophie pushed to her feet and pulled Grace up beside her, laughing when Grace pretended her arms were made of rubber. "Come on, you don't need your arms to use the StairMaster." As they headed for the aerobic equipment, she said, "Lindsay wants a relationship. She's just afraid she won't be good at it because our parents and grandparents are *so* good at it. I think Brett's afraid, too, but for different reasons. Look at his family, and look at mine. From what Amanda has told me, his father lost it when his sister died. He became really mean, and their parents divorced. I'd be afraid if that happened to me, wouldn't you?"

Grace stepped onto the machine and laid her towel over the console. "Sure. I guess you're right. Then there are people like me. My parents are like yours, happily married since the dawn of time, and I'm in no hurry to get into a relationship."

"Because you love your work, and it's demanding and takes weekends and evenings, and a relationship will only add stress. Whereas my job ends when I leave the office."

"True. But even if I didn't work all those hours, I'm not sure I'd want a man in my life. It has nothing to do with my parents."

"And you suffered a heartrending breakup, remember?" Sophie had been there to pick up the pieces after Grace and her first love, Reed Cross, had gone their separate ways. "Oh my gosh. You're right. I could be way off base. Reed ruined you for all other men. Maybe some woman ruined Brett for all other women." She hadn't thought of that. She had no idea what relationships he'd had when he was younger, only of his refusal to have them as an adult.

"Reed didn't *ruin* me. It was my decision to break up. But there are a million reasons people don't want relationships. A person needs to be happy with who they are before they can be in a relationship and have something to offer someone else. So maybe he's not happy with himself."

"Yeah, maybe, but I doubt it. He's more confident than any man I've ever met. I mean, he knows himself well enough to admit he could mess things up between us and that he doesn't want to. That takes confidence." Sophie picked up speed, huffing through her workout. "Why do I feel like, if someone did hurt him, I want to track her down and beat her up?"

"Maybe because you're with a guy who looks and acts like he can do anything. He makes you laugh, makes you *moan*," she said with a lift of her brows. "He's at your house every night and texts you sexy stuff all the time. But he can't give you the one thing you have always wanted."

"Well, I'm not giving up on him. I've never felt this way before, and I—"

"*Trust my heart*," they both said at once.

"You know I love you," Grace said. "But if it were me saying I wanted to try to fix a man, you'd haul my butt into a bar and get me drunk. Then I'd give up, because I don't really want a man in my life. But since we're talking about *you*, and I've never seen you so loopy over a guy before, I'll just say this. If he hurts you, even if it's your fault for wanting something he may not be able to give, I'll kill him, sexually gifted or not."

"You won't have to. He's not broken or in need of being fixed. Just *figured out.*"

BRETT SAT IN the conference room with his management team, reviewing the security details for the upcoming concert and trying not to show his agitation at being stuck in the office at seven o'clock at night. There was no avoiding the late meeting, as coordinating a team of busy managers required flexibility. The concert was taking place in a few weeks, and with the recent attacks on public venues, they had to make sure they had all their bases covered.

"Where do we stand?" Brett pointed to his top guy, Giovanni "Gio" Amato.

Gio had worked for their company for the past seven years. With a background in terrorism detection, a decade in the military, and five years as a private investigator, he never missed a beat. He set a steady gaze on Brett, rubbed his square jaw, a mannerism that gave away his meticulous nature, and said, "We're set. We're taking anti-terrorism precautions on all levels. The facility is in complete lockdown when not in use. Starting three days before the event, we'll be doing bomb sweeps every morning and night, and we've got a team in place to search every package delivered through the day of the event. The venue has already banned carry-in items except for purses, which will be searched. As agreed, we've doubled our security personnel, and every person who enters the building will get a pat-down as well as metal-detection screening. We've added extra camera surveillance and metal detectors on all levels, behind the scenes, and at all entrances. We're also blocking entrances and ramps so nothing wider than a wheelchair can fit through."

"Great, and the staff has all been put through the ringer?" Brett asked Thomas Crull, who managed security for the backstage crew. Brett glanced at his watch, his leg bouncing restlessly beneath the table. He wanted to stop and pick up a bottle of wine and grab a movie from Redbox on the way to Sophie's. When he'd texted her earlier, she'd said she'd had a rough day at work and he hoped it might help her relax.

"We're in solid shape," Thomas answered. "No more hires are going to be made between now and the date of the concert, and the existing staff has been screened and validated. Backstage will be locked down, which the artist isn't thrilled about."

"It means he can't line up his groupies as easily." Brett shook his head. "I don't give a shit if he gets pissed. No one who hasn't been screened gets backstage."

"Did you seriously just say that?" Thomas glanced at Gio, who smirked.

Brett knew he micromanaged the team, but after the recent public bombings, he wasn't taking any chances.

"You should have heard the crap they said when we told them we had to check out the band members," Thomas added.

"The artists are always the worst," Brett said. "They think that because they're the talent, they're clean, but one of these days it'll be a drummer who loses his mind."

"Not on our watch," Gio said.

There was a rumble of agreement and head nodding around the room. Half an hour later they wrapped up the meeting. Brett picked up a bottle of wine and a movie and hightailed it over to Sophie's, worrying whether his staff had felt rushed, or if that was just his impatience to see Sophie getting the best of him.

When he stepped from the cab and raced up the steps to Sophie's apartment building, her voice trailed through his mind. *Don't you ever plan anything?*

He stopped at the entrance, chastising himself for not remembering to call ahead. "Fuck."

"Excuse me?" the doorman said.

"Sorry. Forgot something." Brett jogged back down the steps to the sidewalk and called her.

"Hey."

The smile in her voice took his anxiety down a notch. "Hi. I, um. Are you busy tonight? I'd love to see you."

"Um, I have a standing booty call with this guy I know…"

"Soph," he said, and looked up at the clear night sky. "Don't call it that."

"Sorry. I was kidding. I'd love to see you."

"Great, babe. See you soon." He ended the call, and the doorman pulled open the door. He must have heard Brett's conversation, because he gave him a thumbs-up as he passed through.

Five minutes later Sophie was in his arms, smiling into their kiss, and nothing else mattered.

When their lips parted, her hand snaked around his neck the way he'd come to adore, and she said, "I'm not done yet," in a seductive voice that made his body, and his *heart*, throb.

He deepened the kiss, and the bottle of wine he'd forgotten he was holding slipped. He fumbled for it, catching it just before it hit the floor and slowing him down enough to get a good look at her. Sophie always looked gorgeous, but tonight she had on a pair of cutoffs and a simple white shirt, with a long tan cardigan that hung to her knees. She looked relaxed and comfortable, like the small-town girl she was, and it made him want to experience more of that side of her.

"You brought wine?"

He held up the movie from Redbox. "And *Get Out.*" The shine in her eyes made his heart feel even fuller, which he hadn't thought possible.

She snagged the movie from his hands. "Oh my gosh. You got a movie? Suspense? You hate suspense. Wait. Do you hate suspenseful books *and* movies?"

He chuckled and pulled her in for another kiss. "Both, but you love it, so I can deal with it."

She ran her fingers over the label on the wine, tempered hope brimming in her eyes. *Tempered.* He hated that. He wanted her to *know* how he felt, to count on him and take for granted that he wanted to do things just for her. His pulse quickened erratically with the direction his thoughts were taking him, but he didn't push back. Not this time. Not when pushing back meant seeing that tempered look, which made him even more restless than he was when they were apart.

"Château Lafite Rothschild?" she asked.

"Your favorite red wine from France."

"How did you know?" Her mouth twitched in a surprised and still hopeful smile, giving him another dose of too-much-to-handle.

"You ordered it at Mick and Amanda's wedding, and I heard you tell the girls it was your favorite." Mick and Amanda had gotten married last year at a bar called the Kiss, and Brett and Dylan had taken over as bartenders for part of the evening.

"And you *remembered?*"

"I notice and remember everything about you, even before then and every day since. I noticed the way your cheeks pinked up when I propositioned you all those times before we got together, the way you stood up straighter and your eyes squinted the tiniest bit when you were preparing to turn me down, and the way you make sighing sounds at things that must warm you or something. Why do you think I've got a bottle of it at my place?"

"Wait. You weren't kidding when you said that the other night?"

"I told you I would always tell you the truth, didn't I? I wasn't kidding. I was hoping you'd eventually accept my proposition."

"You bought a six-hundred-dollar bottle of wine on the *hopes* of making out with me?"

"No." He swept her into his arms and touched his lips to hers. "I bought it knowing I'd never give up trying."

"That sounds awfully committed, Mr. Bad." She grinned up at him, and all that hope turned to something he was afraid to name.

"We're not going to use that word, but yes, I was determined to have you, Ms. Roberts. Now, may I interest you in a movie and a bottle of wine?"

"Like a *date*?" She whispered the word *date*.

"What is it with you and labels?"

"I work in a field where we need to be very clear about our intentions." Her expression turned serious. "Besides, a girl likes to know when she's crossed over from booty call to something more."

Brett clenched his hands, scared to take the plunge he avoided like the plague, not because he didn't trust his feelings for her, but because he didn't know how the part of him that ran from commitment like a rebellious child would react if he gave in to them.

One look in her eyes and he knew this was a step he want-ed—*needed*—to take.

"You were never a booty call, Soph. You were always some-thing more."

Chapter Nine

SOPHIE COULDN'T BELIEVE her ears. She'd known in her heart this might eventually happen, but hearing Brett say it was so much bigger than dreaming about it. She had to ask the burning question. "What changed?"

"I don't know. *Everything?*"

He carried the wine into the kitchen, and she wondered if he was avoiding the conversation. *Running. Feeling boxed in.* She handed him two wineglasses from a cabinet.

As he poured the wine, he said, "I hate seeing that look in your eyes, like you don't know if you can count on me, and I know I cause it. But I don't want you to worry about whether I'm your man or if I mean what I say." He turned confident, dazzling eyes on her and said, "I mean every word."

She felt like she wanted to cry and laugh at the same time and had the urge to text Grace and tell her that he was a mind reader after all. "But what about feeling hemmed in and ruining us?"

He handed her a glass and gazed deeply into her eyes with a serious expression. "I don't honestly know. I'm messed up, but my brothers worked through their issues, which gives me hope. I want to try with you, Sophie. If you still want to try with me, that is." He put his hand on hers and said, "You're trembling."

She cleared her throat to try to regain control of her emotions. "I didn't realize how badly I wanted to hear that from you until just now. I want to, Brett. I definitely want to."

The air rushed from his lungs and he pulled her into a tight embrace.

"Can we talk about it?" she asked carefully, feeling his heart thudding against her own.

"Yes, but if you don't mind, right now I'd just like to sit and hold you while we watch the movie, drink a little wine, and come to grips with doing what most people do from the time they are teenagers. This is a huge *first* for me, babe."

"You've never had a girlfriend? Like, *ever?*"

"If a week in high school counts, then sure, but when you grow up in a house where one day you're standing on solid ground and the next everything you've ever known and counted on has been ripped to shreds, *long-term* loses its significance." He kissed the tip of her nose and said, "Think you can give me a little time to adjust?"

It pained her even more knowing how much losing his sister had affected his whole life. The hurt still practically radiated off him. "You know what? I think we just figured out why you have a hard time with commitment."

His face clouded with uneasiness.

Realizing he'd just asked for time to adjust and she'd thrown another life changer at him, she quickly added, "We'll take baby steps."

He captured her mouth in a powerful kiss that rolled through her like thunder. "I don't do anything like a baby, got it?"

"You sure don't, but maybe you should remind me again with another kiss."

"Okay. But you need to know that I'm not ignoring what

you said. You might be right, but I don't want to dissect it tonight, okay?"

"No dissecting. Only kissing."

Several scorching-hot kisses later, they kicked off their shoes and curled up on the couch to watch the movie. Sophie was as shocked by Brett's abrupt change as she was by his confession about the wine. An hour into the movie, she still couldn't stop stealing glances at him, trying to reconcile all the parts of her complicated, emotional man. She couldn't help but wonder how much hurt lingered beneath his tough exterior.

His gaze moved from the television to her, catching her staring. "Come here, babe."

He shifted so they were lying on the couch with him spooning her, and ran his hand along her thigh. His breath was warm on her neck, and when he pressed a kiss there, she closed her eyes and soaked it in.

"I like your outfit. I've never seen you in cutoffs."

His voice brought her eyes open again, and she turned around so she was facing him. "No one wears cutoffs in the city, so I don't wear them out."

"You should wear them everywhere." He kissed her softly and squeezed her bottom. "I take that back. You should wear clothes that cover you up around other guys."

Even though he said it teasingly, she remembered how he'd questioned Charlie and said, "You're a very jealous boyfriend."

"What'd you call me?" He drew back, his tone serious again.

"Jealous, which you are, even if you deny it."

"Hell, babe. I'm not denying it. Wouldn't you be if you were me? You're smart, sexy, and sweeter than honey, and I'm a lucky guy. But that's *not* what I was asking about. You called me your *boyfriend*." A soft smile lifted his lips. "I'm digging *that*."

"Really? But it's a label."

"No shit. Stop reminding me. Just go with it." He kissed her again. "I'm not complaining about this, but you can't see the movie if you're facing me."

"I've already seen it," she whispered, and buried her face in his chest.

"What? Why didn't you tell me?" He grabbed her ribs, tickling her as he swept her beneath him.

She squealed. "Stop! Stop! Stop!" she pleaded.

He lifted her shirt and kissed her belly. "Answer the question or I'll do it again." His hand hovered over her ribs.

"No, please!" She swatted his hand away. "You went to all this trouble. I didn't want to ruin it. I love that you thought ahead and brought a movie over." She pulled him up by his biceps and studied his handsome face. He looked different, happier, *lighter*.

"I need a list of all the movies you've seen," he demanded.

"Why? No one gets Redbox anymore when we can stream movies right to the television. I thought you were a movie guy. You should know that."

He lowered his mouth to her ribs in a series of open-mouthed kisses that made her squirm. "I know how to stream movies." He kissed his way up the center of her stomach to her neck and all the way to her lips, then perched above her. "I admit that I don't have much practice with this, but showing up and saying, 'Let's stream a movie,' doesn't sound as romantic as showing up with a movie in hand."

She pulled him down so their lips touched and whispered, "That's why I didn't say anything. I love that you brought it, and I love that you thought of me and what I'd like. So instead of tickling me, how about we take this into the bedroom and you can thank me properly?"

He was on his feet in three seconds flat, stripping off her sweater. "I'm going to thank you *all night long.* Think you can handle that?"

"I'm game for anything as long as it's with you." She palmed his erection, and he groaned, making her entire body tingle.

"Christ, Soph," he ground out. "Now I can't remember what I was going to say."

"It's a good thing thinking isn't required for what I have in mind." She fumbled with the button on his pants and he grabbed her wrist, stopping her cold with his dark stare.

"Did you hear what I said, babe? I'm not leaving you tonight. Can you handle that?"

Her eyes widened and her fingers curled around the waist of his pants. "You're *staying?* For the *night?*"

"Unless you don't want me to."

"Are you kidding? You're staying!" She leapt into his arms, earning a hearty laugh and another butt grab. "I can handle it, but are you sure you can?"

He strode toward the bedroom with her in his arms. "How about I show you just how well I can handle it." He set her on her feet beside the bed and took her in a slow, sensual kiss. "*All.*" He lifted her shirt over her head and kissed the swell of her breast. "*Night.*" He removed her bra, sat on the edge of the bed, and pulled her over so she stood between his legs. As he lowered his mouth to her breast, he said, "*Long.*"

THURSDAY MORNING BRETT awoke to the feel of Sophie's warm breath whispering over his cheek in soft, repetitive puffs. She was nestled against him in the same position in which she'd fallen asleep, with one knee tucked between his legs and a hand on his neck, as if she didn't want to chance him running away. The thought made him happy and brought a knot to his gut at the same time. How did they end up here so quickly? A few days ago he was spouting off about not being her great love affair and Sophie had accepted him as such. She hadn't pushed, hadn't given him an ultimatum or otherwise tried to pressure him into committing, and she'd managed to reel him right in. He waited for regret to hit, for the restlessness that had chased him his whole life to send him sneaking from the bed and searching for his clothes. It was there, prickling around his edges, trying to get his attention, but there was an even bigger feeling standing in its way. He opened his eyes and found Sophie watching him with a tender, contemplative expression.

"Hi," she said sleepily.

Her sweet, trusting voice doused those prickly edges. "Hey. Did I wake you?"

She shook her head, a smile lifting her lips. "But I'm glad you're still here."

"Soph…" He brushed her hair from her face, feeling a pang of guilt. "Did you think I wouldn't be?"

She shrugged.

"You knew I was leaving all those other nights. You asked me to stay until you fell asleep, I didn't…*Shit.* Was I supposed to read further into that? Why didn't you say something? I told you I had no clue about how to go about this."

"No, you weren't supposed to," she said quickly. "I didn't

mean that. I just wasn't sure if you'd be here *this time*, even though you said you would."

Her words felt like a well-deserved punch to the gut.

"I get why you'd worry, and I'm sorry for that. But you have to know I would never let you think I'd stay and then leave. I haven't been able to go without seeing you for a single day since we've been together. You didn't force me to. I'm here because I want to be with you."

She nodded, brows furrowed, which made that knot in his gut tighten.

"I don't want you to get scared and end this," she said softly. "I'm okay with you not staying over if it's easier for you."

"Why?" came out before he could stop it. "You shouldn't be okay with it night after night. You deserve more."

Her lips curved up at the edges. "I'm glad you see that, but my new boyfriend said he bolts when things get serious, so…"

He rubbed his nose along her shoulder, inhaling the lingering scent of their lovemaking. "I'm not bolting." He nipped at her neck. "I want to be here with you, and if I feel boxed in I promise I'll tell you. I won't just take off or end things."

"Thank you," she said as he kissed his way down her arm. "Because a girl could get used to waking up to this."

"*A* girl?" He dragged his tongue along her side, kissed the dip of her waist and the swell of her hip. "Or *you*? Because I don't give a damn about anyone else."

She squirmed as he kissed his way over her hip to her backside. "*Me*."

"Damn right, *you*." He gave her ass cheek a gentle bite.

She gasped, then glared at him. In the next breath, she curled around his body and bit *his* ass.

"Ow," he said with a laugh. "You are a feisty girl."

Holding his gaze, she rolled onto her back and crooked her finger. He loved how she didn't hold back. Every time they were together he felt closer to her. He grabbed her wrist with his right hand, holding it beside her head as he spread his left hand over her thigh and pinned her to the mattress, then lowered his mouth to her breast the way he knew she loved.

"Brett," she begged. "I want more of you. I want you in my mouth."

"I haven't had my fill yet."

He leaned across her body and circled her other nipple with his tongue. Then he blew cool air over the wetness. She arched beneath him, straining against his hands. He squeezed her thigh as he grazed his teeth over the sensitive nub and moved his hand between her legs, teasing over her slick center. A long, surrendering moan left her lungs.

"Jesus, Soph. You have no idea how good you feel." He brought his lips to hers as he teased between her legs. He traced her lips with his tongue and whispered, "I don't know what I want to do first. Fuck your mouth or sink into you so deep you feel me tomorrow when you're sitting in your pretty little skirt at work and you get wet just thinking about me."

"Ohmygod. Now you *know* that's going to happen."

He grinned down at her. "Want to meet me for a quickie at lunchtime?"

She pressed her lips together, eyes wide, as he slipped his fingers inside. She sighed longingly. He fucking loved that sigh.

"What do you say, Soph? The hotel next to your office? I'll get a room, make you feel amazing." He sealed his mouth over hers, feeling her body tremble as he loved her. "We'll shower together. You like naughty showers." His cock twitched just thinking about being with her in the middle of the day. Her eyes were closed, her lips parted as she panted at his words. "Then I'll walk you back to work, and later, I'll take you out for an incredible dinner, wine and dine you so you know how much I adore you."

Her eyes opened. "I can't...I've never done that in the middle of the day."

"But you want to. With me."

His mouth moved over hers, devouring its softness as he teased over the special spot that made her grab at the sheets and cry out into their kiss, her sex clenching. When she panted for air, he breathed air into her lungs.

"*More,*" she said breathlessly. "More kisses, more *you.*"

He withdrew from between her legs and spread her arousal on his cock, repeatedly moving his hand between her sex and his shaft until it glistened. "Stroke me, baby. I won't come, because I want to be inside you when I do, but I need you to touch me."

Her beautiful mouth spread into a seductive grin. "I like touching you as much as I like kissing you."

He recaptured her lips, more demanding this time as she stroked him and he loved her with his hand. Their tongues danced to the same beat as their ministrations. His hips thrust, her pelvis rocked, and when she grabbed the back of his neck and rose off the bed, her fingernails dug into his skin. She quickened her strokes, and he felt her body flex.

She tore her mouth away and said, "Come with me," then crushed her mouth to his again.

Their kisses were rough and messy. Her hot mouth and the tight grip of her hand on his cock sent him soaring at the same moment she cried out his name. His body thrust with every pulse of his orgasm as he came on her stomach and chest. She didn't relent, continuing to work his oversensitive cock, causing him to buck and groan. He brought his mouth to hers again, feasting on her sweetness. She'd mastered making him hard after he'd come, and minutes later he sheathed his erection. He nudged her legs open wider, and her hips rose to greet him. He lowered his mouth to hers and pushed into her tight heat. Their chests met with sticky warmth, and as they found their rhythm, he cradled her body against his, reveling in their closeness. Amid their hammering hearts and frantic thrusts, he had the overwhelming sensation that they were no longer fucking. When did they stop having sex and start making love? Being with Sophie had been different since their very first time. Was it then? As he surrendered to their passion, everything blurred together and delineations no longer mattered.

When they came back down to earth, Sophie curled into him, as she always did after they were close. He listened to the sweet "Mm" sounds she probably didn't realize she made and he found so alluring. He wanted to do something special for her, to show her that he meant every word he'd said.

"This weekend," he kissed her softly, "I want to take you someplace special. Just the two of us."

She snuggled closer, her hand on his cheek. "I can't. I have to go to my grandparents' anniversary party. I would invite you to go with me, but since last night was such a huge step for both of us, I don't want to put that pressure on you."

He gathered her in his arms. "Where are you going and how long will you be gone?" Monday was Lorelei's birthday, and he knew it would be a rough time for him. She didn't need to witness his grief.

"Back home to Oak Falls. I'm flying out Saturday and coming back Sunday night," she said sleepily.

The thought of not seeing Sophie this weekend brought that

prickly feeling rushing back. He pressed his lips to hers, telling himself he could put in extra workouts and hang out with his brothers to distract himself from missing her. But that sounded like *hell* compared to being with her, seeing her smile, hearing her laugh, and holding her in his arms.

Chapter Ten

SATURDAY BLEW IN with chilly temperatures and gusty winds, mirroring the torrent that had been going on in Brett's head for the past two days. Saying goodbye to Sophie before leaving for his run had been torture. Even the gift he'd hidden in her luggage hadn't relieved the guilt and self-loathing that was pushing him—as if he could outrun his demons. If he could, he'd have done it long ago.

"Want to talk about it?" Carson asked as they ran along the Central Park Reservoir.

"Talk about what?" Brett ducked under a low branch full of orange and yellow leaves. Fall was his favorite time of year, and his most hated. The foliage was gorgeous, and the cooler temperatures made his runs and workouts that much more bearable. But their sister's birthday was on the horizon, and it turned all that beauty into ugly, painful memories.

Carson glanced at him with a worried expression. "Lorelei."

"Lorelei?" Brett's gut seized, but his answer came easily. "No."

With the exception of Dylan, Brett and his other brothers had avoided talking about Lorelei until last year when Dylan and Tiffany had come together. Dylan had suggested they honor Lorelei's memory at their family's annual fundraiser to benefit the Ronald McDonald House. Honoring her at the event had opened the door to conversations that should have happened years ago but had been too painful. He and his brothers spoke of her more often now, but it was still difficult for Brett.

"It's not her," Brett said, glancing at Carson and catching an even more worried expression. "And it's not work."

"Then what's up? You've been in a great mood all week. I figured you finally got your mojo back, but Dylan said you blew out of the bar alone the other night and he hasn't seen you there since."

It felt wrong to hear Carson talk about his *mojo.* "Can I ask you something?"

"Always." Carson motioned to a woman pushing a stroller. "I can't wait to give Addy girl a baby sister or brother. Times have changed, haven't they? This time last year I wouldn't even have noticed a woman with a stroller."

"Times have changed, all right." *This time last month I'd have been checking out every woman we passed.* "You had a thing for Tawny forever, right?"

"Since college." Carson and Tawny had been study partners in college, but they'd also had a secret sexual relationship.

"That's a long time to carry a torch for a woman." Brett didn't know all the particulars, but he knew Tawny had ended things around graduation, and he'd never seen Carson happier than he'd been since Tawny had come back into his life.

Carson glanced over, sweat glistening on his forehead and cheeks. "She's it for me, Brett. Always has been."

"Yeah, I get that. I do." *Hell, I've been pursuing Sophie for years.* "When Dylan met Tiffany, he was all in really fast, too. And Mick has been in love with Amanda since he first met her."

They jogged along the side of the path to let a group of

women who were speed walking pass by.

"That's love, man," Carson said. "What are you getting at?"

"I don't know. I guess I'm wondering how you guys make it look so easy after all the shit we've been through."

"Easy?" Carson scoffed. "It sucked not being able to connect with women on any real level for all those years in between college and when Tawny came back. But you go on. And then Tawny came back, and I swear, that wasn't easy. There was a lot of hurt on both sides. But you know how we struggle to nail down some contracts and others just fall in our laps?"

"Sure." Brett hated analogies, and Carson knew it, which meant this was the only way Carson could spell it out for him.

"The right relationship is a combination of both. You struggle to fit together in a way that's right for both of you."

"*Compromise*, Carson. Cut to the chase."

"That's just it. I can't." Carson grinned and kicked up his speed. "It's not just compromise. It's struggling through to *find* the compromises. Figuring out what battles you want to fight and how much of yourself you're willing to change or give up to make things work."

They jogged in silence for a few minutes as Brett mulled that over. "What if there's something you want to change but you're not sure you can?"

"If that thing is you hooking up with other women, it's pretty much a deal breaker."

"Jesus." Brett stewed over what his brother thought of him.

"What's really going on? There's nothing about us that we don't have the power to change."

"Not true." Anger bubbled up from his gut. "We can't change that Lorelei is gone. We can't change that our lives were ripped apart. We can't change that—"

Carson grabbed his arm, causing him to stumble to a stop.

"What the hell?" Brett wrenched his arm free. Carson was staring at him with a dark expression. Carson didn't do *dark*.

"All that stuff you just mentioned? That's life, dude. And that anger I hear in your voice? It's not about any of that shit. So tell me what's going on because I'm trying to stay out of your business, but you're like a roller coaster waiting to crash. And we've got too much riding on our company for that to happen."

Brett paced. He dragged his forearm over his sweaty brow and said, "I'm with Sophie, okay? I mean, I'm *with* her. Staying at her place the last few nights, and before that, staying until she fell asleep. I'm—"

"Wait." Carson laughed. "You're with *Sophie*? Christ, Brett, why didn't you start with that? I thought you were losing your mind."

"Because I'm so fucking confused, and I'm going to lose her if I can't get my act together."

"Do not tell me you're screwing around behind that woman's back, because I'll kick your ass from here to Mexico."

Carson could no sooner kick Brett's ass than any other man could, but Brett knew he'd damn well try if he thought Brett had hurt Sophie. She was already *that much* a part of their family, and he freaking loved knowing it.

"Can we run, please?" Too edgy to stand still, Brett took off running. "I'm not sleeping with anyone else. In fact, I haven't been with another woman since before your wedding."

Carson's eyes widened. "Seriously? I mean, we've all seen the sparks flying between you two, but...*wow*. No other women?"

"Yeah, *wow*. That's how I feel, completely blown away. I

thought one night would get her out of my system, but I haven't been able to go a single day without seeing her. She's *it*, Carson, but I'm fucked up. You know it. She knows it. I've got enough anger to fuel a 747, and now—"

"Wait. Slow down. Let's talk for a sec. You're spending the night at her place? That's big, man. How's *that* going?"

He and his brothers all had a thing about not staying overnight with women. He always assumed they were as fucked up as he was, but with how quickly they'd fallen for their wives and how easy they'd made it look, he wondered if he'd been alone on the Island for Messed-Up Men the whole time.

"It's awesome," Brett said vehemently. "I wasn't sure at first, you know? I was waiting for that fight-or-flight response, and while I felt something, it wasn't powerful enough to make me leave. I can't wait to see her at the end of each day, and nothing could drag me from her bed at night. She's…*God*, Carson, I've never known anyone like her. She calls me on my shit but doesn't push me to change. I have changed, but that's all me, for her, but not because she demands it. And you're going to think this is insane, but, man, her *kisses*? They fucking wreck me."

He shook his head, remembering how they'd kissed goodbye that morning for so long, he'd had to wait another ten minutes before actually leaving while his erection deflated. Sophie had taken great pleasure in that, traipsing around the apartment in his T-shirt with nothing underneath, bending over to pick up her socks, purposely giving him an eyeful of her gorgeous ass.

"Sounds like things are good," Carson said, bringing Brett's mind back to the moment. "If you're not messing around, what are you worried about going wrong? What do you need to fix?"

"You know me, man. When I feel boxed in, I'll kill to get out. I have the power to ruin us without even thinking about it, and it pisses me off that I don't know if I can handle it." Anger pounded through his veins. "Sophie deserves more. She's incredible, man, and being with her doesn't feel like I'm boxed in. It feels good and right. She centers me, Carson. I don't ever feel like I want to walk away from her. I hate being apart for work, which is fucked up, right? Obsessive or some shit?"

Carson smiled and shook his head. "Dude, you've got it bad. I never thought I'd see the day…"

"Fuck it. You know what? Sophie deserves *me*. If you guys can get over your shit, I can handle mine. I'm three times the man any of you are. And you know what else? We've got to rethink these morning runs, because dragging my ass out of her warm bed isn't worth the workout. I'm outta here. Thanks, man."

After the quickest shower of his life and with a handful of clothes in his backpack, Brett raced through the airport to the kiosk and picked up the ticket he'd purchased on the drive over. He hated crowded airports. If they weren't down to the wire, he'd have taken the company jet, but right now all he wanted was to get to Sophie. He waited forever to get through security, which agitated the hell out of him. By the time he shoved his feet back into his shoes, he was ready to climb out of his skin.

He raced to the gate and came to a screeching halt when he spotted Sophie standing by the windows talking on her phone. Her hair was parted on the side, spilling over the shoulders of her army-green jacket. Her jeans had fashionable holes in the knees, and her white shirt was tucked in only at the center of her waist, giving her a casual-chic look. A big purse hung from the crook of her arm with the grace of a movie star, only Sophie was a million times more beautiful than any celebrity. His heart swelled, and he knew that no matter how hemmed in he might feel this weekend, it would never be enough to cause him to screw up the best and only thing he'd ever truly wanted.

"I'LL TEXT YOU after I escape Nana's setup," Sophie said to Grace as she gazed out the window.

"I'm still bummed that Brett isn't going with you. Imagine the fun Nana would have with him." Grace laughed. "Can't you see her pinching his cheeks?"

"Excuse me, ma'am. Can I see your boarding pass please?"

Sophie spun around, and her heart lodged in her throat at the sight of Brett approaching, looking strikingly handsome in a white button-down and a pair of dark slacks, with a wide grin on his face.

"Grace, I've gotta go," she said as she lowered the phone, too stunned to say any more.

Brett thrust his hand out. "Hi. I'm Mr. Slow on the Uptake, and I need to see your boarding pass, please."

He said it with such a serious tone Sophie feverishly dug her boarding pass from her purse and handed it to him. "What are you doing here?"

"Just a moment, ma'am," he said authoritatively. "I need to take care of some business before I tend to your pleasure." His lips curved up in a sexy smile, which morphed to serious again when he turned and addressed the other passengers waiting to board the plane. "Excuse me. I'd like to sit next to my wife on the plane, and I'll happily give the person holding the ticket for"—he glanced at her boarding pass—"seat number 14C one thousand dollars to swap seats with me."

She was still reeling from *wife* as she processed the rest of what he said. "Brett!" She grabbed his arm as the din of the crowd rose. "You're coming with me? You can't pay that kind of money for a seat! It's a short flight."

He lowered his voice and said, "I'm not spending another second away from you, and I don't care if I have to buy every goddamn seat on the plane. You're worth it." He pressed his lips to hers, but she couldn't temper her smile. "Wait. Is that okay? Fuck, Soph. I should have asked, or planned. I'm sorry."

"Sorry? I'm thrilled." She launched herself into his arms.

"I've got 13B!" a guy yelled. "Maybe you can peer over the seats at her."

Brett scowled at the guy, then turned a softer expression to Sophie. "I should have offered to go with you right away. I was afraid I'd mess things up, but I was a fool. When it comes to you—to *us*—there's nothing I can't handle." He held up a finger and called out, "*Two* thousand dollars to the holder of seat 14C."

"No! Geez! You're so impatient. I feel like I just stepped into *Pretty Woman* or something."

His arms circled her, while more commotion rang out around them. "Baby, you just stepped into Brett-with-no-fear territory. I hope you can handle it."

"I'm ready for the trek if you are." She went up on her toes and touched her lips to his.

"Excuse me."

They reluctantly parted, turning toward the twentysomething guy with a backpack slung over his shoulder standing beside them with a boarding pass in his hand.

He pushed his dark hair out of his eyes and flashed a friendly smile. "Did you say 14C?"

"Yes, that's right," Brett said. "Is that your seat?"

He handed Brett his boarding pass.

Brett looked it over and winked at Sophie. "Looks like we've got a deal." Brett handed him his boarding pass and withdrew his wallet. The people around them cheered.

"First class?" the guy said. "Dude, keep your money. You two just gave me serious relationship goals."

Brett pulled Sophie closer, and when he gazed into her eyes, the joy in his made her stomach tumble. He kissed her cheek, smiling down at her, and said, "If you're lucky enough to get a woman like my Sophie, you'll want to do anything you can to see her smile."

Chapter Eleven

"I'M BEGINNING TO think you're more of a planner than I gave you credit for. Did you plan on turning my world upside down day after day?" Sophie asked as the plane took off.

"You know me better than that." He gave her a quick kiss and said, "I'm not big on planning."

"You planned the movie and the wine." Thinking of the condoms he'd brought over, she said, "And you planned ahead with that *special package* you brought to my apartment the other night."

"As I remember, that one pissed you off."

"True," she admitted, and lowered her voice to a whisper. "But only because I didn't want to be your booty call."

He threaded his fingers into her hair, drawing her closer. "What *do* you want to be, sexy girl? Because you've got me hooked, and I'm falling hard."

"You do everything *hard*," she teased, trying to calm her racing heart.

"That's not an answer." He set his hand on her knee, stopping it from nervously bouncing, and his lips tipped up in the cocky smile that made her swoon. "What do you want to be, Soph?"

She gazed into his eyes, trying to stop the answer that vied for release, or at least temper it and make it less scary, but it was no use. When she opened her mouth, "*Yours,*" came out.

The emotions in his eyes made her chest feel full, and when he took her in a series of slow, sensual kisses, she thought it might burst.

"Then be mine, baby. I want to be yours. No more *what ifs.* Well, other than *what if* I want to kiss you like that when we're with your parents?"

"Mm. I like that *what if.* Didn't I tell you about my ridiculously close family? They'll love seeing us kiss." She laced their fingers together, wondering what Brett would think of her family and her life back home, which was so different from his.

"No, but that's a good thing, because not kissing you would be incredibly difficult."

"Well, you don't have to worry about that, but you should prepare yourself for their anniversary party. My grandmother, Nana, believes life should be celebrated. She throws a party for every anniversary, birthday, every holiday. Nearly the whole town shows up for my grandparents' celebrations. And you know all that 'like mother like daughter' stuff? My mom and my younger sister, Lindsay, are the same way. I'm more like my father. I love going to the celebrations, but I'm not the party planner. Lindsay is a real party planner and photographer. She handles family events. Weddings, baby showers, birthdays. Also like my grandmother, my mom and sister pretty much say whatever they feel—three no-filter women—and they hug *everyone.*"

"That doesn't sound so bad, Soph. What's your father like?"

"He's the best father a girl could ask for. He's supportive and loving. He's friendly, with a quirky sense of humor, and smart, like you, and a little cautious." She didn't tell him that she also thought that was like him, because she didn't think

Brett saw himself as cautious. Then again, he didn't see himself as a man who could commit. "At least he's cautious now. According to my mom, he was pretty wild when he was younger."

He squeezed her hand and said, "Your father sounds like a good man. I look forward to meeting all of them. Is there a hotel close to their house?"

"Hotel? My parents would never let us stay at a hotel. *Ridiculously close*, remember? We'll stay in my childhood bedroom."

His brows went up. "They won't mind?"

"They'll probably throw a party. They haven't seen me with a guy in forever. Oh, that's the other thing. Nana and Poppi, my grandfather, will probably have some single guy there waiting to meet me. But don't worry. I texted my mom a few minutes ago to let her know you were coming, and I texted Lindsay. She'll play interference."

"I'll put a stop to the fix-up thing," he said confidently.

"A little jealous?"

He nuzzled against her neck. "When you're with the prettiest girl in the world, you get used to the idea that you'll spend your days glaring at gawking guys. I can handle it."

"Or, you could just kiss me when you notice someone looking at me."

"Mm. I see a guy looking at you right now." He kissed her softly. "Oh, look, there's another." He kissed her again, longer this time. When their lips parted he said, "Check out that blond guy leering at you," and his mouth came hungrily down over hers.

They talked and kissed throughout the flight. Sophie showed him pictures of her family so he could recognize them. The flight was quick and uneventful—other than Brett suggesting several times that they join the mile-high club—as was the drive into Oak Falls. Sophie hadn't thought she'd be nervous about introducing Brett to her family, but as they drove down the street on which she'd grown up, her nerves prickled. He parked in front of her parents' two-story farmhouse and placed his hand on her leg, which she hadn't realized was bouncing.

"Second thoughts about inviting me?"

"No. Just a little nervous. My family can be overwhelming."

"My father's an asshole. I've got you beat."

She'd met his father. Gerard Bad was stern and appeared perpetually unhappy, but he was also a powerful attorney, and Sophie didn't think he could be a total asshole, considering he'd raised Brett and his brothers, who were all impressive, confident men.

"I didn't really think about how big this was," she admitted. "My mom and grandmother will probably make our relationship out to be much more than it is."

"As long as they're not marrying us off, I'm good, babe." He leaned closer and said, "I told you I'm falling for you. I'm in, Soph. I'm not going to get scared off."

Her thoughts got caught on the not-marrying-us-off part. The legal girl inside her noted that his statement conflicted with the not-going-to-get-scared-off part. She knew she was getting miles ahead of herself, but a sad pang accompanied the reminder that Brett wasn't looking for the same happily-ever-after as she was. That was the planner in her coming out. The side of her who liked to know where she was headed. She wasn't going to let that side of herself rock her happy boat this weekend, especially after how far she and Brett had come as a couple. Her mother's favorite saying came back to her—*Love doesn't come with an agenda. It breaks all the rules, and that's what makes it so wonderful.*

"Hey, Soph? You okay?"

She must have zoned out. "Yeah. Sorry. I'm good."

They both glanced up at the house. Gold and white balloons danced from the railings of the wraparound porch. A long banner was strung above the wide front steps that read, *HAPPY 50TH, NINA AND PETE!* In the side yard, a group of children kicked a ball, and just beyond adults mingled. Sophie could see some of the rectangular wooden tables her grandfather and father had built years ago.

It felt good to be home.

"The party already started?" Brett asked. "Why didn't you come last night?"

"It's a come-when-you-can party. It started at breakfast and it'll go into the evening, but by the time I got off work last night and made the flight and the drive, it would have been really late. It's easier, and less stressful, to come today and not have to worry about getting held up at the office and having to reschedule my flight."

"Ah, my little planner. How on earth do you put up with me?"

She glanced down at his hand on her knee. "Know what's funny? Your inability to plan doesn't drive me as crazy as you'd think. I mean, it did at first, but since the night of the comedy show, when you told me you wanted only me, it's become part of your charm."

"Then tell me this. How did I get lucky enough for you to agree to spend one night with me?"

"*One* night? What about all the other nights?"

Wickedness simmered in his eyes. "Baby, come on. How

could you resist more after one night with all *this*?" He motioned toward his body.

They both laughed, and he gave her a quick kiss before climbing from the car and coming around to help her out. Children's voices and the familiar sounds of celebrations surrounded them as Brett grabbed their luggage from the trunk. She spotted Lindsay and her mother heading their way.

Brett hiked their bags over his shoulder and walked slowly, *purposefully*, toward her, his gaze piercing the distance between them. How did he go from joking to holy-moly hot in only one second?

He placed his hand on her hip and said, "I hope you packed those slinky little cutoffs."

"I wear them all the time when I'm home."

"They won't be on for long."

SOPHIE WAS ADORABLE, trying to blink away the desire in her eyes and school her expression as her mother and sister approached. Brett was surprised he wasn't a nervous wreck as they took their relationship to this new level, but when he took in her mother's bright, friendly smile, it was easy to see where Sophie got her effervescence. While Sophie had womanly curves Brett worshipped, her mother was tall and lean, like Lindsay, and looked closer to forty than fifty, with long dirty-blond hair a few shades darker than Lindsay's. He tried to read the smiles passing between Sophie and Lindsay, but he had a feeling the sisters shared a secret language all their own.

"There's my sweet baby girl and her new beau." Sophie's

mother embraced her and planted a kiss on her cheek. She turned open arms to Brett and said, "Hello, handsome. I'm Angel, and I'm so glad to meet you."

"It's a pleasure to meet you as well," he said as he hugged her.

Lindsay lifted the camera that hung around her neck and took pictures of the two of them. She said something quietly to Sophie, and they both giggled. Lindsay pushed her camera strap over her shoulder and opened her arms. "Come on in here, *handsome beau.*" She was a blond sprite, and obviously shared Sophie's sass.

"Brett, *this* is Lindsay." Sophie pulled the back of Lindsay's peach sweater, prying her from his body. "We also call her *Brat.*"

Lindsay made a show of dramatically flipping her hair over her shoulder and flashed a cheesy smile. "*Brat Roberts* at your service."

"We'll get along just fine," Brett said as he reached for Sophie's hand. "I'm the brat in my family, too."

Lindsay took a few pictures of him and Sophie and said, "Brats rule. And just so you know, Sophie's probably into you because of that nickname. She loves me, so think of *that* every time she puts those lips on you."

"Lindsay!" Sophie went up on her toes and kissed his cheek. "Told you she was a brat."

Her sister could make fun all she wanted if it earned him more of Sophie's kisses.

"Okay, girls. Come on," Angel said. "Let's get Sophie and Brett's stuff put away so we can torture him with the rest of the family."

"Nana's in prime shape today," Lindsay said. "She'll be

pinching Brett *all* over."

"Pinching?" He arched a brow, and the three women laughed.

What had he gotten himself into?

"Don't worry. She's harmless. Still madly in love after fifty years," Angel said as they climbed the porch steps.

"Angel?" a brunette called from the side yard, waving her phone. "My sister is on the line and wants to chat with you." Her eyes drifted to Sophie, then to Brett, where they lingered a beat too long as she stood up a little taller and thrust out her chest. "Welcome home, Sophie! Who's this hot hunk of handsomeness?"

Brett squeezed Sophie's hand.

"He's spoken for, Sable," Lindsay informed her.

Angel patted Brett's arm as she walked by and said, "This is Sophie's boyfriend, Brett Bad. Brett, this is Sable Montgomery."

"Awesome name, dude," Sable said.

"Thank you," he said with a friendly smile. "You're related to Grace?"

"Her sister," Sophie said as Sable handed the phone to Angel. "Sable, we just got in and need to put our stuff inside."

"Stand together," Lindsay said to Brett and Sophie. "I want one more pic for Nana's album, and then I'll get out of your hair, too."

"When you're done making out, come out back and hang with us," Sable said.

"It'll be hours," Sophie called out as she tucked her arm around Brett and smiled for the camera. "Get used to this, Brett. Linds is going to drive you crazy with her camera, and complaining will only egg her on. It's easier just to go with it until she gets bored and finds someone else to look at."

He loved seeing this carefree side of Sophie, and he liked her outgoing family and friends.

"It doesn't take me long to move on," Lindsay said as she lifted her camera and took another picture. "Okay, go make out for hours, but remember to lock your door or you're liable to have visitors."

Visitors?

As Lindsay went after Sable, Sophie leaned against Brett and said, "Feeling boxed in yet?"

"Baby, I'm not sure about *pinching* and *visitors*, but how can I feel boxed in when the box has a hundred different entrances? I have a feeling I'll need to take notes to keep up with you guys."

"That's good, right?" she asked as they stepped inside.

He answered her with a kiss.

Sophie's parents' house had the same country-chic, homespun feel as Sophie's apartment, decorated in creams and white, accented with several hues of pink, peach, and brown. The sofas looked well loved, with indentations proving they weren't just for show. Vases of fresh flowers decorated the mantel and end tables, and happy memories emanated from pictures on every wall. He felt like he'd walked into a warm hug, and it hit him like a bullet to the heart. His mother's house would probably feel the same if she'd moved after his father left. But she'd stayed in his childhood home, and it was riddled with too many painful memories to alleviate the discomfort.

He followed Sophie up the steps, taking in the photographs hanging on the wall. Two little girls, one blond, one brunette, with big blue eyes and pigtails, smiled at the camera in their pink frilly dresses and shiny white shoes. He'd know Sophie's smile anywhere, and the glimmer of mischief in Lindsay's eyes was hard to miss. In the picture beside it, the girls stood in a pumpkin patch making faces at the camera. Above that picture was one of Sophie and a boy. They couldn't have been more than ten or twelve years old, standing barefoot in a creek, eyes closed, lips touching. It was the type of picture that caused women to swoon, like the images he'd seen on black-and-white greeting cards. He wondered who the lucky boy was and how special he was to Sophie now for that picture to be hanging on their wall. But there were so many pictures of Sophie with her arms around girls and boys who could have been friends or family, it didn't seem out of place. He stopped to admire a picture of Sophie and her father standing beneath a sparkly sign that read 7TH GRADE FATHER-DAUGHTER DANCE. She wore a navy dress, and he looked handsome in a dark suit with a navy tie. In another frozen memory, Sophie wore a short pink dress and a pretty corsage on her wrist and stood between a handsome boy and her parents. Brett was torn between the jealousy of wanting to be the boy who had been there with her and happiness that she'd had a night worthy of her dazzling smile.

"That's Shane Jericho," Sophie said casually. "He might be here later, and his brother Justus—we call him JJ—is bartending for the party. You can't miss them. They wear cowboy hats day and night. Even their sister, Trixie, wears one most of the time."

"You keep up with your old boyfriends?"

"Our town is about as big as my fist. I don't have much choice. But Shane wasn't a boyfriend. He was just a friend."

They made their way to her bedroom, and he set their bags down by the door. He wasn't surprised to see white furniture, a pink bedspread, and a beautiful picture window overlooking the backyard. There were several pictures stuck in the frame of the mirror above her dresser of her and Grace, Lindsay, and groups of friends. His heart warmed with the realization that Sophie must have had a charmed childhood.

She dropped her purse on the bed and wound her arms around his neck. "You'll be the first guy to share this bed with me."

"Your bed's pretty small. I might have to sleep *really* close to you."

"That's the plan," she whispered.

He gathered her in his arms and gazed into her happy eyes. "Thank you for letting me come with you. I should have offered right away."

"Nope. That's not how my guy works. My guy needs time to process things, to figure out what he *really* wants. I get that, and you're here now, which is all that matters."

"I really want *you*, Soph. I hope you know that above all else." He kissed her then, pouring his whole heart into it and hoping she knew he meant every word he said. He wasn't running, and he wasn't restless. He was exactly where he was supposed to be.

Chapter Twelve

AFTER NOT NEARLY enough toe-curling kisses, Sophie and Brett forced themselves to stop making out and went to join the party. Sophie had a feeling she'd spend the next twenty-four hours hot, bothered, and flustered—and she wouldn't mind it one bit!

As they stepped outside, Brett said, "Wow," under his breath.

Even though it was daytime, lights were strewn above the patio, which was lined with buffet tables that were covered with dishes overflowing with food and decorated with gold and white streamers and balloons. The rectangular wooden tables her father and grandfather had built were lined up, creating a U shape around the middle of the expansive yard, above which more lights were strung from tree to tree, meeting in the middle, where the grass was mowed extra low to serve as a dance floor.

"Is that Axsel, the lead guitarist for Inferno?" Brett motioned toward Sable's brother, playing his guitar beneath the big oak tree where a swing had hung when she was young.

"Yes. He's Grace's younger brother. He's really nice. You'll like him." Axsel wore one of the knit caps that had become his signature style when he was a kid. Though he was gay, the girls in town swooned every time he visited. He was surrounded by a number of them now. Blankets were spread around the yard, and on them, couples cuddled, children played, and friends mingled. Lindsay was chatting with two of Grace's sisters and a handful of other people down by one of the weeping willows that anchored the property by the creek's edge. All the pieces inside Sophie felt as though they exhaled at the familiar, comforting scene, and when Brett put his hand on her lower back, she realized he didn't seem nervous at all. That made her feel even happier.

"Your family throws a party like this every year for their anniversary?"

"Yes. Isn't it fabulous?" She took his hand and led him across the patio to a table where a large chalkboard announced, LEAVE A FOND MEMORY OR AN ENCOURAGING WORD FOR NINA (NANA) AND PETE (POPPI). Beside the chalkboard was a red velvet journal, like the one her mother got for her grandparents every year. Photographs of her grandparents hung from clothespins on a line that ran the width of the patio.

"Everyone who attends writes something to Nana and Poppi." She flipped open the journal and wrote, *Nana and Poppi, I hope this is your happiest year yet and that I'm lucky enough to find love as pure and immense as yours. I love you, Sophie.* She handed the pen to Brett. "Would you like to write something?"

"I'd love to." He put pen to paper and hesitated, glancing up at her with a strange mix of emotions she couldn't read, and then his pen moved swiftly over the page.

She was dying to see what he wrote, but her father's voice boomed through the yard, catching them both by surprise.

"There's my city girl." Her father was a dead ringer for Dennis Quaid, soft around the edges, unless you messed with his family. Then hell hath no fury like Del Roberts.

"Hi, Daddy."

He drew her into a hug, then held her by the shoulders and took a good hard look at her, as he always did. "Sugarplum, whatever this Brett guy's got going on looks good on you." He winked at Brett and said, "Don't make me regret saying that, ya hear? Because if you hurt my baby girl, I'll take you down like a hurricane."

Brett stood up a little straighter and said, "Yes, sir. Understood." He held a hand out in greeting. "Brett Bad. It's a pleasure to meet you."

"Del Roberts, and right back at ya, son." He swatted his hand away and pulled Brett into a manly embrace. "You a football fan, Brett?" he asked as they parted.

"Yes, sir." Brett's arm swept around Sophie's waist. "For as long as I can remember."

"Well, good, because my girl loves football, and she can't be with a sissy city boy." Her father ran a scrutinizing gaze down Brett's body.

"Dad!" Sophie glared at him. "Brett is manlier than any farm boy out here."

"Thanks, baby," Brett said. "Del, I might be a city boy, but I'm into sports, working out, driving my Harley, and *most importantly*, your daughter. What else would you like to know?"

Her father crossed his arms and said, "Can you ride a horse?"

"Oh my gosh, *Dad*." Sophie rolled her eyes. Her father was an accountant, but his heart would always be on her grandfather's farm, where he still helped out when he could. He'd been heartbroken when Sophie had left home for college and still held on to the hope that she might come back and settle down there ever since. She didn't think she ever would, but she loved coming back for visits, and one day, when she had children, she'd like to spend more time there.

Brett shook his head. "I have never ridden, but that's not to say I can't, or I'm not willing to. And I'd put money down that if you give me a week, I'll be roping cattle."

"A man with no fear," her father said with a slap on Brett's back. "That's what I like to hear."

His gaze moved over their shoulders, and a spark of love rose in his eyes. Sophie knew that look so well, she wasn't surprised when her mother pushed between them and looped her arms through each of theirs.

"Brace yourself, sweethearts," her mother said conspiratorially. "Everyone wants to meet Sophie's beau."

"Mom, can't you give him a chance to—"

"It's okay, baby. I want to meet your friends," Brett assured her.

Her mother turned toward her with a smile in her eyes and mouthed, *Baby!*

Sophie laughed. "Mom, please don't make this awkward."

"Me?" She pulled them toward the crowd. "Awkward doesn't exist in this family. We have to find Nana and Poppi before Nana bursts from nosiness. When she heard you two were inside putting your things away, she wanted to charge up those stairs. But I told her, 'Nana, they're young, and they're going to want some alone time. Besides, Sophie needs to butter up her beau with kisses before bombarding him with friends and family.'"

"Mom! Sorry, Brett. I haven't brought a guy home since high school. I forgot just how embarrassing it could be."

"Oh, honey, please. Remember that time you snuck all the way down the creek to kiss Mikey White?"

"Oh my gosh. Please put me out of my misery before it gets any worse," Sophie pleaded.

Brett smiled and said, "I'd like to hear the creek story."

"She was ten years old," her mother said, "and it was at one of Nana and Poppi's anniversary parties. She and Mikey snuck all the way down the creek because Sophie didn't want anyone to see them. Well, what she didn't know was that Lindsay, who had taken after me with her love of photography, was stalking them. You see, Sophie made the mistake of telling her younger sister that she was going to get her first kiss. And Lindsay, being the thoughtful girl she was, wanted to get it on film so Sophie would never forget."

"Did she get the picture?" Brett asked. "Did you get your first kiss, Soph?"

"She got her kiss all right. And Linds got the picture," her mother answered.

"It's hanging by the stairs," Sophie said flatly. "Screwed into the wall by my grandfather, because I've taken it down so many times."

Brett laughed. "That's adorable. So, what happened to Mikey White?"

"He's gay and married to the man of his dreams," Sophie said. "His one and only girl kiss is forever commemorated on our walls. And no, I did not *turn him gay*. If I hear that joke one more time I'll punch someone. As if you could turn a person one way or another."

"I think it's adorable." Brett reached behind her mother and touched Sophie's back. "I just wish I were your first."

"Oh boy, do I like you," her mother said.

Her mother dragged them around the yard, introducing Brett as *Sophie's beau* to friends and neighbors and explaining how she knew each one. *Clare was Sophie's second-grade teacher* and *Sophie babysat Bobby when he was a boy*. Brett went with the flow, shaking hands and reciprocating embraces, and he was quick to reach for Sophie after he was released from their clutches. The way he reached for her, keeping her close, and the tender kisses he pressed to her cheek, or hand, or head in between each introduction made her warm all over.

As they neared her grandmother, they stopped to greet Grace's mother, Marilynn Montgomery. She had been like a second mother to Sophie, Lindsay, and many other kids in town. With seven children of her own, her house had been a gathering place for all ages.

Marilynn hugged Brett, then settled her hand on her hip and said, "My Gracie told me about you."

Brett flashed a nervous smile. "Should I start apologizing now?" He reached for Sophie and said, "I am really sorry that what you heard is probably true, but it turns out I'm a little slow on the uptake. I'm a much better man with Sophie in my life."

"Oh goodness. You are charming. Do you by any chance have a few single brothers for my girls?" Marilynn asked.

"Sorry. They're all taken, but I'll keep my eyes open."

"Well, that's okay," Marilynn said. "I'd really like to get Grace and her sister Pepper back to Oak Falls. I think we need some new male blood in this area."

"If you find some, let's get my Lindsay in on the dating game," her mother said. "That girl's got no interest in settling down with one man."

"Maybe she just hasn't met the right one yet," Brett suggested, eyeing Sophie.

Sophie caught that shooting star and hung on for the ride.

Her mother guided them through the crowd toward her grandmother. "You picked a good man, Sophie. Let's hope your grandmother doesn't scare him off."

Her grandmother looked up from the phone she and three of her friends were studying. She set her blue-gray eyes on Brett and said, "What is this I hear about scaring someone off? Are they telling lies about me?"

"No, Nana." Sophie hugged her, inhaling the familiar scent of her perfume. "Nana, this is my boyfriend, Brett." She loved saying that. *My boyfriend.* And she loved the proud look in Brett's eyes when she said it even more.

Nana waved a hand dismissively, mischief dancing in her eyes. Her grandmother looked as sweet as could be, with layered white hair that still had strands of blond mixed in and just enough makeup to appear younger than her age but not like she was trying too hard. Her smart linen blouse and slacks gave her an air of properness that was often obliterated when she opened her mouth. Sophie loved Nana even more for her lack of filter, despite the fact that she might embarrass her.

"I know who this is, and so does everyone else on this lawn. You, my dear"—Nana pointed at Brett—"are the talk of the party. And now I see why. Tall, dark, and delicious is not a difficult way to go through life. We were just checking out a few Tumblr pages, and those boys have *nothing* on you."

The women behind her nodded and murmured in agreement.

Sophie exchanged an amused glance with her mother, who said, "Brett, this is my mother, Nina, but you can call her Nana."

"Thank you for the compliment, Nana. It's nice to meet you." Brett opened his arms, clearly catching on to the Robertses' way of greeting friends.

"Is Bad your real last name?" Nana asked.

"Yes, ma'am," Brett said. "I guess the naming gods had a sense of humor." He put his arm around Sophie and pressed a kiss to her temple. "But I assure you, as far as your granddaughter goes, I have only the best of intentions."

"Well, that'll get you in her father's graces, but I don't think it'll get you very far in the long run." Nana leaned closer to him and said, "Women like to be loved up, if you know what I mean."

"Nana!" Sophie chided her.

Brett drew his shoulders back with a half-laugh, half-shocked sound and said, "Happy anniversary, Nana. Fifty years is quite a milestone."

Sophie breathed a little easier, thankful he'd redirected the conversation.

"Fifty years is just enough to get to know each other's hot spots." Nana elbowed Brett and added, "If you know what I mean."

"Nana!" Sophie slipped her arm around Brett's waist.

"I can see you've finally figured out how to use those feminine wiles of yours. Now I understand why Lindsay dragged that hunky guy I brought for *you* down to the creek."

Thank you, Lindsay. "Okay...Where's Poppi?" Sophie scanned the crowd. "I'm afraid you might drool on my man if we stay here too long."

"Now, there's an idea," Nana said, laughing loudly and making the rest of them laugh, too. She leaned in closer to Brett and said, "I like you. A good man doesn't get embarrassed. He takes the ball and runs with it."

"Thank you, Nana. I like you, too." Brett chuckled.

Nana pointed across the yard. "Poppi's over by the barn with Chet Hudson and his nephew, Scotty. Such a nice man. They're teaching Scotty to hike the ball."

"Nana and Poppi had a small kitchen fire a few years ago, and Chet was one of the firefighters on duty," Sophie explained. "He's been like family ever since."

Nana touched Sophie's hand and said, "Look at Poppi, tossing the ball to that boy. Isn't he the sweetest?"

"I see a love of football runs in the family," Brett said.

"You don't think Sophie picked it up out in the city, do you? We might be country folk," Nana said, "but we have our priorities straight, and football is right up there with Sunday brunch." She reached up and touched Brett's biceps, then patted his cheek. "I bet you played football. With all those muscles, it'd be a shame if you didn't." She peered around him, checking out his backside.

"Nana, stop!" Sophie said with an incredulous laugh. "That's my boyfriend's butt."

"*Tsk.* I was checking out his hamstrings. Although his derriere is quite nice."

Sophie hugged her and said, "I love you, Nana, but I'm taking Brett to meet Poppi before you start talking about leaving his balls on the field."

"Don't be silly, sugar. The way he's looking at you tells me they're right where they belong."

"About those Tumblr pages…" her mother said to Nana, pushing her away from Sophie and Brett.

"Sorry. I told you my family members have *no filter*."

"Soph, I love your family. My grandparents aren't around anymore, and I'd give anything to have them in my life, even if they made inappropriate comments like Nana. I think she's adorable, and it's easy to see where you get your sass from."

"You really don't wish you'd stayed in the city?"

"No, not even a little. Let's conquer your grandfather so we can sneak off and make out by the creek. I might not be able to be your first boyfriend kiss, but maybe I can be your last."

A STEADY STREAM of visitors came and went throughout the day, each taking time to chat with Sophie and Brett. He had met so many people he needed a roster to keep track. The party was markedly different from the events he was used to attending. No one was checking their phones or rushing to get to the next thing on their agenda. It was like he'd stepped into another world, where nothing mattered except catching up with friends and family and enjoying the moment. And what a beautiful collection of moments it was. Long after meeting Sophie's grandfather, who was just as much of a jokester as the rest of her family, the sun dipped from the sky, and guests danced as Sable and Axsel, who was about as laid-back as Carson, played their guitars.

Brett stood by the makeshift bar gazing at Sophie and her father dancing beneath the lights. A few feet away, her grandparents danced cheek to cheek, swaying with the grace that told of a long, loving history.

"How long have you and Sophie been going out?" the bartender, Justus "JJ" Jericho, asked. He was a nice guy with an affable personality and a shock of dark hair poking out from beneath his cowboy hat.

"Not nearly long enough," Brett said thoughtfully. Something had happened to him today, or maybe it had been happening for a week, or two years. He had no idea how long, or why, but his worries about being in a committed relationship with Sophie seemed like a distant memory. He wondered if it was because they were away from the constant reminders of his family falling apart, which came at him from all angles when he was in the city, or if this was enough of a break to let him finally remember what it felt like to be truly happy. There was so much joy all around them, and he knew this was only a moment of time, a snapshot of their lives, but it reminded him of happier times. And man, had he missed them.

He returned his attention to JJ and asked, "How about you? Do you have a girlfriend?"

"Me?" JJ scoffed. "I wish, but no. Too many women have money signs in their eyes when they hear I own a bar."

"I can relate to that. My brother and I own an international security firm." He'd seen those dollar signs JJ mentioned too many times to count, but never from Sophie.

"Drink or date?" JJ asked as Lindsay and his sister, Trixie, approached. Sophie had introduced Brett to Trixie earlier. She was a quick-witted, long-haired brunette, and looked every bit the cowgirl in her jeans, boots, and a plaid shirt tied at the waist.

"Gross. I'm your sister," Trixie teased. "And I'm pretty sure Sophie would kick my ass if I tried to hook up with her man."

"*Drink*," Lindsay said to JJ. "Something fruity, please. Brett, are you and Sophie sticking around after Mom and Dad go to bed?"

Sophie had mentioned that after the older generations had turned in for the night, she, Lindsay, and whichever friends were still around, would hang out and catch up over drinks. As anxious as he was to get Sophie alone, he was enjoying getting to know more about her through her friends and family. "Whatever Sophie wants."

"Well, considering my very proper sister brought a guy home for the first time in forever and your stuff is in her bedroom," Lindsay said, "I'd say we all know what she wants."

Trixie high-fived Lindsay, and they both laughed.

Brett chuckled. He gazed out at Sophie dancing with her father and made his way around the dance area, taking in the vast number of friends still there. His mind traveled to his own family. He was close with his mother and brothers, but he'd never seen so much love in one place as he had over the past few hours. It was no wonder Sophie wanted it all. This was what she knew, what she expected of the world and of relationships. A life full of endless love and family, a husband she could count on for fifty-plus years.

Her voice sailed through his mind. *One day you'll wake up and realize I'm the best there is.* There was no doubt Sophie was the *best* there was. But the word *best* didn't sit well with him. What he felt for her had nothing to do with how she compared to anyone else. He was falling for the woman she was, and today he'd been privileged to see another side of her. The country girl who threw her head back when she laughed and blushed at stories of her childhood. The girl who danced with the young man she'd once babysat and the adoring daughter who looked at her father like he was bigger than life.

There had been a time when he'd looked at his own father that way. A time when his sister had looked at him that way, too.

"She's always been a daddy's girl," Angel said as she came to Brett's side.

Brett smiled, blinking away the emotions he was struggling with. "Your daughter is an incredible woman. I should have led with that when I met you, but—"

"You were shell-shocked?" Angel gazed out at her husband and daughter. "Our family can be a bit much."

"Your family is exactly as a family should be. My mother would fit in well here." Even after all his family had endured, his mother's walls had never gone up the way his, and the rest of their family's, had.

"And your father?" she asked carefully.

Brett clenched his jaw, his emotions roiling again. "Maybe at one point, but…" *After my sister died, we all changed.* "Life's taken its toll on him. He's not a happy man."

"I'm sorry to hear that." She tucked her hair behind her ear and tilted her head, as if she were thinking.

He saw Sophie in her expression.

"You know, Sophie's pretty tight-lipped about her personal life, but she's mentioned you to me quite a few times over the last couple of years."

"She has?" A wave of pleasure swept through him and just as quickly he cringed inwardly, thinking of all the times he'd propositioned her. "I'm afraid to ask…"

Angel patted his arm and said, "Let's just say that she saw right through you. I tried to tell her to be careful with her heart and that if you were a playboy, you might always be. But my Sophie is as stubborn as her father, and she's also quite intuitive. She said, 'Mom, sometimes you know there's more to a person than even *they* see.'" Angel put her hand over her heart and looked lovingly at Sophie. "The little rascal threw my own words back at me. It's exactly what I said about her father."

"I don't know what I'm more shocked by. Sophie seeing so

much in me, or knowing her father hasn't always been perfect."

"Oh, I never said Del wasn't perfect. He might not have been perfect for some women, but he has always been perfect for me. What do you say we dance over to my perfectly flawed husband and your brilliant, all-knowing girlfriend and cut in?"

He offered her his arm. "Angel, I like your style."

Sophie watched them approach with a soft and adoring gaze. Could he give her everything she wanted and deserved? He sure as hell would do everything within his power to try.

"You know, there are all types of people in this world, and if we judged everyone by who they were before they met their special someone, why, even I might not be such a gem in some people's eyes," Angel said as they danced toward Sophie and Del. "Don't ever apologize for who you've been. Whatever you've gone through has made you the man you are today, and you make my daughter happy. I see it in her smile and the way she is with you. That tells me what I need to know."

"Thank you, Angel. Now I see where Sophie learned to be so forgiving."

"We're only forgiving of those who deserve it," she said with a smile. "You're also a very good dancer. But my little girl looks like she's ready to be in your arms."

"And that guy over there has been eyeing you all night." He motioned toward Del, who was looking at Angel with the same emotional gaze Sophie had locked on him. They danced over, and Brett and Del exchanged a silent nod of appreciation.

As Angel and Del danced away, Brett lifted Sophie's hand and kissed the back of it. "Sweet Sophie, may I have this dance?"

A tender smile lifted her lips as she walked into his arms. "There's no one I'd rather dance with."

Sophie rested her head on his chest, one hand around his neck, the other resting half on his jaw, half on his cheek. He felt himself leaning into her familiar caress as they danced beneath the lights.

He touched his cheek to hers and whispered, "I can't get close enough."

"Me, either," she whispered.

He closed his eyes as emotions whirled inside him. "What have you done to me, sweet Sophie? I don't ever want to let you go."

"Be careful," she said so softly. "I might believe you."

Chapter Thirteen

AFTER THE GUESTS and Sophie's grandparents left, Sophie and Lindsay helped their mother put away the extra food, while Brett, JJ, Sable, Trixie, and Axsel folded chairs and gathered trash. Sophie loved that their friends stuck around to help after parties. They'd been doing it for so many years, they no longer asked if they were needed. They simply pitched in.

She stood by the kitchen sink watching her father and friends through the window as Sable directed the others. She was bossier than Grace, and as the owner of an auto shop and lead guitarist in a local band, Sable was good at making things happen. Sophie caught sight of Brett and her father carrying chairs to the shed. She liked seeing them together. Brett seemed a lot more relaxed than he did in the city. But then again, didn't everyone?

"He's really taken with you, sweetheart," her mother said, joining her by the window.

"I know," she said softly. *He's my forever kisses, and I want to be his.*

"It's a scary and wonderful thing watching my little girl give her heart to a man." She tucked Sophie's hair behind her ear, her lips curving up in a warm smile.

"Oh my God, you guys." Lindsay pulled open the refrigerator and set a platter inside, then joined them by the sink. "I swear I live in a Hallmark movie." She grabbed a piece of celery from a tray on the counter and bit into it. "Can't you just celebrate the hot sex and steamy kisses and then move on to another pasture?"

"No," Sophie said sharply.

"Just because you don't want to settle down one day, Lindsay Anne, doesn't mean it's wrong for Sophie to dream of more with her man."

"I never said I was dreaming of more." *At least not out loud.*

Lindsay rolled her eyes. "You didn't have to. It's written in those starry eyes of yours."

Their mother put an arm around each of them and said, "And there's nothing wrong with that. We all know that you like to play the field, Linds, which I'm pretending means you *only* kiss the men you go out with and *only* after very nice dates."

"I hate to burst your bubble," Lindsay said with a laugh. "But I think I must be adopted."

Their mother shook her head. "I assure you, you're not, and I think I'd know after twelve hours of labor. You're just more like your dad than me when it comes to settling down. You need to sow your wild oats first. But Sophie's heart doesn't work that way. She gives her all. I think she fell for Brett long before now."

"Mom," Sophie pleaded. "Can we not dissect the Secret Life of Sophie Roberts tonight?"

"Well, it's true." Their mother kissed Sophie's cheek and finished wrapping the last tray of food. As she put it in the refrigerator she said, "I'll go grab your dad so you kids can have some fun."

"That won't happen until later, when Sophie shows Brett

the hayloft," Lindsay teased, ducking out of reach when Sophie tried to swat her.

"Brat!" When Sophie was in high school, her father had caught her in the hayloft kissing the boy who had later broken her heart. She'd found out the next day that Lindsay had been mad at her about something and she'd told their father where she was.

"You love me." Lindsay put her arm around Sophie and whispered, "You should totally do it. I'll send Dad out with a flashlight." She took off out the door with Sophie on her heels and ran through the yard, both of them laughing.

JJ caught Lindsay around the waist, and she squealed.

Brett intercepted Sophie. What else could she do but barrel into his open arms? They laughed into the kiss as he twirled her around.

His eyes glittered in the moonlight. "Gotchya, beautiful."

"What are you going to do now that you caught me?"

All that glitter turned to steam. "If I weren't afraid of embarrassing you, I'd carry you into the barn, strip you down, and take you every which way you'd let me."

Oh, how she wanted that! But Lindsay and the others were already heading to the barn with their arms full of blankets and a cooler full of beer. "Later," she said as her toes touched the ground. Then she remembered why she'd been running in the first place and added, "But not in the barn."

They followed the others down to the barn and sat on blankets draped over hay bales. Sable played her guitar as they caught each other up on their lives and her friends got to know Brett. Time moved like a dream as she and Brett swayed to the music and Lindsay told them about the wedding she was planning for a couple in a neighboring town. She wished Grace could be there. She was the one who had pushed Sophie over the hurdle toward Brett, and she knew Grace would like seeing how happy they were.

"Seriously? Who has a cotton-candy-themed wedding?" Lindsay pulled her legs up beside her on the hay bale. "It's weird, but it's going to be cute. The bride's gown is pale pink, which reminded me of Sophie's homecoming dress."

"Oh, Soph," Trixie said. "I forgot to tell you Shane said he was bummed he couldn't make it to the party, but he got held up picking up a horse with Trace in Maryland."

"Trace is another of Trixie and JJ's brothers," Sophie explained.

"Does Brett know about you and Shane?" JJ asked.

"You mean that he took me to homecoming? It's not like he could miss the picture on my parents' wall." She smiled up at Brett, and he leaned in for a kiss. She loved that he was comfortable enough around her friends and family to be affectionate. She'd worried when he'd said he was coming with her that he might suddenly realize he'd made a big commitment and freak out. But he clearly hadn't, and if anything, she felt even closer than she had when they'd arrived.

"I think he means the *after-party*," Sable explained.

She should have expected her friends to try to embarrass her. "Geez. Really, you guys?"

"*After*-party?" Brett's brows lifted.

"He doesn't know?" Lindsay dramatically flipped her hair over her shoulders and sat up pin straight. She turned toward Trixie and, speaking in an animated voice, as if she were a younger Sophie, said, "I had a wonderful time at homecoming. Thank you for taking me."

Trixie leaned forward to kiss Lindsay, and Lindsay moved

out of reach, causing Trixie to fall off the haystack. Everyone laughed, except Brett, who was trying to suppress his smile, and tightened his grip on Sophie.

Sophie felt her cheeks burning. "That was a hundred years ago!"

"*Who* doesn't kiss their homecoming date good night?" Lindsay teased. "I would have kissed him."

"Of course you would," Sable said. "You'd also kiss my homecoming date, or Grace's, or Trixie's…"

"True," Lindsay said.

"Why wouldn't you kiss him good night?" Brett asked.

"Because!" Sophie glared at Lindsay. "He was a friend, not a *boyfriend*. But if I had known what would happen by not kissing him, I would have done it. He told a friend, who told another friend, and by the end of the next day, the whole town knew I didn't kiss him."

"Aw, my poor virtuous girl." Brett pressed his lips to hers. "I feel insanely lucky right now."

"Don't you ever forget it," Sophie said sassily.

"But Shane *did* get his kiss," Axsel reminded her. "I wasn't even in high school yet, and by the time I was, their midgame kiss was legendary."

"*Midgame kiss?*" Brett asked.

"The whole town was talking about me," Sophie said. "What was I supposed to do? I had to shut them up."

"Shane was the quarterback for our high school team," Lindsay explained. "At the next game, Sophie marched out onto the field right after he'd thrown the ball—in the *middle* of the game—yes, *middle*—and she ripped off his helmet and kissed him smack on the lips."

"Then she curtsied and sauntered off the field like she

hadn't just turned my brother's world upside down," Trixie said.

"No boys tried to kiss me after that," Sophie said, feeling mildly embarrassed by that fact, even though there were no boys she'd wanted to kiss. "But I did get a standing ovation."

Brett cradled her face in his hands and said, "I would have wanted to kiss you. You're the gutsiest girl I know, and I love that about you."

He lowered his lips to hers, and Axsel strummed his guitar *loudly*. "Hey, *I've* kissed your girl."

"I thought I heard you were into guys," Brett said.

"My sister has a history with gay men." Lindsay winked at Sophie, who rolled her eyes.

"I am into guys," Axsel said. "I was eight and Sophie was babysitting. She brought stuff to make Christmas cookies, and there was this moment I'll never forget. She was smiling, and her hair was falling over one shoulder. She was just so beautiful, and I wanted to kiss her." He shrugged and said, "It wasn't a sexual thing. I mean. I was *eight*. But I kissed her, and she said, 'Axsel, you're really sweet, but you can't kiss me.' I said something like, 'That's okay. It wasn't as fun as I thought it would be,' and we went back to making cookies like it never happened."

"You guys are dead set on embarrassing me, aren't you?" Sophie leaned over and touched Axsel's hand. He had the kindest hazel eyes, and while he could hang tough with the best of them, he had a gentle soul. "You know I love you."

Axsel blew her a kiss. He began strumming his guitar and sang, "If you're going to break my heart, just break it," earning more smiles.

"Did you babysit everyone in this town?" Brett asked. "Your

mom introduced me to at least three people you babysat, and you danced with one of them."

"Just about everyone who was younger than me. I *loved* babysitting," Sophie admitted. "I was always booked weeks in advance."

"She was the best," Axsel said. "She'd come armed with crafts or baking paraphernalia and would let me stay up late. And she used to practice for the school plays and pretend I was her audience. It was fun."

"You know she loves scary books, right?" Sable asked. "We used to tease her about becoming the sweet grandma who secretly wreaked terror on people's lives in other towns."

"You guys were mean to my girl." Brett pulled her up to her feet and said, "Axsel, do you know the song 'Last First Kiss'?"

"Heck, yeah." Axsel began playing the song.

Brett drew Sophie into his arms, right there in front of everyone, and began singing the song word for word right along with Axsel.

"Dance with me!" Lindsay grabbed JJ's hand, pulling him to his feet.

Sable picked up her guitar, playing along with Axsel. Trixie jumped up and began dancing around them.

As Brett sang about wanting to be Sophie's last first kiss, her emotions soared, and she was thrown right back to when they'd danced on the sidewalk in the city, and before that, when they'd danced in the bar.

When he pressed his cheek to hers and changed the lyrics to—*Baby let me be your last first everything*—she knew in her heart they were meant to be together all along.

AFTER SOPHIE'S FRIENDS packed up and called it a night, Brett and Sophie went for a walk. Moonlight cut through the trees and tangled branches, glistening off the slow-running creek water. The smell of damp earth and lush greenery accompanied by sounds of crickets and other night creatures scurrying through the brush brought a peacefulness that the city didn't offer. Between the close-knit community he'd met tonight and the serenity of Sophie's parents' property, Brett finally understood the draw of rural life. He'd always considered himself a city dweller, but with Sophie he could imagine sitting on a front porch overlooking acres of farmland, with a hint of family and livestock hanging in the air.

"You know about my first kiss and my homecoming nightmare," Sophie said as they walked along the creek. "But all I know is that you haven't had a long-term girlfriend until now. Tell me about your first kiss. Where was it?"

"It's been a long time since I thought about it, but I was in seventh grade, and it was after art class. The prettiest girl in the whole school was Shelby Grand. She had long dark hair and big blue eyes, like you, only not nearly as beautiful." He leaned down and kissed her cheek. "Every guy in school wanted to go steady with her, but I didn't. I just wanted to prove that I was better than all the other guys."

"That's awful."

"Probably, but it's the truth. I was so angry back then, Soph, I could barely keep my head on straight. After art class I saw her at her locker surrounded by all her friends. She was one of those girls who was friends with everyone, not fake or too good for the unpopular kids. I liked that about her. Anyway, my buddy Cooper Wild liked her."

"Heath's brother?" Heath was married to Amanda's sister, Ally. Sophie knew all four of the Wilds and their families.

"Yeah. I saw him coming up the hall, and we were friends, but you know, as guys we were always competitive. Plus, back then I was a bit of a prick. Always ready for a fight, even with friends. I have no idea how anyone put up with me, but I'm thankful they did. I strode right through the circle of girls and kissed Shelby right on the lips."

"That's *so* you. Kind of like my midgame kiss, except my guy had already tried to kiss me once. What did Shelby do?"

"She smacked me, then Cooper punched me, and we ended up in the principal's office. My mother made me apologize to Shelby, but I won the fight and I got the kiss."

Sophie laughed. "Of course you did."

He stopped beside a weeping willow that bowed out over the water and drew Sophie into his arms again. It struck him that he was always doing that, trying to get closer to her. "Speaking of kisses…"

She tipped her chin up, and when his lips touched hers she made one of her sensual sounds, and as always, it sailed through his body like warm liquor, soothing and stirring at the same time.

"Baby," he whispered against her lips. "Your kisses destroy me. I never really enjoyed kissing until you, and with you, I never want to stop. When we first got together you said you didn't want to rush our kisses, and that was so different from anything I'd ever known. You opened my eyes to how incredible kissing can be."

"Sex without kissing is just sex, and I didn't want that with you. I wanted to feel closer to you, even if only for one night, and to me, kissing is the most intimate thing you can do. It lets me feel everything you feel. A good kiss feels nice. But when *we* kiss, I feel it all over my body, like it, and part of you, becomes part of me."

"Baby—" His voice got choked by emotions. "I've never felt closer to anyone in my life. Your kisses are unforgettable. They're there even when we're apart."

"Forever kisses," she said softly.

"What, babe?"

"That's what our kisses are. They stay with us forever. *Forever kisses.*"

"That's exactly what they feel like." He had the urge to make their forever kisses more permanent, to memorialize this moment, the time she'd given him with her family and friends, so they'd never forget it. "I wish I had a pocketknife. I'd carve our initials in that tree. That's a small-town thing to do, right?"

"It is, and it's a family thing to do, too. But we're already on here." She took his hand and led him around the tree, pointing to an area that had been stripped of bark, where two hearts with initials were carved. One of the hearts had DR + AR carved inside it, and the other had SR + FK.

"My parents call this the Tree of Forever Kisses. Nana and Poppi have one in their yard, too. When I have kids, I hope to do the same thing. Lindsay doesn't ever want to get married, so her initials aren't on here, which makes me sad. But maybe one day she'll change her mind."

She pointed to the first heart. "This is my parents' heart." She pointed to the heart with her initials in it. "And this is mine. I carved it into the tree in middle school. Sophie Roberts and FK *Forever Kisses.* That's you."

He laughed and kissed her again. "That's *any* man, baby. I need a knife to fix that up."

"It's not *any* man. You're wrong. Only one man can be my forever-kiss guy. My father is my mother's, and my grandfather is my grandmother's. My uncles are my aunts' forever kisses. It's how things work."

She was so sweet, but she wasn't naive, and he felt compelled to ask a difficult question. The question that made him think about his own parents and the relationship he'd seen between them before Lorelei died. "What about marriages that don't last? Those people who think they've found their soul mate, but their relationships fall apart? Are they out of luck?"

Her brows knitted, and she sank down to the grass. He sat beside her as she said, "Not out of luck, no. Relationships can go wrong for so many reasons. Sometimes it doesn't matter how strong your love is. The things that tear the relationship apart are too hurtful or too big to see your way around. But that doesn't change the love that was there. Lots of marriages fall apart because of outside influences. The husband or wife gets off on the wrong path, or they grow apart, or they're tempted by someone else."

"That's messed up," he said too sharply. "Think about it, Soph. *Temptation?* Cheaters need to grow up. If a man or a woman commits to marriage, temptation shouldn't mean shit. And growing apart? Yeah, I can buy that to a point, but if your partner is doing new things, get off your ass and do them with her. I think those are poor excuses people use when they've grown bored with their partner or to give validity to their insecurities when they need an ego stroke and reach outside their marriage."

"So, what do you think is an acceptable reason for divorce?"

she asked.

"I don't know. I'm sure there are some. If you find out your spouse isn't the person they led you to believe they were. Why do you think I've never committed to a relationship before this? Committing to anything means something to me. Marriage isn't supposed to be disposable. The last thing I want to do is let down a person I care about." The topic made him think of his parents, which caused him to be edgy. He pushed to his feet and paced.

"But your parents are divorced."

"And? Do you think I agreed with that? They lost their daughter. A child they created *together*, a child they loved and raised for eight years." His voice escalated. "How does tearing the family apart help?" He paced beside the tree, trying to get a grip on his mounting anger. "How can you turn your back on your other children? Or holler at your grieving wife until she's ready to lose her mind?"

Sophie went to him, but he stormed away, splaying his hands like a warning. "You should give me some space to get this out of my system."

"Brett, why are you so upset? I'm sorry I hit a nerve, but is it because you lost Lorelei? Or because your parents divorced?"

He looked up at the sky, trying to calm the rage eating away at him. "I'm sorry," he finally said. "It's both, and it lives right there beneath the surface. You didn't need to hear all that. I'm sorry."

She closed the distance between them and wrapped her arms around him.

"Sophie, please give me a minute." He tried to step back, but she held on tighter.

"Talk to me," she said softly.

He ground his teeth together, upset with himself for burdening her. "You don't need to hear any of this ugliness."

She leaned back enough to gaze into his eyes. "No, Brett. *You* don't need to hold it in. You committed to me, and communication goes hand in hand with commitment. I want to help and understand what you've gone through. My mom had a brother who died when he was young, and she said it was the worst kind of sadness she'd ever known but that talking helped."

"Jesus. I'm sorry for your mom and her family."

"Thank you. I can't imagine losing a sibling, or what that would feel like. But please talk to me. Help me to understand so I can be there for you."

He looked away, but he didn't want to shut her out. "I don't...I've never really talked about it."

"All the more reason to," she said with a small smile. "I'd love to hear about Lorelei. I know it'll be hard, but I'd like to know what happened with your family."

"Soph, it's all awful."

"It's awful that you lost Lorelei and that your parents didn't stay together, but it must have been wonderful to have had a sister for all those years. Were you close to her?"

He felt a pained smile tugging at his lips. "Yeah. Really close. She's the reason I know how to dance."

"She liked to dance?"

"Lorelei liked *everything*. She had a personality that was bigger than life, and she wanted to be famous for about a hundred different things—acting, modeling, dancing, baking, trapeze..." He felt a knot that had lived in his chest forever loosen the slightest bit. "She loved old movies, musicals, and plays. She watched all the old Fred Astaire classics, and she took dance lessons down the street from our house. I used to walk her there twice a week. Her teacher wrangled me into being Lorelei's dance partner." Memories flew through his mind at breakneck speed, bringing a smile. "I haven't thought about that for a long time. My family doesn't know. I remember thinking about how my brothers would give me shit for dancing."

"And yet dancing helped you reel me in. I always wished I had an older brother. Lorelei must have felt so special to have that secret with you."

"I hope so. She liked to pretend I was her bodyguard. A few months before she died, my parents took us to a Broadway show, and she wore this fancy dress. She was so excited, and she made all these plans about her *big debut*. My parents bought each of us boys dark suits." His throat clogged with emotions. They were the suits they'd worn to her funeral. He cleared his throat to try to regain control, struggling to find his voice again. "She, uh, she wanted to pretend she was an actress. When we got into the theater, I put my arms out to the side and walked ahead of her, clearing the way, and said, 'Lorelei Bad coming through. No autographs, please.'"

Sophie laughed softly, her eyes glistening with tears.

"She ate it up, waving as she walked through the lobby. Can you imagine? I don't know how she did it. The girl had more guts and confidence than I could have dreamed of at her age. I haven't been to a show since…Anyway, after we lost her, the whole bodyguarding thing tore me up."

"Because you couldn't protect her?"

He nodded. "We lost her so quickly after her diagnosis. That was the beginning of the end. We went from being a loud, happy family to not knowing what we were. My mom cried day and night, and my father worked all the time, and when he was home he completely lost his shit."

"It must have been awful for all of you. I can't imagine what your parents went through. They not only lost their daughter, but they had four grieving children to try to help through it."

His chest constricted. "Yeah, it was tough, and the way my father handled it pisses me off. He was the man of the family, the one we looked up to. The man who was supposed to protect us. As stupid as it sounds, at ten years old I blamed *him* for her death. I knew then I shouldn't blame him, but I was so angry and so fucking sad. I didn't know what to do with it." The words fell from his lips like bombs, exploding around him.

"Everyone grieves differently," Sophie said empathetically. "You must have felt as helpless and lost as your parents did."

He paced again, unable to stop the truth from coming out. "We couldn't talk about it. We didn't know what would set my father off. The overwhelming pain of losing Lorelei burrowed deep inside me, turning dark and ugly, until it was all I felt."

He faced her again, taking in the pain in his sweet Sophie's eyes. In that moment, the darkness of his past collided with what he wanted for his future, and for the first time in his life he wanted to own up to his part in their family's destruction. With his heart in his throat, he stepped closer to Sophie, holding her gaze to be sure she would hear every word he said and hoping like hell she would still want him afterward.

"Sophie, as awful as that time was, the truth of our family falling apart is even uglier. I wanted to blame someone. I wanted to *kill* someone, and I'm damn lucky that I didn't. I went out and got in as much trouble as I could. Fighting, causing shitstorms in stores, doing anything and everything to try to get that rage out of my system. Two years after she died, right before my father moved out, I was picked up by the police for trying to beat up a guy who owned a convenience store because he wouldn't sell me cigarettes. I didn't even smoke. I just wanted a fight." He laughed at how stupid he was as a kid, but the reprieve was short-lived. The truth came slamming back like a boomerang.

"You were hurting," Sophie said as she reached for him again. "You were only a kid."

He kept her at arm's length, steeling himself for the truth. "But I wasn't a stupid kid, Sophie. You need to hear the truth before you give me any more of that sweet heart of yours. My father used his connections to get the charges dropped, but all that trouble I caused was misdirected. I knew it then, and I'm ashamed of it now. At first I was honestly trying to get past the gaping hole inside me. But as time passed my reasons changed. You know how I said I blamed my father? I turned that blame into hatred, feeding off of it. I thought if I got him and his anger out of the house, I'd feel better and my mom would feel better, but that's not how things work. All that shit I did made things a thousand times worse for my parents. I destroyed him and decimated our family."

A tear slid down Sophie's cheek, nearly dropping him to his knees.

"I'm sorry, Sophie."

"Sorry?" She swiped at her tears.

"That I'm not the man you thought I was."

"You're right. You're not the man I thought you were." Her expression turned serious. "Because the man I thought you were before we got together was a man who would never admit to something like that. He'd make a joke about it, or get pissed if someone accused him of it. And the man I've come to know? The man I trust with my heart?" She stepped closer. "That man has been slowly opening up to me, and everything I've learned about him has surprised me. That man *owns* his strengths and his weaknesses. That man is brilliant. But like the rest of us, he wasn't born that way. You were a kid when you lost your sister. I can't imagine how devastating that must have been for all of you, but to the ten-year-old boy who secretly danced with her? The boy who protected her and loved her?" More tears slid down her cheeks. "There are no words for how horrific and sad that must have been and must continue to be when you think of her. You might have been a really smart kid, but as you said, everything you knew was upended when you lost Lorelei. You can't blame yourself for what happened between your parents. You weren't acting rationally, and chances are neither were they."

He wanted to take that lifeline and run with it, but he knew better. He needed to be sure she fully understood where his head had been.

"I knowingly did things that would make my father angry, and that's shameful."

"That's a *hurting child*," Sophie insisted. "I'm sure your parents knew that."

He shook his head. "Do you understand the ramifications of what I did? My mother lost her *forever-kiss* guy because I couldn't keep my shit together long enough for him to get through his own grief. She's alone now, Soph, because of me."

Sophie studied his face, and he wondered what she saw. The new pain slicing through him as he bared his soul? Or the relief he was ashamed to feel, because revealing that secret felt like he'd released a hundred ghosts from the cavern of his chest?

"People get second chances, Brett. You asked if broken marriages meant the couple was out of luck." She shook her head. "There are more opportunities to find love and even to fall back in love with an old partner. If your mom is still alone, maybe she wants to be. Or maybe she's waiting for your father to become the man he once was, or some rendition of that person. What I'm saying is, you're carrying an awful big burden that you picked up as a kid. I wonder if you've added to it over the years as you became stronger and felt you could carry more weight?"

He folded his arms around her and touched his forehead to hers. His rational mind knew he'd only been a grieving kid, but the guilt he'd harbored had magnified. He'd kept that secret for so long, he expected others to feel the weight and shame of what he'd done, too. He'd feared that confessing would unleash demons he'd always believed could drag him so far under he'd never resurface. But just as Sophie calmed him, she made everything seem clearer.

"I don't know. Maybe. It feels good telling you, and that makes me feel guilty, because you don't need to be brought down."

"You're not bringing me down. You're letting me in. Now I understand more about who you are, how deeply you hurt, and how intensely you love."

"Sophie..." He was at a loss for words. He never realized how good it would feel to finally have someone to talk to about this.

"It's not surprising that you didn't want to get close to anyone for all this time." She placed her hand on his cheek, drawing those feelings right out.

"And now I can't get close enough to you."

Chapter Fourteen

SOPHIE AWOKE TO the sound of voices outside her bedroom door. Brett's arm was wrapped tightly around her as he slept. She wondered if he was having a bad dream or was afraid she might run away. The thought made her smile. Like she'd ever run away from him? When they'd come to bed last night they'd made slow, sweet love, and then they'd made wild, frenzied love, and she knew they'd crossed another bridge and taken their relationship to another level.

Her bedroom door flew open, and Brett bolted upright, putting his arm out in front of her like a barricade.

"Rise and shine!" Nana said as she burst into the room and threw the curtains open.

Brett turned his face away from the bright light.

Sophie's mother was on Nana's heels. She closed the curtains and said, "Sorry, baby girl! Nana! We talked about this!"

Brett's arm dropped, and he flopped onto his back with a groan, pulling Sophie against him, and whispered, "Thank you for making me sleep in my underwear."

"I told you. Personal space does not exist in this house." Nana and Poppi lived only down the road, but she wondered how long they'd been waiting for them to wake up.

Nana opened the curtains again. "Wake up now, kids. The day is waiting."

Lindsay leaned against the doorframe in her pajamas, her blond hair a tangled mess. She didn't live far from their parents, but when Sophie was in town, she always stayed over. She covered a yawn and said, "Welcome home, sis."

"Nana, we're tired. We got in late last night," Sophie pleaded as she glanced at the clock. Holy cow, it was already *nine*? Brett usually woke up at the crack of dawn. Had their talk helped ease his conscience so he slept better? Or had they simply worn each other out?

Nana set her hand on her hip with an amused expression. "My sources tell me that you two lovebirds were up all night. These walls aren't soundproof, you know."

Brett's eyes widened. Sophie wanted to disappear.

"My apologies," Brett said as he tightened his grip on Sophie and sat up, bringing her with him.

Could this get any more embarrassing?

Nana waved a hand. "No apologies necessary, but now it's time to greet the day."

Poppi appeared in the doorway and put an arm around Lindsay. He kissed the top of her head. His dark eyebrows and white hair made his blue eyes look as if they were painted on, and his easy smile warmed Sophie's heart despite the craziness of the last few minutes.

"Nana, how about you leave these kids alone? Who's ready to help make brunch?" her grandfather asked.

"Come on, Mom," Sophie's mother said as she dragged Nana toward the door. "How about we make sausage and eggs?" She looked over her shoulder and whispered, "Sorry. You two rest."

Brett laughed. "We're up for the day. Don't worry."

Lindsay sauntered closer to the bed and said, "I think you

should skip your morning sausagefest and come down for breakfast with *real* sausage." She hurried toward the door, giggling.

Sophie threw her pillow at Lindsay.

Brett tackled Sophie to the mattress, grinning like a fool while she tried to recover from her embarrassment.

"I love your family," he said, and her heart soared.

"They're freaks." Embarrassed, she couldn't believe he said he loved them.

"They're *real*, baby. Like you." His eyes were warm and loving, making his words even more meaningful. "I don't want to leave today. Let's stay for a few more days."

"You want *more* time here?"

"Yes, more time with you, around your family, in your world. I want to see where you went to school, the field where you kissed and curtsied. I want to see your grandfather's horses and that hayloft Lindsay told me about."

"She told you?" *I'm going to kill her!*

"She did, and I want to replace that flashlight in the dark with a memory of us." His gaze turned serious, and he said, "Tomorrow is Lorelei's birthday, and usually the days around it are horrible for me. It was one of the reasons I was hesitant about coming here. But being here has made it easier, and our talk last night really helped me get out from under some of the guilt I've been carrying around. Being here with you makes me happy, Sophie. It reminds me of what a family should be like, and I want to experience more of it."

She felt like her heart might explode. "I want to, but I have to work."

"I'll call Mick. He'll understand. I'm sure Carson has told everyone about us by now. I won't jeopardize your job. If he needs you back, that's cool, or if you'd rather not stay, that's okay, too. I just…" He pressed his lips to hers. "I want *more* with you, Sophie."

"More time?" she asked softly.

"More *everything*."

SOPHIE SPENT THE morning on cloud *eleven*, because when she got to cloud nine, she kept on soaring. She was filled with nervous energy, *good* energy, the type she hadn't ever felt before. After helping her family cook, she and Brett skipped breakfast and went for a run, jogging into town. She showed him her elementary school, the café where she used to ride her bike to meet her friends when she was in middle school, and the eclectic clothing shop Grace's sister Morgyn owned. They jogged by the library and kissed on the stone steps. Brett wanted to hear stories and memories about each place, and she loved how intently he listened to each and every one.

When they reached the high school, he took her hand and led her out to the middle of the field. It was a brisk morning, and his hand was cool to the touch, despite the sweat on his brow from their run. He tucked a few strands of hair behind her ear and lifted her hand to his lips, placing a kiss on her knuckles. "I keep asking myself, if we had met when we were younger, would we have been this connected? Would you have been able to slow me down, to make me think and feel, the way you do now? Or did I need to go through all that I have for us to find each other?"

"You were such a bad boy, I might have been intimidated

by you," she answered honestly.

"Which would have made me that much more drawn to you," he said with heat in his eyes. He hauled her against him, a sinful smile curving his lips as he dipped his head and nipped at her neck. "Do I intimidate you now?"

She tilted her head to the side, allowing him better access for the kisses he was lavishing on her. "No. You thrill me."

He cradled her ass in his hands, holding her against him. "Do you worry I'm not all in?"

"Not anymore."

"Are you still all in, Sophie? Even knowing about my past? My fuck-ups? Because I'm falling hard and fast for you, and I don't want to stop."

She felt her eyes widen, her pulse quicken, and managed, "Yes, I'm all i—"

Her words were smothered by the hungry press of his lips. His strong hands moved over her back and into her hair, angling her mouth so he could take the kiss deeper. She went up on her toes, and he lifted her into his arms. Electricity radiated from his body, arcing through her as he showered her with kisses—her cheeks, her chin, the tip of her nose, and *finally*, her mouth, flooding her with uncontrollable passion. She held his face, not wanting him to end their kisses, but he seemed in no hurry to do so. One hand slid beneath her bottom, cupping it. His touch sent bursts of passion pulsing through her.

"Think anyone would mind if I took you right here?" he asked between kisses.

She got excited at the mere thought of it. "Well, you know Nana wouldn't mind!"

His mouth swooped down, capturing hers, muffling their laughter until it turned to greedy noises, and he kissed her breathless. By the time her toes touched the ground, her body vibrated with liquid fire, her legs were weak, and her heart was racing.

She clung to him. "I'm not sure I can walk."

"Then I didn't kiss you thoroughly enough. Let's make sure you can't walk." He pressed his lips to hers again, kissing her beyond the point of return.

His eyes gleamed with desire. "Better?"

"Uh-huh" was all she could manage.

He turned around and crouched in front of her. "Climb on my back, sweet Sophie. I'll be your chariot."

He glanced over his shoulder as she wrapped her arms around his neck, and she leaned forward and kissed his lips.

"Take me for a ride now," she said seductively, "and I'll take you for one later."

"Baby, I'll carry you all the way home."

Sophie thought Brett was joking about the piggyback ride home, but no matter how many times she asked him to put her down, he refused, insisting they'd get home faster if he carried her. *The faster we're home, the faster we get to play.*

When they reached her parents' house, she could hear everyone out back and said, "Hurry!"

Brett carried her to the front steps and set her down, then proceeded to kiss her so thoroughly, she didn't care who was out back. She needed him, and she needed him *now.*

"Whose good-night-kiss memory am I deleting?"

She took his hand and led him toward the front door. "Every good-night kiss I've ever had."

"There you are," her father said as he came around the side of the house with her grandfather.

Sophie's stomach sank.

Brett must have seen the disappointment in her eyes, because he pulled her closer, whispering, "It's okay, babe." Then to her father, he said, "How's it going, Del? Poppi?"

"Good," her father said. "But we could sure use your help hanging the front porch swing I bought for Sophie's mother."

"Daddy, we were just going to shower," she said quickly, still hoping to get a few minutes—or an hour—alone with Brett.

"That's okay, sugarplum. You go on up and shower," her father said. "The three of us will have this up in no time. Then you and Brett can have yourself a nice afternoon ride in the new swing."

That wasn't the kind of ride I had in mind.

"Y'ALL HAVE A nice run?" Del asked as he marked the spots on the porch ceiling where they needed to drill holes in the beams.

"Yes, sir. The town is charming." Brett reached for the drill and was hit with a memory of helping his father fix the porch railings the summer before Lorelei died. She'd danced around the front yard calling out to them, *Look at me!* Then she'd do a cartwheel or twirl in circles.

He thought about what Sophie had said last night about how wonderful it must have been to have had a sister for all those years, and for the first time in ages, he didn't try to push those memories aside. He wanted to honor them as they had honored Lorelei at the fundraiser last year.

When Del climbed down from the ladder, Brett took his

place. "I'll drill the holes." He screwed the hooks into the beams thinking about calling Mick and wondered if his brother had more memories of Lorelei that Brett might have blocked out.

"I've lived here all my life," Poppi said as they attached the chains to the hooks in the chair. "I saw street corners give way to phone booths, and now those are gone and we've become impatient and moved on to cell phones. But for the most part, it's the same close-knit town it's always been."

Poppi stepped toward the ladder, and Brett said, "Why don't you and Del prop up the chair and I'll climb up and lift it with the chains."

Poppi stepped onto the ladder. "*Pfft.* You city folk think age means you can't work as hard. I've got news for you. I'll be climbing ladders, mucking stalls, and riding my horses until the day they bury me six feet under."

Brett held his hands up in surrender. "I have no doubt you will. I was just trying to help."

"Did you see that smile on my granddaughter's face?" Poppi asked as they lifted the swing into place. "That's the only thing that matters to me. Sophie is a special girl, and she's been waiting a long time to find happiness."

A wave of pride and gratitude washed through Brett. "Then I hope you won't mind if we stick around for a few more days. If Sophie can get off work, that is. We can get a hotel room, if you'd prefer, but I'd like to spend more time here with Sophie, if that's all right."

Del and Poppi shared an approving smile.

"We'd like that very much." Del patted him on the back. "No hotels necessary."

"But you might want to lock that bedroom door tonight," Poppi suggested. "Unless you want my wife barging in again.

She loves that girl to pieces. I don't know if Sophie told you or not, but Nana celebrates love every chance she gets. She just about climbed out of her skin waiting to see you two this morning."

Brett felt the same way about being with Sophie. Every minute with her was better than the last.

"Thanks for your help, son," Del said, putting an arm over his shoulder.

A pang of longing for all the years their family had lost, and still stood to lose, hit him like a bullet. "I'm happy to help, anytime."

"You must be starved after your run. Come around back and we'll fix you a plate."

He was starved, all right. *For Sophie.* But first he needed to call Mick. "Thanks. I've just got to make a phone call first, if you don't mind."

While Del and Poppi headed for the backyard, Brett pulled his phone from his armband, walked into the front yard, and called Mick.

"Hey," Mick answered.

"Hi. How's it going?"

Mick chuckled. "I think I should be asking you that. Carson said you took off after telling him you and Sophie were a couple. Is that true?"

"Yeah, it's true, bro. I'm at her parents' house in Virginia. That's actually why I'm calling."

"Her *parents'* house. You went to the anniversary party?"

"How did you know?" Brett gazed down the street. Tall trees bursting with colorful leaves lined the rural road. The air was crisp and clear for as far as he could see. There was no exhaust, no crowded sidewalks. *No anger pushing me toward a two-hour workout.*

"She talks about her family a lot," Mick explained, "which means you two must be serious for her to have taken you to meet them. How the heck did that happen?"

"The night of Tawny's grand opening we went out for drinks with her friend Grace, and…" He paused, thinking about how long he'd been unable to think about anyone but her. "No, that's not true. That's not when it happened." He glanced over his shoulder and caught sight of Lindsay standing in the side yard, her camera focused on him. He waved, wondering if he'd get a spot on the wall by the stairs. "It was at Carson and Dylan's wedding. Near the end, after I'd hit on her so many times she rolled her eyes as I approached."

"Doesn't she always?" Mick teased. "You're not exactly marriage material, and Sophie's like Amanda. She's been dreaming of Mr. Right forever."

"I know. I mean, you've told me that, but the last time I approached her at the wedding, she shut me up before I could say a word. She said, 'There are a million girls in the world. Why do you want me?'"

"Sounds like Sophie. She likes to know why things happen and where she's headed," Mick said. "It's one of the things that makes her so good at her job."

"I'm sure. Mick, I gave her some half-cocked answer because I didn't understand all the reasons myself. But that question stuck with me, and then she was *all* I could think about. And now I'm drowning in love for her, man. I'm not a wordsmith, but I'm beyond happy when we're together. I told her things I haven't told you or anyone else about Lorelei and Dad. And about myself."

Mick was silent for so long, Brett feared he didn't believe

him. He couldn't blame him. He'd never committed to a woman in his life.

"It's true, Mick."

"I don't doubt it." Mick's voice was thick with emotion. "I'm just so damn happy for you it's got me choked up. I worry about you, Brett. I've seen how you and Sophie look at each other. I knew what she felt for you, but I had no clue if you were even capable of…" He exhaled loudly. "I thought we'd lost that part of you."

"You and me both," Brett admitted. "Talking with her has helped me to realize a lot about myself. I have some shit to take care of before I can be the man she deserves, including an apology to you and everyone else in our family."

"What the heck are you talking about? You're one of the best men I know. You are every bit the man she deserves."

"Not really. All that trouble I got into after we lost Lorelei? I think I wanted to punish Dad. I had a stupid kid's perspective, but I blamed him for not protecting her."

"Jesus, Brett. We all did. We were kids. We didn't know any better."

"Maybe so, but I was the one getting into trouble, and that had to piss him off even more. I think I pushed him over the edge."

"My ass you did," Mick said sternly. "Dad was on his way out the day we lost her. Nothing any one of us could have done would have kept him in the house. He was an adult, Brett, and he had a choice—fight for his family and hold them together, or check out. He checked out and spent all that time at the office. Don't you remember? He was never home, and when he was, he was a mess."

"I remember, but I added to it."

"We *all* added to it. How could we not? A piece of each of us died right along with Lorelei, but don't you dare take responsibility for him. Look, you see yourself in him because you have all that anger inside you, but you're nothing like him. You've found ways to channel that anger away from the people you love. You're twice the man he could ever be. And I hope that if Amanda and I have boys one day they'll be as strong as you are."

Brett swallowed hard against the emotions that stirred. "That's really hard to hear. I don't know if I should warn you not to want that or thank you for making me feel better."

"Thank me, man. You deserve Sophie, and you've got to let that misplaced anger go. That's water under the bridge."

"Yeah, I'm working on it. Being here with Sophie and her family has reminded me what family should be like. She's so relaxed and happy here, so loved...I need to be here with her, Mick. It's healing in a way I can't seem to heal back home. It feels good to see a family that's still intact and not weighed down by the ghosts of their past, you know?" He thought of what Sophie had said about her Nana and Poppi losing a child and realized how true his statement was.

"I do. It's giving you faith in family again, buddy. That's huge."

"It is. I'm wondering if you can spare Sophie for a few days? We can fly back Wednesday. She'll be at work Thursday. She's not asking for the time off. I am. I'll pay for a temp to replace her. I'll pay her salary. Whatever you want. I need this time with her so I can get my head on straight and be the man I want to be for her."

"Are you seriously asking me for help? Hang on. I've got to write this day in my calendar."

"Smart-ass."

"Brett, Sophie texted me a few minutes ago and asked if she could have a few days off. She said someone she cared about needed her. I had no idea it was you. I already gave her the time off."

Brett turned toward the house, catching sight of his sweet temptation closing the distance between them. Sophie's high ponytail swung with each step as she approached wearing a pair of sexy cutoffs and a New York Jets sweatshirt. She lifted her hand and crooked her finger, beckoning him to her.

"Thanks, Mick, I appreciate it. I'll call you when I'm back in town." He ended the call and reached for Sophie. "There's the girl who makes my briefs fit tighter."

She put her arms around his neck and said, "I'm very talented that way. But you are talented in many ways, too. Like making my heart go crazy at a particular picture I found in my suitcase."

"You found the gift I tucked away. I've had it on my nightstand at home since the wedding." The picture of him and Sophie toasting his brothers and their new wives was taken by Jackson Wild, Cooper and Heath's brother. Cooper and Jackson were two of the most sought-after photographers in the city, and they had photographed the wedding. The picture was taken from a distance, looking through the altar after the ceremony in his mother's backyard. Jackson had caught Sophie leaning in, her hand on Brett's lapel, his hand resting possessively on her hip. The picture told of an intimacy he hadn't thought they'd shared at that point, but he now realized it had been there all along.

"Next to your *bed*? That makes me kind of giddy. If I had known that, I might have taken you up on your propositions sooner."

"Damn, baby. I would have filled my room with pictures if that's all it would have taken." He patted her butt and said, "You look sinful in your shorty shorts."

She set her hands on her hips, scrunching her face in feigned anger. "Says the man who left me high and dry up there."

"I doubt you were dry when you went up those steps after our scorching-hot kisses." He pressed his lips to hers, obliterating her feigned anger.

"Okay, you left me hot and bothered."

"I'd say sorry, but…" He kissed the corner of her mouth. "I was helping your family." He slicked his tongue along her lower lip the way he knew she loved, earning a sexy sigh. "And I called Mick, but you beat me to him."

She grabbed the front of his shirt and pulled him closer, bringing his lips just above hers as she said, "I felt funny about you doing it."

"Thank you for taking time off for me."

"For us."

"I want to make up for leaving you hot and hungry. We could sneak upstairs, or behind a tree, in the barn, the backseat of the rental car…"

She laughed softly, but her hands pressed against his chest, and he knew she was considering their options, the same way he was. He nuzzled against her neck, pressing another kiss there.

"I want you, Soph. I want to bury my face between your legs until you come." Her breathing hitched, and he said, "I want you to ride me while I love your breasts and watch as I disappear into you." She made a whimpering sound, and his cock swelled. He held her hungry stare and said, "And after you come, I'm going to take you from behind so you feel me *everywhere.*"

As he lowered his lips to hers, Lindsay's voice cut through their heat. "There you are. Nana's on her way up to your bedroom, wondering if you two are fooling around instead of visiting with her."

Sophie groaned.

"Shit." Brett held her against him to hide his arousal.

Lindsay looked through the lens of her camera and said, "Smile pretty. I'm going to call this one 'In Need of a Cold Shower.'"

Chapter Fifteen

SUNDAY PASSED IN a whirlwind of stolen kisses and hidden caresses as Sophie and Brett watched the football game with her family and played in the family's half-time touch-football game in the yard. Sophie's father and grandfather had both played football in high school, and they liked to relive the good old days with touch-football games whenever they could get family and friends to indulge them. Brett had eagerly jumped right in, and they'd had a blast. When Sophie got the ball, he picked her up and carried her to the other end of the field, while her father and mother—his teammates—cheered him on and the others gave him grief.

She watched him now, moonlight kissing his handsome face as he sat on the patio talking with her family, and she swelled with love for him. She'd gone out with her mother, Nana, and Lindsay to pick up a few things from the grocery store, and when they'd returned, the three men were just coming up from the barn. Brett had helped replace the old, rusted locks with new ones. He'd pitched in all afternoon and evening. He'd helped set the table and barbecue dinner and had helped clean up afterward. He and her father had even done a security check on the house. Brett was not pleased that they didn't have motion-sensor lights and planned to install them while they were in town. He even told Poppi they would help him on the farm tomorrow. Sophie wondered if he had any idea what that really meant. The thought of Brett mucking stalls brought a smile.

"You have that Hallmark look in your eyes," Lindsay said as she came out the patio doors with a glass of wine.

"I'm wondering how many stars had to align for me not to get burned when I jumped in with Brett on a hope and a prayer." She had never realized how all-consuming love could be, but he had taken up residence in her mind and in her heart.

"I don't know, but everyone loves him. Nana's practically planning your wedding. She said I should ask you what kind of theme you want, as if I haven't been taking notes for the last twenty-five years."

"You won't believe this, but things are so good, marriage isn't on my mind. I want tomorrow, and next week, next year…But I don't care if there's a ring on my finger or not. I love him, Linds. I really, truly love him."

Lindsay gazed at Brett with her brows knitted. "I'm not a marriage girl, but I want that for you, because you are one. But"—her voice rose with the hint of a tease—"I took some great pictures of you guys and of Brett with the rest of the family, in case you scare him off with your dreams of forever."

"That was thoughtful of you. *Not*," Sophie said to the sister she'd loved, protected, and had gone head-to-head with her whole life. They thought differently and they wanted different things out of life, but when Sophie was talking with Brett last night about his family, she realized that none of that really mattered. What mattered was that they had each other. Period. She knew the pictures were Lindsay's way of supporting her love for Brett. "That *was* thoughtful of you, Linds. Too bad there's no room on the wall for more pictures."

"You never know. I do know how to use a screwdriver." Lindsay patted Sophie's shoulder and said, "I've got your back."

"Maybe you could have used that screwdriver five years ago."

Brett looked over from his perch on the chair across from Poppi. His gaze moved slowly down the short dress Sophie had changed into all the way to the tips of her cowgirl boots, leaving a trail of fire in his wake. He reached a hand in her direction with an alluring look in his eyes.

Sophie lowered her voice as they went to join the others and said, "I wish everyone would go to bed already. I want some time alone with Brett."

Lindsay guzzled her drink as Brett pulled Sophie down onto his lap.

"I missed you," he said, warming her all the way to her toes.

Lindsay feigned a yawn and looked at her watch. "It's after eleven. I have to go to bed. I have a long drive tomorrow." She bent to kiss their mother's cheek, and Sophie caught wind of whispers.

"Oh, goodness, it *is* late. We have to work in the morning," her mother said as she shot an encouraging glance to Nana. She got up and reached for Sophie's father's hand. "Come on, honey. The alarm goes off mighty early."

Thank you, Lindsay. Sophie and Brett got up to say good night.

Poppi pulled Brett into an embrace and said something too quietly for Sophie to make out. She liked that they had their secrets.

Nana hugged Lindsay, then Sophie, and whispered, "Maybe you should play around out here so you don't keep your mama up all night."

We all have our secrets. Sophie hugged her harder, thankful for who she was, no filter and all. She'd welcomed Brett into their lives without question, even knowing about his playerlike past. "I love you, Nana. Thank you for teaching me about love."

"I love you, too, sugar. Now, go put all those lessons to good use." Nana patted Sophie's butt, nudging her toward Brett's open arms.

"There's my girl." Brett embraced her as Nana and Poppi headed for their car and the rest of the family went inside. "I have been waiting to get you alone all day."

"Tell me about it."

His eyes smoldered. "Come with me." He took her hand and led her off the patio.

"Oh, I plan on *coming* with you," she said seductively.

"Many times. Guaranteed. But first…"

He led her across the lawn toward the creek, picking up his speed to a jog. She laughed as he pulled her along. When they reached the willow tree, his mouth swooped down to hers so passionately, she knew he'd been waiting all day to do it, just as she had.

"Hey there, beautiful," he said as their lips parted, and he cradled her face in his hands.

She loved when he did that. It was like he didn't want her to miss a word, but she'd noticed today that those looks had become penetrating, as if he didn't want to miss a second of *her*.

"I think it's time we let the world know that I'm your forever-kiss guy, and that starts here."

He reached into his back pocket, and her mind raced through all the things he might mean. Before she could hold on to any one thought, he opened his hand, revealing the pocket-knife her grandfather always carried in his back pocket.

"Are you going to do what I think you're going to do?"

"Oh, yes." He opened the blade and went to the side of the tree with the hearts carved into it. He set to work carving another heart beneath them.

"But I told you, you're *FK*." She couldn't suppress her smile as he glanced at her with a don't-you-know-me-by-now expression.

He continued carving, forming his initials. Afterward he paused long enough to kiss her, then went back to work. She stood behind him, one hand on his shoulder, feeling his muscles pulse against it as he carved, ever so slowly and deeply, L-O-V-E-S beneath his initials.

Oh God!

He paused, brushing away tiny pieces of bark, before carving her initials below.

"Brett," she whispered, her eyes filling with tears.

He retraced every letter until it was etched so deeply it would never go unseen. He closed the knife and put it in his back pocket before turning and taking her face in his hands again. He gazed into her eyes for a long, silent moment. The air between them pulsed with emotions so strong they drew her against him. She soaked in the love in his eyes, the strength of his hands, and when he touched his lips to hers as soft as a feather, she could barely breathe.

"I'm not just falling for you, baby. I've fallen in love with you, and I know I'll only fall deeper in love with you tomorrow, and the next day, and the next."

"You *love* me" fell from her lips full of disbelief. Her world was officially spinning.

"More than I ever thought possible. I think I've been falling for you for a long time, but I fought feeling anything for so many years, I was blind to it." He kissed her again, leaving her mouth burning for more.

"I love you, too, Brett. So much!" She pressed her lips to his, fast and impatient, and squealed, "Oh God! You *love* me."

She laughed out of sheer elation, and in the next breath, she was in his arms, his hot mouth devouring hers, their tongues probing and their hands groping as they stumbled in the moonlight toward the barn. When they reached it, she remembered the new locks.

"I don't have a key," she said between kisses.

He shoved a hand into his pocket and withdrew a shiny silver key. "Think I'd leave you hanging?"

She shook her head. "Does my dad know you have the key?"

He gave her a sly look and unlocked the door. The scent of hay and old wood filled her senses. Brett closed the doors behind them and pulled her into his arms again. His tongue slid along her lips in a slow sensual path as his hands moved over her bottom, and he ground his hips against hers.

"Kiss me," she pleaded. His hands slid lower, his long, hot fingers playing over the backs of her thighs beneath her dress.

"Oh, I'm going to kiss you, baby, in due time."

He dipped his head and kissed the swell of her breasts, his tongue delving into her cleavage, sending heat between her legs. She palmed his hard length, stroking upward through the rough denim, and he grabbed her wrist. His eyes blazed right through her. *Blaze, baby, blaze.* She wanted to feel all that heat inside her, over her, beneath her. He pressed her palm lower, cupping his balls through his jeans.

"I want your hot little hands all over me tonight, baby."

"Hayloft," she said urgently, and led him up the old wooden steps she hadn't climbed in years.

He groped her from behind as they ascended the steps, one hand between her legs, the other caressing her breasts.

"You're so fine, sexy girl." He sealed his teeth over her neck as they stepped into the loft, and she closed her eyes as he sucked *hard*.

Her back was pressed against his chest, and he slipped his fingers beneath her panties. His other hand dove into her bra, and he masterfully teased her nipple as he entered her down below.

"*Oh God*," she panted out.

He sucked harder on the curve of her neck, pinching her nipple until a sharp, scintillating mix of pain and pleasure shot between her legs. She reached back with both hands, one holding his head in place, the other pushing between them so she could squeeze his cock. He groaned, his hips bucking forward.

"Come for me, baby," he said, and used his thumb to bring her swollen nerves to the peak of pleasure. She whimpered as her orgasm mounted, filling her veins, making every muscle flex and swell.

"Suck on my neck," she pleaded.

And he did, hard and perfect, sending her spiraling over the edge. She clenched her teeth, trying to stifle the sounds of pleasure streaming from her lungs. He continued sucking, continued teasing over her sensitive nerves as she gasped, climbing up, up, up again, until her eyes slammed shut and his name flew from her lips like a prayer.

As the clutches of pleasure eased, his mouth claimed her neck again, taking her back up to the clouds. His hand pushed beneath her panties, holding her bottom, his fingers still wet from her arousal. That touch, this kiss, brought her right up to the edge again, as he turned her in his arms, roughly claiming her mouth. He was like a drug, lulling her into a high, and *Lord have mercy*, she wanted to overdose.

They kissed so long, his rough, strong hands moving hungrily over and inside her, by the time their lips parted, her entire body was vibrating and her legs felt like rubber.

Brett gazed into her eyes with the arrogant smile that made her stomach flip. "Have we obliterated that flashlight kiss yet?"

"I can't remember kissing anyone but you. *Ever*," she said, earning the hottest smile yet.

He reached over to the wall and flicked the light switch. Soft country music filled the air. Sophie felt like she'd walked into a dream. Strings of blue lights hung from the rafters, illuminating the loft. Hay bales were set up like a bed, draped in thick, fluffy floral comforters, with pretty pink and lace pillows. Vases of fresh flowers were set up around the floor, and the picture of her and Brett that he'd hidden in her luggage, alongside three mason jars with colorful lights inside them, sat atop a small wooden table she recognized from Lindsay's bedroom. White sheers hung from the rafters, separating the lovely makeshift bedroom from the rest of the loft.

"How...?"

"I had a little help from a blond fairy."

She turned to him, struggling against happy tears. "You planned this for us?"

"I planned this for *you*," he said lovingly. "I wanted you to remember this night forever. This is only the beginning, babe. Every thought of you, every time I see you, touch, or kiss you, my love for you grows."

"Oh, Brett—"

He reclaimed her mouth, crushing her to him, whispering

sweetness between hungry kisses as they undressed each other and fell to the blankets in a tangle of limbs and greedy gropes. He pinned her hands to the blankets as he nipped and kissed her neck, tasting his way lower. Every graze of his teeth made her wetter, and every slick of his tongue scorched down her body like a river of fire. His hard length pressed against her skin, hot and tempting, and when he sucked her breast, she arched beneath him, holding his head to her. He took the hint, sucking harder, and shifted his weight. The length of his cock rested against her sex, and he began rocking with deadly precision, time and time again, until she was unable to hold on to a single thought. He pushed his other hand beneath her bottom and teased over her most private area. Lust *zinged* through her, ricocheting like bullets and exploding through her core. She bucked and panted as her orgasm crashed over her in relentless waves. And then his mouth was on her sex, his fingers sliding into her. He withdrew them quickly, replacing them with his tongue as his lubricated fingers teased over her bottom. She lifted her hips, giving him the approval he sought, and he pushed his finger into her bottom.

"Ah! Brett!" She rose off the blankets.

His hand stilled. "Too much?"

The concern in his voice made her love him even more. "No. Never. Just *so* good."

He loved her with his hands and mouth, taking her higher with every orgasm, until she lay boneless and panting. Then he loved and tasted her entire body again, from the tips of her toes to the shells of her ears and every sensitive spot in between. His touch was divine. His hands moved slowly and eagerly. His cock brushed over her belly, her thighs, her bottom. She was dizzy with desire. He perched above her again and took her in a series of slow, intoxicating kisses that sent her stomach into a wild swirl, leaving her dizzy and panting. He rose and sheathed his length. She ran trembling hands along his muscular thighs. Her heart was full to near bursting as he came down over her slowly, aligning their bodies. Her hips rose to greet him, and his lips curved up in a heartrending smile.

"How did you become my entire world so fast? You own me, Sophie, and I adore you."

Chapter Sixteen

IN ALL HIS years, Brett had never watched a sunrise. He'd been awake through sunrise, he'd ended his evenings at sunrise, but he'd never actually sat and watched the dawn of a new day crawling across the sky. He'd never seen the grass go from dry to dewy or heard the crow of a rooster—until today. He and Sophie made love for the umpteenth time—yes, *made love*, because what he had with Sophie was so far beyond sex, he couldn't even think in those terms anymore. After washing up in the barn bathroom, they bundled up in blankets in the yard to greet the day. He was sure they'd witnessed the most glorious sunrise that had ever occurred, but that might have had something to do with watching it with the woman he wanted to spend every minute with.

Hours later, as the morning sun warmed the air, with Nana and Poppi's burly old retriever, Breeze, by his side, Brett carried a bucket of fresh eggs out of Sophie's grandparents' chicken coop and reached for her hand. She looked beautiful in a pair of skinny jeans, red rubber boots, and a flannel shirt tied above her belly button. Her grandparents lived on fifty acres down the road from Sophie's parents, in a quaint yellow farmhouse surrounded by beautiful gardens. They had two barns, three horses, a few cows, and a handful of chickens. He and Sophie hadn't arrived early enough to take part in the milking, but

Nana promised to drag them out of bed tomorrow so Brett could experience it firsthand. He was actually looking forward to it.

"I think we need a farm. I'm having farm-girl fantasies that we have no business acting out on your grandparents' property."

She wound her arms around his neck and kissed him. "Does this mean you're done with your city-girl fantasies?"

"You don't think I'm that limited, do you?" He set the bucket down, and Breeze shoved his nose into it as Brett gathered Sophie in his arms. "We're only getting started, baby. I have office fantasies, Sophie-in-the-snow fantasies." He kissed her deeply. "Car and truck fantasies, elevator and poolside fantasies." He licked the column of her neck.

"I love when you do that." Her fingers pressed into his side. "I have fantasies, too."

"Do tell." He gazed into her eyes, loving the lusty look in them.

Her cheeks flushed and her gaze skittered around them, as if she needed to make sure no one would hear her. Nana was up at the house, and Poppi was with the horses. There wasn't a chance in hell anyone could hear them.

"It's okay, Soph. You don't have to share them with me. I'll enjoy discovering them all on my own."

"But how can you if I don't tell you what they are?"

He waggled his brows. "I'll just have to try *everything.*" He slid his hand beneath her hair and pulled her closer so he could speak directly into her ear. "You said you wanted everything with me, remember? I have a very good imagination."

"Yes, but some of my fantasies aren't sexual, like walking around all day naked with you or taking a bubble bath together."

"Baby, I love that you don't think those are sexual." He pressed his lips to hers, then whispered, "Remember our *shower?*"

Breeze pushed his nose between them. Brett stole another kiss before giving in to the needy dog and kneeling down to love her up.

"What do you think, Breeze?" he asked the dog. "Can I walk around naked all day with Sophie and keep my hands to myself?"

The dog answered with a *woof!*

He grinned at Sophie. "If those are your nonsexual fantasies, I can't wait to hear the ones you're too nervous to tell me."

She looked around again as he rose to his feet and picked up the bucket of eggs.

"I've never been blindfolded," Sophie said tentatively as they headed for the house with Breeze on their heels.

"Now we're talkin'. Good thing I brought a tie."

She bit her lower lip.

"What else?" he urged.

She shrugged, blushing a red streak. "I've never done it outside or made out in a theater. This isn't sexual, but I've never ridden double on a horse with a man, and I think that would be romantic."

He draped an arm around her shoulder and said, "I'm going to make all your fantasies come true, and from now on we're implementing Naked Saturdays."

"I like the sound of that. I have another fantasy." She gazed up at him with those trusting baby blues, and his heart thumped harder. "I would like to see your place. We always stay at mine, and I want to see you in your natural surroundings."

"Like an animal at the zoo?" he teased. "Baby, I want you in my apartment, in my bed, on my couch, on my dining room table." He nuzzled against her neck. "When we leave we'll pick up a few things from your apartment and stay at my place. Sound good?"

"Sounds perfect," she said as Nana came out the side door and Breeze trotted off to greet her.

Nana crouched to pet the dog, looking spry in a pair of jeans and a white sweater. "I thought you two got lost in the henhouse."

"I wanted to, but your granddaughter refused me," Brett teased.

"Silly woman." Nana shook her head. "You've got to seize the moment! *Every* moment!"

"He was kidding, Nana." Sophie hugged her. "Want help making breakfast?"

"I would love that. I'd like to make banana bread, too. How hungry are you?"

Brett shrugged. "I can wait as long as it takes. Or if you'd prefer, I can run out and grab breakfast from someplace in town and bring it in for everyone."

Nana pursed her lips together. "We're going to break you of that restaurant habit, city boy. While Sophie and I make a breakfast worth eating, would you mind checking on my husband and making sure he didn't overdose on sugar? I swear eating poorly runs in male genes. He thinks I don't know about his secret stash of Ho Hos or the ridiculous number of sports magazines he hoards in the tack room. As if I don't realize it doesn't take two hours to muck out three stalls. That man would eat sugar and read sports all day long if he could." She sighed with the same dreaminess Sophie did and said, "I do love that man, though he's a sneaky Pete."

Brett gave Sophie the bucket of eggs and a quick kiss before heading down to the barn. He found Poppi pushing a wheelbarrow toward a stall. The pungent aroma of manure and damp straw greeted him.

"Grab a pitchfork, son. Lemme show you how country boys build muscle."

Brett reached for a pitchfork. "I could use a few tips. The gym's getting old."

"Somehow I doubt that." Poppi opened a stall and said, "Taking care of a horse is a lot like taking care of a good woman. You want to make sure she's got a clean bed, a roof over her head, and every once in a while you've got to take her out for a nice long ride."

He proceeded to show Brett how to muck the stalls. Brett had never been around horses, but mucking stalls was pretty basic. Pitch the soiled bedding into the wheelbarrow, toss it in the manure pile out by the woods, and then replace it with clean bedding.

"Are you from the city or…?" Poppi asked.

"Born and bred. My family is there."

"Then I guess there's no sense in trying to get you to convince Sophie to come back to Oak Falls permanently."

Brett smiled at that. "She loves the city, but she also loves being here. I think she's found a happy medium."

"That she has."

Thinking of Sophie, he said, "I wonder if you might be willing to teach me how to ride."

Poppi set aside the pitchfork and grabbed a shovel, using it to scoop up the remaining wet bedding. "Sounds like my granddaughter has gotten under your skin. I thought I saw the look of love in your eyes. That unmistakable look that makes smart men appear a bit...*vacant*."

"I'm not sure how I should take that." Brett laughed. "Vacant?"

"You know, *delirious*, like you don't know why you're doing what you're doing. The heart will make you forget things you never thought you could and remember things you never wanted to."

"Ain't that the truth," Brett said as he tossed a load of wet straw into the wheelbarrow.

"When you're a young man, another organ takes over your brain for a while. But in the end the heart leads you where you're supposed to be. I'd be honored to teach you to ride, especially for Sophie. Round these parts, kids learn when they're tykes. Let's get this chore done. Then we'll saddle up and see if we can make a real man out of you."

After they mucked the stalls and put the tools away, Poppi disappeared into the tack room and returned with two Hostess Ho Hos. He handed one to Brett and winked. "Don't go yappin' to my wife about these. She's got this thing about food that isn't made from the heart." He tore open the wrapper and bit off a hunk of the pastry. "Tastes mighty good to me."

"I have to admit, I've never had a Ho Ho." Brett bit into the spongy treat. "Not bad." *But not nearly as good as a slutty pumpkin bar.*

"Not bad my ass. These are delicious." Poppi pointed to the door at the back of the barn. "Go in there and put on my leather boots. I've got Ruthie all warmed up. I took her out for a short trail ride just after dawn."

"Really? You rode that early?" Brett asked.

"Absolutely, as I've done for many years. Now, get those cowboy boots on so I can make you into a real man."

Brett did as he asked and then followed Poppi out of the barn to a small riding ring, where a beautiful chestnut-colored horse was waiting.

"She's gorgeous. Can I pet her?"

Poppi made a clicking sound with his mouth, and the horse sauntered over and pressed her muzzle into his sternum. "How's my girl?" He stroked her jaw. "Ruthie's been with us twenty years. Get on over here and give her some love."

Brett came to his side.

"Talk to her like you might a potential lover."

Brett tried to figure out what that might sound like, and once he did, he wasn't sure he wanted to say it to a horse.

He must have taken too long to respond, because Poppi said, "I hope you weren't this nervous when you asked my Sophie out."

"I didn't get nervous with Sophie until I realized how much I liked her. Only then did it mess with my mind."

"That's that heart thing. It gets ya right in the britches." Poppi pet the horse and said, "Well, son, you gotta make friends with Ruthie before she'll let you ride, so go to it."

The horse appeared to be looking at Brett warily, as if she knew he was nervous. He didn't know why he was nervous, except maybe because he wanted to learn to ride because it was a part of Sophie's life and he didn't want to screw it up. It couldn't be harder than revealing his secrets had been.

"Hi there, Ruthie," he said, feeling a little silly for his hesitation.

"Get your hand up there and give her some love." Poppi took Brett's hand and set it on the horse's cheek. "Atta boy. She feels your hesitation. How on earth did you rope my granddaughter? Pull out your swagger, Brett. Make this girl feel safe.

Let her know you can handle her."

He'd never met a woman he couldn't handle, but he wasn't about to say that to his girlfriend's grandfather. Thoughts of Sophie brought a surge of confidence. "Don't you worry, Poppi. I'm a master at safety. I've got this." He gazed into the horse's big brown eyes and stroked her cheek. "Hey there, sweetheart. Think you can teach a city boy to ride?"

Ruthie's big head swung toward him, and he continued petting her. "That's a girl. I can ride a Harley, but Harleys don't buck, so you be good to me and I'll be extra nice to you." He turned to Poppi and asked, "What do you give a horse to thank them afterward?"

"Huh. You are good," Poppi said with a warm smile. "We brush them down real good, love 'em up."

"Great. I can do that." He continued talking with Ruthie, moving to her side as he pet her thick, strong neck. "What do you call this kind of horse?"

"She's a chestnut quarter horse with a flaxen mane and tail, but we call her part of the family." Poppy chuckled. "Some people choose their horses. Ruthie chose us. A friend was having financial problems and had to give up his farm. I went over to check out some equipment, and this little lady wanted all my attention. Once Nana saw that, she decided it was time to celebrate our newest family member."

"Nana's something else. Her zest for life is contagious."

A faraway look came over Poppi, and he cleared his throat. "Losing a child will do that to you."

"I'm sorry." Brett's gut clenched. He continued petting Ruthie as he said, "Sophie mentioned that you had a son you lost when he was young. I don't know if she told you, but I lost a sister, Lorelei, when she was eight. She would have loved your farm, and I imagine she'd be like Nana, squeezing every last drop of enjoyment out of every day."

"Sophie didn't share that with me. I'm sorry for yours and your family's loss. There's no greater pain than losing a loved one at any age." Sadness rose in Poppi's eyes. "Our Joey was a special boy, as I'm sure your sister was. He was with us for six wonderful years. He had a heart condition that went undetected. He was running with some boys after school and dropped on the field. They tried to revive him, but..." He shook his head.

Brett's throat thickened. "I'm sorry. We lost Lorelei to leukemia. It happened fast, and it tore us apart." He hesitated for only a moment before sharing, "Our family didn't make it through so well. Do you mind me asking how your marriage survived?"

Poppi leaned against the hitching post and pushed his hands into the front pockets of his jeans, gazing thoughtfully up at the house. "I used to wonder that myself. Joey was our firstborn, and as you can imagine, that boy was the light of our lives. When we lost him, Nana cried for four straight days. I was sure we were destined to live under a dark cloud. But one day she woke up and said, 'Joey was an amazing boy and we need to celebrate him. We need to appreciate all the things he can't.' She saved me with her outlook, that's for damn sure. I wanted to hole up and disappear. And then, like a miracle sent from the heavens, two weeks after we buried our son, Nana found out she was pregnant."

"Angel?" Brett said softly.

"Angel Josephine. Another reason not to disappear into grief." He stroked the horse's neck. "I'm sorry to hear your family didn't come through it whole."

"A piece of each of us was lost when she died, but it destroyed my father. Short of dying himself, I don't think anything could have kept him from falling apart."

"And you?" Poppi asked.

"I was a mess, too. Got into a lot of trouble between ten and twelve years old. I'm sure I added to my parents' grief."

"You were a boy dealing with a loss. Can't place blame on you for that. Losing a loved one can make you stronger, braver, more able to appreciate things in life, like Nana, or it can gnaw away at you like a wild animal. The middle ground is confusing as hell. When I found out Nana was pregnant with Angel, I wondered if I could handle it." He squared his shoulders. "If I had to do it all over again, I would, even knowing we'd lose Joey. Nothing and no one could have given us what Joey did in those six years."

Brett thought about Lorelei twirling in the front yard, holding her head up high as they paraded into the theater with him playing bodyguard. Dozens of memories flew at him at breakneck speed. Lorelei was one of a kind. He'd never thought in terms of whether he would go back and relive the same life again, because it was so painful to know what lay ahead. But now, hearing Poppi's confession, he thought he'd choose the same. But he'd work like hell to change his own behavior after she died. The trouble was, he knew he couldn't have changed it then, which meant he'd live the same troubled life over again. Sophie didn't deserve a troubled life, and he sure as hell didn't want one.

It was time to lay those ghosts to rest once and for all.

"What do you say we get you on this horse?" Poppi patted the saddle, pulling Brett from his thoughts.

"Sounds good to me." He felt closer to Poppi, and that made him feel closer to Sophie. "Thanks for talking with me and letting me into your family. I appreciate it."

Poppi put an arm around Brett's shoulder and said, "Son, we can let you in, but whether or not you choose to stay is up to you. Now, let me give you the lowdown on riding so you don't fall on your keister."

"Do I need to wear one of those awful helmets?"

"If you were on someone else's horse, or if I thought you were stupid enough to try to ride hard or bully Ruthie, yeah, you would. But I trust my girl here, and I trust you. Plus, I know how young guys like to look manly." He winked and said, "In my day, kids rode without saddles. Just don't do anything dumb."

After receiving a very thorough explanation about riding and safety, Poppi put a saddle on Ruthie, and then Brett mounted the horse. He gripped the reins the way he was told, aligned his body, and stroked Ruthie's mane. "How about this, girl? Make me look good, and I'll give you a nice rubdown when we get back."

Poppi said, "I used that line on my wedding night. Let's go make a man out of you."

"NANA, WE'VE BEEN cooking and baking for almost *two* hours. Brett's probably starved. I'm going to run breakfast down to him before he passes out." She grabbed a banana muffin.

"He's a man, honey. When he's hungry, he'll come knock-in'."

"Unless Poppi decided to have him build a new barn or something." She kissed Nana's cheek. "This has been fun. I can't wait to go pick apples at the orchard tomorrow. I wonder if Brett's ever done that."

"Doubt it. There aren't many orchards in the Big Apple." She laughed at her own joke and pulled a bottle of juice from the refrigerator. "Take some orange juice, and give me two seconds to wrap up some egg sandwiches for *our* men. They need protein."

Breeze went paws-up on the windowsill and barked.

"What is it, Breezy?" Sophie gazed out the window. Her grandfather was standing on the porch looking out at the yard. Her heart stumbled at the sight of Brett riding a horse toward the house. "Holy cow. Nana, you've got to see this!"

Nana sidled up to her as she put the wrapped sandwiches into a bag. "Well, look at that. Your city boy's looking a lot like a hunky cowboy right now."

"You're telling me!" Sophie pulled open the door and hurried outside. Brett Bad was a panty melter all on his own, but riding a horse? Wearing a black Stetson and cowboy boots? He scorched those panties right off.

"Hey there, darlin'." His cocky smile brought even more butterflies to her stomach.

She put her hand on his leg, feeling his muscles strain against the denim. "You're riding!"

"No, babe. *We're* riding."

Poppi put a hand on Sophie's back and set one of the chairs from the porch on the grass beside the horse. "Your man could have been born here, sweetheart. He's a quick learner and a damn good rider. Climb on up."

"I can't believe it!" She climbed onto the horse behind Brett and put her arms around him. He smelled like the summer days of her youth, familiar and happy, with a hint of pure, masculine yumminess.

"Do you want to take breakfast?" Nana held up the paper

bag.

Poppi put his arm around her and said, "I think these two could survive on the love between them."

"True, but we might be out for a while and need the nourishment." Brett reached for the bag. He turned and kissed Sophie. "Ready, beautiful?"

"For *anything*." She held him a little tighter.

His hand covered hers as he tipped his hat to Poppi and Nana and said, "Pretend we're riding off into the sunset."

They rode through the pasture to the trails Poppi had taken Sophie on when she was a girl. When they came to the meadow where she did her first cartwheel, Ruthie slowed to a walk.

"Whoa, girl," Brett said, bringing her to a halt. He dismounted and reached up to help Sophie down. "We survived."

"We more than survived. That was the hugest aphrodisiac *ever*."

"Mm," he said against her neck as he placed a kiss there. "I told you, I'm going to fulfill all your fantasies, sexy girl."

She pushed her hands beneath his shirt. His skin was hot, his muscles hard, and when she gazed into his eyes, she saw just what her touch was doing to him—and loved it.

"Careful, baby. There're no trees around here. I've got no place to tie up the horse."

"Who needs to tie her up? All you have to do is stand there." She dragged her hands down his abs and hooked her finger into the waist of his jeans. "Have I told you about my cowboy fantasy?"

His eyes smoldered.

"Don't let go of the reins, big boy…" She unbuttoned his jeans and pressed a kiss to his stomach, then proceeded to fulfill a steamy fantasy she hadn't even known she possessed until her panty scorcher rode up on the horse.

Chapter Seventeen

BRETT PACKED HIS clothes Tuesday evening, listening to the sounds of Sophie and her family floating up from downstairs. They were leaving the next day, and the end of their visit was bittersweet. After being woken up at the crack of dawn by *Nana the Curtain Opener*, Brett had learned how to milk a cow. He'd helped with the barn chores, and Nana had made an elaborate breakfast. He and Poppi put up motion-sensor lights on their house and on Sophie's parents' house. They spent the rest of the day picking apples at an orchard with her grandparents and baking. Brett thought Dylan, who loved to bake and who Brett loved to tease about it, would get a kick out of hearing he'd spent the day in the kitchen. The banter between Nana and Poppi had Brett in stitches, but it was the intimate moments he and Sophie shared as they worked side by side cutting apples and measuring ingredients, pouring love into the food, that made him want even more than they already had together.

"Daydreaming? Isn't that my sister's job?" Lindsay walked into the bedroom carrying a small stack of his and Sophie's clothes.

"Shoot. We forgot to throw those into the dryer. I'm sorry." He took the clothes and put them in his bag.

"No worries. Mom threw them in for you." She sat on the

edge of the bed and tucked a sock that was hanging over the edge of the bag back inside. "I heard Sophie talking to Grace on the phone earlier. You know she's head over heels for you, right?"

He zipped up his luggage. "It's mutual, Lindsay. You don't need to read me the protective-sister act. I promise I'm not going to hurt her."

"I wasn't going to." She rose to her feet again, and her gaze softened. "I just wanted to be sure you knew."

"I can't hide my feelings either. How could I miss hers?"

"From what I've heard, you can be a little slow on the up-take." She smiled with the tease. "Seriously, though. I'm glad you're in her life. I've never seen her this happy. And what you did for her in the barn? It *almost* makes me wish I wanted a long-term relationship."

Brett laughed. "I couldn't have coordinated that night without your help. Thank you. And as far as forever goes, love hits when you're busy trying to avoid it, so watch out."

"I'm pretty love repellent. Hurry down or you might not get any dessert. Your girlfriend has a thing for whipped cream and hot apple pie."

As she left the bedroom, he mentally added whipped cream to his grocery list.

He went to the window and gazed out at her backyard, thinking about what he'd said to Lindsay about avoiding love and realized it wasn't really true. When he'd rushed to the airport, avoiding anything having to do with Sophie wasn't anywhere near his radar screen. But there was one thing he *had* been avoiding for too many years to count, and he wouldn't have imagined it had anything to do with falling in love. But he would have been wrong, because the more deeply in love he fell with Sophie, the more he wanted her world to be everything she'd ever dreamed of. If he had a hope in hell of offering that to her, he needed to deal with the ghosts of his past.

He needed to deal with his father and try to mend the fences he'd broken. His mother had long ago forgiven him for his recklessness, but he'd never even tried to heal the pain he'd caused his father. Mick was probably right about the demise of their family, but that didn't negate the truth of how Brett had acted in the years following Lorelei's death. There was a great deal of shame that came along with that confession—including the thing that hurt most. If Lorelei had been able to see him in those destructive years, she'd have seen a brother she wouldn't have looked up to.

He set his bag on the floor beside Sophie's, determined to right his wrongs, and headed downstairs. He went slowly, taking in the pictures of Sophie and her friends and family. He recognized a few more faces now. He stopped midway down the steps at the sight of the picture he'd given Sophie of the two of them standing in his mother's backyard. His chest constricted, but now he knew that was love, a feeling that no longer felt foreign. He didn't think it was possible to fall in love with a family other than his own, but it was happening just as effortlessly as he'd fallen in love with Sophie.

The smell of baked apples and cinnamon surrounded him like an embrace as he came to the bottom step, and his heart took another hit. Hanging on the wall was a picture of him and Sophie standing beneath the willow tree, moonlight raining down on them. He was cradling Sophie's face in his hands, gazing into her eyes. How had Lindsay captured the moment he'd told Sophie he loved her? He took a moment to soak it all in. He was in love, and it was as real and undeniable as Lorelei's death.

He followed the sounds of the others into the kitchen and found Nana and Angel chatting while they sliced pie and doled out ice cream. Lindsay was ladling dollops of whipped cream on top. Del and Poppi stood by the patio door talking, and Brett spotted Sophie heading up from the creek with a handful of wildflowers.

"Thank you for hanging up the pictures of me and Sophie," he said to Lindsay.

Lindsay smiled. "I don't think we'll need screws for those."

"I have no idea how you timed it so perfectly, or how you could have gotten out there without us seeing you, but I'd really like a copy of that picture for our house."

"*Our* house?" Lindsay arched a brow, and the kitchen grew quiet.

He hadn't even realized he'd said it. He didn't want to go back to two separate residences, not after spending this time together. He shrugged and smiled. "Slip of the tongue."

"We like tongue slips," Nana said as Sophie came in the door.

He imagined his brothers there, eating pie and making snappy retorts to Nana, and it made him almost as happy as Sophie walking into his arms.

"Hey, flower girl. You've been busy. Did you see the picture Lindsay took of us?"

"Yes. It made me cry."

"Aw." He brushed a kiss over her cheek. "Happy tears are good tears."

"Tongue slips are even better," Nana said as she passed by on her way to the table carrying two plates of pie.

"Nana!" Sophie gave Brett a chaste kiss and put the flowers

in a vase her mother had filled with water. "Thanks, Mom."

Angel set the vase on the table and everyone sat down. "I can't believe you guys are leaving tomorrow. I'm really glad we got this extra time with both of you."

"I've had a wonderful time. Thank you." Brett pulled out a chair for Sophie, then sat beside her.

"You'll be back in a few weeks for the Halloween shindig," Nana said.

"Halloween shindig?" he asked.

"Celebrate every holiday, remember?" Poppi said with a confirming nod.

"And then there's Thanksgiving and Christmas. Oh, and New Year's Eve. That's a biggie around here." Nana ate a forkful of pie "Mm-mm."

"Nana, Brett might want to spend the holidays with his family," Angel reminded her. "But, Brett, I hope you know you're welcome to join us. In fact, you're welcome to bring your family here and we can all celebrate together if you'd like."

Brett reached for Sophie's hand and squeezed it gently. "Thank you. I guess we have some decisions to make."

"Don't feel any pressure to—" Sophie said.

"*Feel* pressure," Nana interrupted. "Pressure to be included in family celebrations is good! We already got one slip of the tongue."

"What…?" Sophie's brow wrinkled in confusion.

Brett lifted a forkful of pie to Sophie's lips in an effort to change the subject. She took the bite, and he caught Nana chuckling.

They ate too much pie, talked about Nana and Angel's plans for upcoming celebrations, and Lindsay made Nana promise not to bring any prospective suiters to future parties.

Even knowing Nana for the short time he had, Brett had a feeling Nana was already making lists of men for Lindsay, who was probably next on her matchmaking list.

A while later, they stood on the front porch saying goodbye to Lindsay, Nana, and Poppi.

"Swing by for a brown-bag breakfast." Nana gave Brett a hug and pinched his cheek. "My friend Cora did an online search of you. It seems you're even more impressive than you are charming. A real *catch*. But so is our Sophie. I'm glad you two have found each other. Take care of her in that big city."

"I'm not sure I'm such a catch, but I only need one woman to believe I am." He gathered Sophie in his arms and said, "She's my number one priority, Nana, but Sophie's a strong, capable woman. She did fine before I came along."

"Of course she did," Lindsay said. "You can't grow up here and not be a badass." She hugged Sophie. "But unlike me, most people like knowing someone's watching out for them."

Brett embraced her. "I guess you want me to send a security crew to your house to shore up your windows and doors?"

"Why on earth would she want that?" Sophie asked.

He winked at Lindsay and said, "We wouldn't want anything sneaking in while she's trying to avoid it."

Chapter Eighteen

AFTER RETURNING FROM Virginia Wednesday afternoon, Brett and Sophie stopped at her apartment to pick up a few things for the next couple of nights before heading over to Brett's. Usually when she returned home she flopped on the couch and called Grace, happy to regain her footing in her own space. But this time she couldn't wait to submerge herself in Brett's world, although as he opened his front door, butterflies swarmed in her belly.

The scent of leather and something spicy greeted them. Sophie's gaze swept over the rich, hardwood floors and rough brick walls, brown leather couches that sat low to the floor, and an enormous granite coffee table. Around the perimeter of the living room, several heavy floor lamps had metal casings that looked like scaffolding, interesting wooden bases, and spotlight housings. Spotlight-type sconces were placed along the far wall, where a metal staircase ran up to a second story. A black leather armchair and ottoman sat beneath a tangle of lights in a corner by one of the nearly floor-to-ceiling windows. Beside it, a wooden crate with heavy metal clasps was home to a few workout magazines.

"Why am I so nervous?" she asked as Brett dropped their bags by the door. She saw the kitchen through an archway in the brick wall, all clean lines and lighted cabinets. Several potted plants sat atop one of the expansive counters beside a bank of windows. The kitchen looked as big as her apartment.

He put his arm around her, nuzzling against her neck, and said, "Because you know I want to do dirty things to you on every surface."

"Nope. I counted on that, though." She pressed her lips to his, then glanced around the room. Every piece of furniture, even the walls and floors, appeared substantial and elegant, yet subdued, not showy. His home wasn't intimidating or terribly inviting, and she wondered if that was because he had been so unsettled his whole life. She had the sense that he lived here, but he'd never put down roots and made it his home.

"Then why *are* you nervous, babe? You know I don't bring women here, so it's not like there's anything to be jealous of."

"Maybe because of *that*. Not jealousy, but this is your private space and you're letting me in. That's *huge*."

"Not as huge as meeting your parents. Or making love to you in their barn. Or telling you I love you under their forever-kiss tree."

He brushed his lips over hers. She closed her eyes and whispered, "I love you."

She felt him smiling and went up on her toes to steal a real kiss. His mouth pressed firmly against hers, warm and hungry.

As he trailed kisses along her cheek, his husky voice swaggered into her ear. "I have something *huge* to show you."

He sank his teeth into her earlobe just hard enough to sting deliciously. She heard him groan. Why, oh why, was that such an aphrodisiac? She drew back, meeting the inferno in his eyes.

"Are you trying to distract me from being nervous? Because it's working really well."

"I can't help myself around you. Maybe we should go for

Naked Wednesdays instead of Naked Saturdays." He lifted up the edge of her sweater and pushed his hand beneath, palming her breast.

"I'm not sure Mick will think that's appropriate since I work on Wednesdays." That earned a brooding stare and he tweaked her nipple. She gasped and tugged him down by the collar of his T-shirt. "You're so jealous. It's kind of cute."

"I'll show you cute." He swept her into his arms and looked around the room like he wasn't sure where he should *take* her. Mumbling something about a theater, he carried her down a hallway.

She kissed his neck, then the prickly scruff along his jaw, and he made another greedy noise as they entered a dark room. He lowered her to an enormous couch that felt cold like leather and came down over her.

His eyes shimmered in the darkness. "You have never made out in a theater, right?"

"You have a home theater?" She leaned up, surveying their surroundings as her eyes adjusted to the dark. There was a row of recliners behind them, which sat higher than the couch. An old reel-to-reel projector sat off to the side on a tall table, and the walls were covered with old movie and Broadway posters set in elaborate frames. "Wow."

"I'd rather hear that when I take my clothes off."

"Oh, you will," she promised, still looking around.

He touched her cheek, bringing her attention back to him. "Would you like to see the room, baby? Maybe watch a movie?"

"Yes, I'd like to see it. You can't take me into your private theater and expect me not to want to see this secret side of you."

"I was getting ready to show you the secret side of me." He picked up a remote lying on a table beside the sofa and pushed a button, illuminating a blank wall in front of them and several artistically angled, dimly lit fixtures throughout the rest of the room.

"Your *secret* is about as safe as Victoria's," she said as she pushed to her feet.

He pulled her down onto his lap and kissed her passionately. "I happen to like Victoria's Secret." He pushed his hand beneath her dress, running his fingers over her panties. "And from the lingerie you wear, I believe you do, too."

"Maybe so," she whispered, "but I like your not-so-secret secret much better. I've seen enough movie room. *Secret* now, please." She straddled his lap as the room went dark.

SEVERAL INCREDIBLE ORGASMS and one pizza delivery later, Sophie lay in Brett's arms on the couch watching a movie, their bodies intertwined. Dylan had called earlier and invited them to watch football at his place on Sunday. Sophie couldn't get over how happy Dylan was about the two of them coming together. It felt like ages since she'd seen everyone, even though the perfumery opening was only two weeks ago. She felt like they'd been away for a month. A very long, wonderful month, and she wasn't ready to go back to real life. She hated the idea of spending several hours apart when she'd gotten used to seeing and kissing Brett anytime she wanted. They'd become so in sync and comfortable with each other, she wondered if anything would change once real life crept in.

"Have lunch with me tomorrow?" he asked. "I can't go cold turkey for eight-plus hours."

He nipped at her shoulder. She couldn't get enough of those love bites!

"I'd really like that." She turned toward him and said, "Careful, Mr. Bad. Your commitment is showing."

He tightened his hold on her. "I'd like to put it in lights, or on a billboard. 'Sophie Roberts is Taken.'"

"Only if I get one claiming you as mine, too." She closed her eyes, snuggling closer. Real life could creep in all it wanted. It had nothing on them.

Chapter Nineteen

THE NEXT FEW days moved by too slowly, and the nights too quickly. Sophie and Brett had been staying at his place ever since they'd gotten back in town. Sophie was the joy at the end of his workday, the light to his dark, worrying thoughts about going to see his father. She'd even become his workout partner, which usually ended up with them rolling around naked, and he realized he no longer felt the need to beat his body into submission. But yesterday morning Sophie had gone to work out with Grace, and he'd gone running with his brothers. He'd almost told them about wanting to go see their father, but he'd held back because he knew they felt their father was, for the most part, a lost cause. Now, as they rode the elevator up to Dylan and Tiffany's apartment to watch the game Sunday afternoon, Brett second-guessed himself. He didn't like keeping secrets, especially from his family.

Sophie put her arms around his neck and he crushed his mouth to hers, hoping to escape the worry and stress of his decision, but she drew back almost instantly.

"What's wrong?" Sophie gazed deeply into his eyes. "You've been edgy all week, and that kiss…" She touched her lips to his again, softer, like a test, and shook her head. "Talk to me."

He should have known better than to try to escape his torment with kisses from his forever-kiss girl. He'd told her the other day that he was thinking about talking to his father, and she'd thought it was a good idea. She'd even offered to go with him. But this was something he needed to do on his own, though her support meant the world to him.

He took her hand as the elevator doors opened, and they headed for Dylan's apartment. "I was thinking about telling my brothers that I might go see our father."

"Oh, you should. They love you, and I'm sure they'll support you."

Brett stopped walking and said, "Baby, we talked about this. My father has been an ass for years. You think love and support comes easily and unconditionally because it's all you know, but there are so many hurt feelings between him and all of us, it's not like that. If it feels right, I'll tell them. If not, I'll go see my father and figure it out from there. I'm sorry I've been edgy, but I have a feeling I might be until I deal with this."

She took his face between her hands, went up on her toes in her skintight jeans and pretty black sweater, and kissed him passionately, taking his edginess down a notch.

When their lips parted she said, "It's a good thing I like edgy sex."

He chuckled and claimed her luscious mouth again, reveling in their closeness.

"You know hearing those words from your sexy mouth makes me hard." He pressed his hips to hers, and she grinned like a Cheshire cat.

"I like edgy sex," she said tauntingly, running her hands over his pecs. "*Dirty* sexy." She grabbed his ass. "Sweet sex, movie-room sex—"

He grabbed her hand and dragged her toward the elevator.

"What are you doing?" she asked through her laughter.

"Adding—and checking off—another item to our fantasy list." He pushed the elevator button repeatedly. "Elevator sex."

He backed her up against the wall, claiming her mouth again, his worries forgotten, replaced with white-hot desire. When the elevator doors opened, they stumbled toward it—and bumped into Mick and Amanda. Sophie drew back so fast you'd think she'd gotten burned.

"Mick," she said, her cheeks flaming.

Brett hauled her against him again. "It's okay, baby. He might be your boss, but he's also a husband. He gets it."

Mick was more reserved and refined than Brett. Where Brett would have instantly made a joke had he found one of his brothers in the same position, Mick casually put his arm around Amanda, who looked sweet and embarrassed in a pink sweater and jeans, and with a careful expression, said, "He's right, Sophie. I told you at the office I was okay with this. No need to be embarrassed."

Her eyes shifted nervously. "There's a big difference between being okay with me and Brett as a couple and seeing us practically tearing each other's clothes off."

"It was totally hot," Amanda said, breaking the tension.

"We are hot," Brett said, and tried to joke away Sophie's embarrassment. "Now that elevator sex is out, we might as well head to Dylan's."

"Elevator sex?" Amanda said softly. "You'd have to push the stop button or be *very* fast." She wrinkled her nose as if she were analyzing the possibilities. Rumors had it that when Amanda had wanted to learn how to seduce a man, she'd thoroughly researched the topic before taking her chances. She was the perfect woman for Mick, who was as academic as he was sexual.

Mick's dark eyes heated up. He kissed the top of Amanda's

head and said, "We'll conduct our own research."

"Oh God." Sophie turned away, her cheeks pinking up again. "Can we go see the others now, and move on to a subject where neither my boss nor I have to think about the other one in compromising positions?"

"You know Brett saw Tiffany naked, right?" Amanda asked as Mick knocked on Dylan's door.

"Thanks, Amanda." Brett shook his head, remembering the awkward situation. Tiffany had hoped to surprise Dylan by showing up at his apartment wearing nothing more than a belted coat. She had opened the belt to flash Dylan, but unfortunately, Brett had answered the door. Her seductive surprise had gone downhill from there. But she'd earned a level of respect from Brett. He wanted happiness for his brothers, and Dylan had needed a woman who could own up to embarrassing moments, as Tiffany had the next time she'd seen him.

"Can we please let that unfortunate incident be forgotten?" Brett asked. "That image has already been deleted from my memory."

"I heard about that, and I felt bad for Tiffany," Sophie said as Dylan answered the door.

"Hey, you guys. Glad you could make it, Sophie." Dylan hugged her and said, "It's about time my brother got his head on straight."

"Dude, I can hear you," Brett said flatly, though Dylan was right. He followed Sophie in, while Dylan greeted Mick and Amanda. Carson and Tawny were in the kitchen, filling bowls with chips and pretzels. Adeline was with Brett's mother, having a grandmother-granddaughter day, and Brett was sure they were both having the time of their lives. His mother doted on Adeline like she used to dote on them.

Tawny's eyes moved between Brett and Sophie, and she did a little shimmy dance, grinning from ear to ear. "I'm so happy right now." She hugged Sophie. "I saw Brett watching you at the grand opening of Cashmere, and I told Carson there was no way you two wouldn't end up together."

"They were about to have sex in the elevator," Amanda said as she and Tiffany joined them in the kitchen.

Sophie turned beet red. "Amanda!"

Brett took a step forward, wanting to rescue her, but Dylan put a hand on his arm and dragged him into the living room. Brett looked over his shoulder.

"Elevator sex?" Tiffany said incredulously. "That's old-school. You should try the roof of the building. Or the balcony!"

Speaking low, Dylan said, "You've got to let them induct her into the world of Bad women."

"She doesn't like to talk about this stuff," Brett snapped, and tried to return to Sophie's side, but Dylan grabbed his arm and glared at him.

"You have no idea what women talk about, Mr. Control Freak. She's a big girl. Let her be."

Brett's gaze darted to Sophie, who was now talking privately with the girls. She looked completely comfortable, which put him at ease. "I just don't want them to make her feel weird."

"I'm sure you do enough of that yourself," Carson said, and set a bowl of pretzels on the coffee table. He handed Brett a beer. "It looks like going home with Sophie did you a world of good."

"Yeah, you could say that." *It was life changing.* Brett sat down on the opposite side of the couch from Mick, who was doing something on his cell phone. Dylan sat in the recliner, and Carson claimed the love seat, his gaze darting to his beautiful redheaded wife in the kitchen.

"The guys said you didn't check in once while you were away." Carson brought his attention back to Brett. "Good job. Maybe Sophie can break you of your micromanaging ways."

Brett scoffed. "When I'm with Soph, not much else matters."

Mick looked up from his phone with a serious expression. "That's how it's supposed to be."

"Says the man giving his full attention to answering emails on his phone," Dylan chimed in.

Mick set his phone on the coffee table and glanced into the kitchen. "Just arranging a weekend away with Amanda." He held a finger over his lips.

"Don't let Adeline hear you're planning to go away or she'll ask if she can go with you," Carson said with a warm smile.

"Adeline was a big eye opener for me," Mick said. "Amanda and I have decided to try to start our family."

"Seriously? That's awesome." Brett held Mick's gaze for an extra beat as Dylan and Carson congratulated him. Before proposing to Amanda, Mick had told Brett he was afraid to take their relationship further because Amanda wanted children, and like Brett, Mick didn't. He thought about how easily his response had come, and how quickly he'd judged his brother. *Of course she does. She's a chick. She's got ovaries and a uterus and hormones that make her want all sorts of things. A white picket fence. A dog. Flowers and shit.* He'd told Mick he was being absurd.

Brett glanced at Sophie, leaning against the counter with a wineglass in her hand, talking with the girls. She must have felt the heat of his gaze, because she looked over with that sweet, trusting look in her eyes that turned his insides to mush. *God, baby. I love you so much.* It was no secret that Sophie wanted children—or that he didn't. He felt sick at the thought of loving a child and possibly losing it. But after spending time with Sophie's family, he realized how short-sighted that was.

Tawny said something that drew Sophie's attention, and there was a collective laugh, followed by a hushed conversation.

Brett's gaze moved over each of his brother's faces. They were talking about having kids and what life was like with Adeline. Dylan said he and Tiffany were also thinking about starting a family. Their father had been at their wedding, though he'd left shortly after the ceremony. Maybe Sophie was right and they'd support his need to clear the air.

"So, um," Brett said, curling his hands into fists. "I wanted to let you guys know that I'm thinking about going to see Dad."

Silence descended on the living room, and three sets of dark eyes and serious, doubting faces turned toward him. Brett's statement hung in the silence like a ghost that had come back to haunt.

"Brett, we talked about this," Mick said as sternly and confidently as only an eldest brother could. "You don't owe Dad anything."

Brett held his stare, but it was like looking in a strange mirror that included the image of their father, as he and Mick both shared their father's deep-set eyes and strong, square jaw. "I think you're wrong. I might not owe him what I thought I did, but I owe him an apology. I was a prick after we lost Lorelei, and whether or not that made him worse doesn't really matter. What matters is that if I'm ever going to give her"—he glanced into the kitchen, then quickly back at Mick and lowered his voice—"the life she deserves, I have to deal with my own shit."

"Wait," Dylan said. "What are we talking about? *Owing* Dad what?"

"I don't know exactly," Brett said. "An apology for being a prick, I think, but maybe more. Or maybe I'll get there and feel what I've felt all these years, too much resentment to say anything nice. I don't fucking know. Maybe I'll go off on him. Whatever happens, *happens*, but I need to try to bridge the gap between us."

His brothers stared at him without saying a word. Brett's chest constricted as the seconds ticked by, but he wasn't going to be waylaid.

"I'll go with you," Carson offered, causing all those stares to shift to him. He shrugged and said, "I don't think it's a bad idea. We lost Lorelei as a family, and whether we like to admit it or not, Dad's family. *Our* family, and knowing how cutting he can be, I'm not letting one of us face him alone."

Brett cleared his throat in an attempt to move past the emotions clogging it.

"You're right," Dylan said. "Dad's softened since the fundraiser, so maybe it's not a bad idea. I'll go with you, too, but don't expect miracles."

"If he and I both come out of the room alive, that'll be a miracle," Brett said, shifting uneasily on the couch. "But I need to go alone. With you guys around I'll feel caged, and I either won't say what I want to say, or I'll blow up. I appreciate the offer, though."

Mick stewed in silence.

"Mick, I'm doing this for me and Sophie, not just for Dad."

"I was there, Brett, remember? I saw and heard everything he did. You are *not* to blame for a damn thing." Mick cracked his knuckles and leaned forward, elbows on knees. "I get why you're doing it, and I'll admit that Amanda and I talked about my doing the same thing."

"I don't want to talk, Mick. I need to do this for my own sanity." Brett leaned closer to him, holding his gaze, and said, "You know Sophie wants kids. How can I be a good father if I still resent my own?"

Mick put an arm around Brett and pulled him closer. "I get it, brother. I should do the same."

"How about we see if I survive first?" Brett cleared his throat again as the girls came into the room, and he pulled Sophie down beside him. He kissed her, then whispered, "Missed you."

"What were all the serious faces about? Is Brett worried he isn't going to survive coupledom?" Tiffany teased as Dylan pulled her down on his lap.

Brett kissed Sophie again, already feeling more at ease, and said, "Survive it? I'm going to be Sophie's great love story."

SOPHIE HAD WONDERED if things would be weird around Brett's family now that she and Brett were a couple, but the girls were as excited about them as she was, and his brothers acted like they were a given. The afternoon flew by amid laughter and smart-ass banter as they watched the football game. It wasn't so different from watching football with her own family, except that Brett's brothers and sisters-in-law were kissing and touching as much as she and Brett were. Love resonated off of each couple, but Brett's love felt more intense, like she was a million times more important than the football game or anything anyone else said. He was constantly whispering in her ear about what he'd like to do to her later and running his hands along her leg. She spent the entire football game hot and bothered, and the darkness of Brett's eyes told her it was exactly what he'd hoped for. Two could play at that game, and she made a mental note to torture him next time they were around her family.

He brushed her hair over her shoulder and whispered, "You. Me. Bathroom." Then he whipped out his phone and pulled her in for a selfie. She was sure her cheeks were bright red. He took another picture, kissing her smack on the lips this time. All three of his brothers looked over. As if he couldn't have cared less, he put his hand on the nape of her neck, drawing her cheek to his, and whispered, "You on the bathroom sink, me on my knees. Meet you in there."

Lust seared through her.

"Selfies?" Dylan said with wide eyes. "Never thought I'd see the day when you took selfies."

Brett held Sophie's gaze, his eyes simmering with heat.

"Leave him alone," Tiffany said. "You always complain that he's not in touch with his feelings. Now he is."

"I've always been in touch with my feelings, just not the girlie ones Dylan is in touch with." Brett squeezed Sophie's hand and said, "I was thinking, how about if Sophie and I host football next weekend? Is that all right with you, Soph?"

"Yeah, great." She loved the idea of hosting the get-together. *Maybe then we can sneak into your bedroom...*

"Really?" Carson asked, snapping her from her fantasy.

"Do you even know what *hosting* means?" Dylan teased. "Do you have enough plates and silverware for more than one person?"

Brett scoffed and pushed to his feet. "I'm going to use your bathroom instead of smacking you in the head. You can apologize when I get back." He blew a kiss to Sophie and headed down the hall.

Everyone looked at Sophie with inquisitive expressions. *Shit.* Had they heard what he'd whispered? "What? Hasn't he ever had you guys over for football before?"

Mick and Amanda said "No" in unison.

"Brett can't take off if we're all at his place," Carson explained. "He has a hard time staying in one place for too long. We were all pretty surprised that he went to your parents' house, much less stayed longer than he'd planned."

The girls had told her that Brett had never brought a woman with him to watch football and that he usually left early. None of that surprised her, because she knew how he was about feeling boxed in. *Or rather, how he used to feel about it.* She fidgeted nervously with the seam of her jeans, wondering why Brett thought she'd be able to meet him in the bathroom without everyone knowing *why*. The elevator was beginning to look mighty good.

Dylan hiked a thumb over his shoulder toward the hallway. "I don't know who that guy is, taking selfies, offering to host next week, whispering in your ear, but he reminds me a lot of the brother I had many years ago."

"He does?" Sophie asked, giving up on the idea of meeting Brett in the bathroom. She'd seen so many changes in Brett since they'd first come together, she knew she was seeing even more of the real Brett on a daily basis. He was still the same sexual, confident man he'd always been, but his arrogance had morphed to heightened confidence, and he smiled more often. It was almost as if that arrogance had been a shield to keep people out as much as it was to draw them closer to his boundaries—close enough to get what he wanted and far enough to walk away afterward.

His brothers murmured in agreement as Dylan got up and surprised her with a hug.

"Geez," Mick said with a chuckle. "Sit down, you fool."

"What?" Dylan went to sit with Tiffany again. "You can't tell me he's not different."

Mick sipped his beer. "I was laughing at your dramatics, not whether he's changed. We're all thrilled you're in Brett's life, Sophie. You're obviously just what he needed, and you've gotten to him in a way no one has for a very long time."

"Thank you. He's such a good person," Sophie said. "I love his intensity, his impulsiveness, his sense of humor, and the way his brain is always churning. He's got the biggest heart of any man I know, and I realize he thinks he hides that well. But when I look at him, sometimes it's all I see."

"You really do see him for who he is beneath all the show-manship, don't you? I've never seen him so happy," Carson added, "or so—"

"Determined to figure my shit out?" Brett interrupted, his eyes locking on Sophie as he strode down the hall looking ridiculously sexy.

Would she ever get used to the fact that the fine specimen of a man was *hers*? She felt greedy, wanting to go home and tear off his clothes so they could drive each other crazy.

"I was going to say *settled*, but..." Carson lifted his beer in a toast. "Determined works."

As if he'd read her mind, Brett reached for her hand with a devilish look in his eyes.

She adored that look!

He pulled her up to her feet and said, "Sorry to cut our visit short, but we've got to take off." His hand slid to her butt, and he held on tight. Luckily, she was facing the others and they couldn't see his hand moving lower, playing between her legs.

She tried to mask her desire as everyone got up to say good-bye.

Brett pulled her toward the door. "I'll text you about next Sunday, but count on being at our place for the game."

Then they were in the hall and his mouth was on hers, her back against the wall as they made out like they'd been apart for months. They kissed their way to the elevators, and when the doors opened, they both drew back and stared into each other's eyes. Desire and naughtiness erupted between them. Brett took Sophie's hand and pulled her into the elevator. Adrenaline surged through her veins.

The door closed, and Brett hit the stop button. Sophie slammed her eyes closed, expecting an alarm to sound. When no alarm came, her eyes flew open and a secret agreement passed between them. He crushed his mouth to hers, devouring her as they worked the button on each other's jeans and tugged them down. Brett fished out a condom from his wallet and rolled it on in record speed. He lifted her in his arms, and then he was buried deep inside her.

Brett groaned, low and sexy. "Christ, baby. I want to live inside you."

"I'm so nervous we'll get caught. Kiss me until I can't think."

He stopped short of kissing her and said, "I want you to think, and feel, and be so consumed with us you remember every second of this."

"Then you better not kiss me. Because I lose myself in your kisses every time."

His eyes smoldered, and he lowered his mouth to her neck.

"Oh, Lord. It's not just your kisses. It's your mouth," she said breathily.

"The hell with remembering."

He pulled her mouth to his, and she couldn't have held on to a thought if she were given a leash.

Chapter Twenty

BRETT WENT ALL out on his heavy bag Thursday morning while Sophie got ready for work. She had an early meeting, which was just as well, because he was seeing his father at ten, and his body was all knotted up, like his pre-Sophie days. As he took out his anxiety on the heavy bag, he told himself Sophie was worth every freaking painful minute of what was yet to come. And he knew it would be painful, which was probably why his father had suggested his office when Brett called to ask for a meeting. Not a bad idea with two hotheads. Then again, when had an office environment ever stopped Brett from a damn thing?

He heard the familiar clicking of Sophie's heels approaching and wiped the sweat from his brow. She came into the gym carrying a bath towel and a jug of ice water, looking smart and sexy in a pair of killer heels, a tight gray skirt, a white blouse, and a blue blazer. Her hair looked in need of his fingers. Oh wait, that was just his itchy fingers talking. A sweet smile played at her lips. She didn't wear a lot of makeup, but she usually wore lipstick to work. This morning her lips were bare, which meant he could kiss her to his heart's content.

That could take all day.

All year.

A lifetime.

"Hey, babe?" She set the jug of ice water on the floor and began dabbing the sweat from his cheeks with the towel.

"Is this a hint that I should shower right this second?"

She laughed softly and shook her head, easing the knots inside him as she continued dabbing at the back of his neck and shoulders. Her eyes flicked up to his as she slowly, sensually, wiped down his chest.

"You know what this does to me," he warned as she moved around him and wiped his back and shoulders, then returned to the front and crouched as she wiped down his legs. His cock twitched eagerly. "Soph, if you have to be at work early, this isn't a good idea."

She stood and began taking off his fingerless gloves. She held them up between her fingers and thumb, her baby blues locked on him, and dropped the gloves to the floor. Then she wound her arms around his neck, and a dreamy sigh slipped out. He knew it was a purposeful sigh by the heat flaming in her eyes.

"I know you're anxious about seeing your dad today, and I also know that our kisses help calm you down."

She brushed her lips lightly over his, then ran her tongue along the seam. Lust blazed through his core, and he captured her mouth in a hungry, possessive kiss. She was light and lightning, sweet and spicy. She was goddamn mind-blowing.

"You've got me all fired up, baby."

"I counted on that, too."

She kissed a trail along his jaw, and then her lips met his again in a kiss so needful and hungry he couldn't resist fisting his hands in her hair and tugging hard enough to earn an erotic gasp. Christ, he was so hard he ached to be inside her.

He tore his mouth away and said, "Baby, getting me all hot

and bothered isn't going to help me relax."

"I know…" She splayed her hands on his chest and kissed his shoulder and then the center of his chest. "I thought a little morning workout fantasy might go a long way."

She licked his nipple, then sucked hard.

"Fuck," he ground out.

Her skillful hands caressed and groped. Her nails dug into his flesh as she tasted his ribs and abs, the muscles by his hips. When she kissed the skin just above his shorts and bit into it, his hips bucked.

"Sophie, if you do that, you're going to be late," he said through gritted teeth. "Please tell me that ice water isn't for dousing me."

"It was in case you were too upset to let me touch you."

Damn, his girl thought of everything. Didn't she know that time would never come?

"Never," he growled.

Her brows lifted, and then her eyes narrowed, darkening like the sea. She yanked down his shorts, freeing his erection. "And look at this." Her fingers circled his shaft. "I've just arrived at my morning appointment."

Holy. Fuck.

She crouched lower, licking his balls and dragging her tongue along his shaft repeatedly, until it was nice and wet. Then she returned her attention to his balls, loving him with her mouth as she stroked his cock. His eyes closed, legs tensed, his fingers still buried in her hair as she licked and sucked, making one sinful, appreciative sound after another. When she lavished the head of his cock with that hot mouth of hers, he opened his eyes and couldn't hold back.

"Suck me, baby. Take me hard and deep."

What a sight she was, her full lips spread around his cock, her tongue slicking out along the head, one hand fondling his balls, the other following her mouth up and down in a mind-numbing rhythm.

"Sophie—" He pulled her up by her arms and captured her mouth in a plundering kiss. "Need you, baby."

She shook her head as they kissed. "No."

"No?" He drew back, flabbergasted. "Why?"

She moved lower, kissing as she went. "Because I want you to have motivation to be strong today."

"Fuck," he panted out. "Baby, you make me weak."

She giggled. "You're so wrong. I've never known a man stronger than you. That's why you're going to come in my mouth now." She lifted her gaze to his as she took his hard length in her hand. "And come inside me later."

She swallowed him deep, obliterating his ability to think or speak, or do anything other than enjoy the pleasures she was giving him. She quickened her pace, knowing all the tricks to throw him over the edge. He grunted out her name, his hips bucking with every pulse of his release. She lovingly accepted everything he had to give. When his body went slack, she rose again, claiming his mouth with the same fierceness she'd taken his cock. Adrenaline pushed through inside him. He tugged her skirt up to her hips, and holy mother of God, she was pantiless. He sank to his knees, feasting on her sweetness. She was so aroused, so hot, when he sucked her clit and thrust his fingers inside her, she spiraled out of control, shattering against him. He loved her breathless, then he made her come again. Only then did he rise and possess her lovely mouth, pouring his soul and a well full of promises into her.

"Baby, you're incredible. You're—"

"Wait," she panted out. "I need you to know something first. I know you're talking to your dad for us, and I love you so much for that. But even if you decide not to, I'll still love you more tomorrow, and the next day, and the next."

He pressed a series of kisses to her swollen lips, so overwhelmed with emotions, he grasped for the right way to convey them. "Sophie, love isn't a big enough word..."

"I know. *Kiss me.* I feel it in your kisses."

If she felt it in his kisses, he wanted to put them everywhere. He pressed his lips to the middle of her chin, the hollow of her neck, the tender spot beside her ear. He could kiss her all day long, every inch of her flesh, and still he wouldn't have kissed her enough. Anxious to love her again, he lowered his head and pressed his lips over the special part of her that had changed his world—*her heart.*

Gazing into her eyes, he said, "You are my forever kiss, Sophie," and lowered his lips to hers.

AT EXACTLY TEN o'clock, Brett followed his father into his posh law office, steeling himself against the chill settling into his bones and the anger simmering beneath his skin. There were no hugs, no warm glances, only awkward silence. Brett rooted his feet in the expensive carpet as his father pushed the door until it was strategically ajar. Gerard Bad was a leading criminal attorney and one of the most manipulative, cunning men Brett had ever known, but Brett had never been intimidated by him. It would be difficult to feel intimidated by a man he'd once seen as weak.

His father strode across the room in his Armani suit and motioned toward a leather chair in front of his desk, before sitting in the taller, more commanding chair behind the desk.

"I'll stand, thanks." Brett crossed his arms, needing the barrier between them. He'd purposely dressed in jeans and an old favorite blazer, wanting his father to see he didn't take after him at all. It was the rebellious punk in him coming out. Brett owned that punk-ass attitude. Lord knew he needed it today. The cold glint in his father's deep-set eyes told him the clothes he'd chosen didn't matter. There was no hiding from the truth.

His father nodded, holding Brett's gaze. Just one of the damn mannerisms Brett had picked up from him. Like the cold stare, the anger, and the ability to live behind a wall of ice. Those traits had haunted Brett for too long. At least he no longer existed behind those fucking barricades. *Thanks to Sophie.*

The thought brought his mind back to the reasons he'd come. If only he knew where to start. It seemed silly to try to hash out what happened all those years ago. He wasn't a child needing his father's approval. Fuck that. He was a highly respected businessman, had more money than any five men needed, and he had the woman of his dreams waiting for him at the end of the day.

He didn't need to be here.

He eyed the door.

"I assume there's a reason you've come?" His father's deep voice was as commanding as his presence.

He met his father's gaze, expecting to see the same cold stare as always, but his gaze was thoughtful, concerned even. Fine lines feathered out from the corners of his eyes. His forehead was etched with worry lines, his hair more silver than black. His shoulders were thinner than Brett remembered. The longer he studied his father's features, the clearer reality became. He no longer knew who his father was, or what was going on inside his head. For the second time in as many weeks, Brett thought of his sister looking down on him from the heavens above, seeing the two of them acting like strangers, and the thought of disappointing her slayed him.

Brett uncrossed his arms and said, "I came to apologize. I was an arrogant kid, and I'd like to say I didn't know what I was doing when I got into all that trouble. But the truth is, I did." He paced, the weight of his father's stare trailing him like a shadow. "I blamed you for Lorelei's death." He crossed his arms again and met his father's gaze.

His father didn't flinch. "Go on."

"I shouldn't have blamed you, and I'm sorry that I made things harder for you and Mom." He'd expected to feel anger or relief after getting it out in the open, but he didn't. He felt overwhelmingly *sad*. Sad that their lives had turned out this way. Sad that his father didn't seem surprised by what he said. He sank down to the leather chair, leaned his elbows on his knees, and stared at the carpet, trying to wrap his head around the grief.

"I'm sorry you felt the need to apologize." His father's voice was a little unsteady.

Brett lifted his gaze and saw regret staring back at him, pulling him deeper into the darkness.

"I'm sorry I couldn't save her," his father said as he rose to his feet and paced—another similarity Brett couldn't deny. "I'm sorry I was too wrapped up in building this fucking company to realize she was so sick. We thought she had the flu. Kids get sick. It's part of life. And you kids were like little petri dishes.

Someone always had a cold or a stomach bug."

Brett opened his mouth to speak, but his voice was lost in disbelief.

His father leaned against the edge of his desk. "After the fundraiser last winter, when you guys had all those pictures of her up…" His eyes dampened and his voice escalated. "I went home and tried to get lost in work, but it was like she was right there all over again. Crying, *pleading* with me with her pretty little eyes. 'Daddy, please make me better.' My baby girl lay dying, and I couldn't do a damn thing but hold her hand and *lie* to her."

Brett felt gutted. He'd had no idea…

When he'd been allowed into Lorelei's hospital room for the last time, he'd crawled into the bed beside her and told her a story about *Lorelei Bad, the greatest actress who ever lived.* Midway through his story, she had spoken in labored, exhausted breaths, and said, *And she had the best bodyguard in the world.* She'd nodded off to sleep right after that, and Brett had lain there until his parents had dragged him home for the night.

His father strode across the room again and pushed the door closed, turning the eyes of a tortured man on Brett. "Do you know what it's like to tell your little girl that everything's going to be okay when you know damn well it's not? Nothing you could have said or done could have made mine or your mother's lives harder than they were back then. You were an arrogant kid, but damn it, Brett, you kids fed off *my* emotions. You and your brothers hid out in that goddamn fort in the woods at a time when you should have been taken care of. But what did I know about grief? I had no clue. All I knew was that I needed to stay away from everyone for fear of dragging you all down with me."

"But you *did* drag us down." The words flew from Brett's

lips with such venom, they propelled him to his feet.

"No shit," his father spat. "I get it. I'm not denying it. I made your lives harder, and I will regret that until the day I die. I'm sorry. I wish I could go back and learn how to deal with our loss and start all over. But I was too mired in my own self-pity to know where to turn. I did the only thing I knew how to do. I worked myself into the ground in an effort to *never* forget a second of the pain. I'd have drilled it into my bones if I could have. I'd have given my own life for her."

"But not for us!" Brett clamped his mouth shut, angry at himself for letting the old hurt derail him. "Sorry," he snapped. "I didn't mean that. I didn't come here to accuse you."

"Bullshit. You meant it, as well you should have. I fucked up, Brett. I fucked up everyone's lives, and I have no excuse for it. Hell, I'm only now starting to grasp the depth of my failures." He swallowed hard and said less vehemently, "When I went to that fundraiser and saw the pictures of my baby girl, of your sister. Of *Lorelei*..."

Brett's throat thickened. He hadn't heard his father say his sister's name since she died.

"When I saw her smiling down at the world, it tore me up." Tears streamed down his cheeks. He turned away and leaned on the windowsill, his head falling between his shoulders. "I tried to get lost in work, and when that didn't cut it, I tried drinking. But I wasn't weak enough to disappear into a bottle." He scoffed. "Too weak to save my family, too strong to become a drunken bum. Senseless."

He turned around, his face a mask of devastation. "That was the night I called your mother."

"What?" Brett's protective urges surged forward. His fingers curled into fists. He and his brothers had protected their mother from their father's wrath ever since his father moved out.

"I understand why you look like you want to kill me," his father said. "But please, hear me out. I didn't call her to cause trouble. I called her because finally, after all these years, I hit rock bottom. She always knew I would, and she left that door open. I know it doesn't seem like it, but I never stopped loving her. She came over the next day, and I won't give you all the details, but she convinced me to see a therapist."

What the hell? Brett wanted to grab hold of the beacon of hope his father's confession held, but he'd been burned too many times. "All these years you would lose your shit if we brought Lorelei up, and now you're suddenly ready to deal with it? *Why?* What's in it for you?"

His father held his steady gaze, the loaded question hanging between them like a line drawn in the sand. "What's in this for you, Brett? Why are *you* here after all these years?"

"Because I can't move forward carrying all this anger and guilt around, and I don't want to end up"—*like you*—"alone and angry, making people walk on eggshells." Brett squared his shoulders, thinking about Sophie and her family and how wonderful it was to be part of that. "And because even though I know we'll never be a close family again, that doesn't mean we can't be *something*."

His father's eyes misted over again. "Common ground. That's where I'm coming from, too."

Emotions bowled Brett over, momentarily stunning him into silence.

"I'm still seeing the therapist," his father said. "It's been a process, building up to do what you had the courage to do today. To apologize. I didn't think any of you would accept an apology from me. *Too little too late.* I've been putting off reaching out and trying." His mouth twitched, as if struggling over what might come next. "Another weakness of mine, avoiding failure."

Failure? Brett hadn't thought his father even knew the meaning of the word. What else did he have wrong?

"But you're here, Brett," his father said. "And you're more of a man than I could ever be. I'm sorry, son. I'm sorry I wasn't the father you and your brothers deserved. Or the husband your mother deserved, and I'm sorry we lost Lorelei." His jaw tightened, just as Brett's already was. "But I hope your being here means it's not too late for us to salvage some kind of relationship."

Brett nodded, for fear that if he tried to speak, the tears he'd been holding back for decades might break free. His father took a tentative step closer, and the boy who'd lost his sister, his father, and the family unit he'd once counted on bullied his way through, closing the distance between them and stepping into his father's open arms.

Chapter Twenty-One

"I'M GOING TO become a pro at this," Sophie said as she tossed a piece of popcorn into the air and dove to catch it in her mouth Sunday afternoon. "Darn it!" She bent at the waist, wearing Brett's favorite cutoffs, the ones he usually tore off her the minute he noticed them, and tried her best to get Brett's attention. But he was busy making two different types of dip. She hadn't even known he could make toast, much less dip.

Brett's eyes shifted to her for only a second, then back to the vegetables he was cutting, which was how she knew her badass boyfriend was a nervous wreck. He hadn't yet told his brothers that he'd invited their father to stop by and watch the game with them. He'd found out that Carson and Tawny were bringing Adeline, and he'd been worried ever since. He didn't want there to be any trouble in front of his niece, but he also didn't want to cancel the invitation, especially since his father had said he wasn't sure he was ready to see everyone, and he might not even show up.

She ran her hand along Brett's side and kissed the back of his neck, hoping to distract him and help him relax before everyone arrived. She went up on her toes and whispered in his ear, "What other *secret* talents do you have?"

He smiled and tossed the vegetables into a bowl, then set to work crumbling bacon.

"That looks delicious." She moved beside him, her back to the counter, and picked up a carrot. "I do love having things in my mouth." She slid the carrot between her lips and moved it in and out. "Mm."

He cleared his throat, his jaw clenching. She ducked under his arm, moving in front of him, and lifted his shirt, kissing her way up his tense muscles, slowing to suck the spots she knew drove him wild, over his ribs, and around his nipples.

"Play with me," she said between kisses. The song on the radio changed to "Love Me or Leave Me Alone" and she swayed seductively, rubbing her body against him.

His arms stilled as she sang about magic between them and his eyes *finally* met hers. She ran her hands along his thighs, singing about him loving her or leaving her alone, and his lips curved up in a lecherous smile. He swept her into his arms, holding her tight as they danced across the kitchen floor, and he showered her with tantalizing kisses. When he deepened a kiss, a groan rumbled up his throat, sending her girly parts into a celebration. They danced around the island, and he clutched her hips, holding her tight. Passion brimmed in his eyes. She loved the way he looked at her as he lifted her up and set her on the counter with a predatory stare.

"They'll be here any minute," he said, running his hot, rough hands up her thighs.

She palmed his hard length through his jeans and said, "Then we better be quick."

"Fuck," he growled. "Sophie…" He lowered his mouth to her neck, sucking hard enough to kick off the celebration in her panties. "You know I can't resist you."

"I'm not sure why you ever try."

She unbuttoned his jeans and made a lusty noise as she

licked the palm of her hand and then stroked his cock. Just touching him made her wet, and he was right there with her, hard and eager, eyes as dark as night, breathing heavily. He captured her mouth in a punishingly intense kiss as he pushed his fingers beneath her shorts and directly into her needy center. She gasped into their kiss as they drove each other wild.

He pulled her to the edge of the counter with his free hand. "I want to fuck you."

She slid off the counter, mourning the loss of his fingers inside her but knowing it was only momentary, and quickly stepped out of her shorts and panties. She turned, bracing her hands against the counter as he sheathed his cock. "Hurry."

"Christ, baby, you are stunning. Hurrying is *not* on my agenda."

He pushed into her, and they both made greedy sounds as they found their rhythm. She looked over her shoulder, taking in the man who had captured her heart, hoping today went well, and knowing if it didn't, their love was strong enough to carry them through.

"Kiss me—"

"Always," he said as his mouth came hungrily down over hers.

His hands pushed beneath her shirt, groping and teasing her nipples and driving her out of her blessed mind. When one hand moved between her legs, a long, surrendering moan left her lips.

"Come with me, baby." He sealed his teeth over the base of her neck, and she felt his thighs flex.

The doorbell sounded, and they both stilled. *No!* She didn't want to stop.

She grabbed the edge of the counter with one hand and

reached between her legs, fondling his balls the way she knew would make him come. Knowing her man could live up to any challenge, she said, "Come with me in thirty seconds or less and tonight we'll try *any* position you want."

He rammed into her, their hands and bodies working their delectable magic. They gasped and cried out as their orgasms hit—and the doorbell sounded again. *Repeatedly.*

"Hang on!" Brett hollered toward the door, staying inside her until the last pulse of her release. They reluctantly separated, and he turned her in his arms and took her in another soulful kiss, then smiled down at her. "You look freshly fucked."

"Feel better?" she asked cheekily.

"Much. Go get cleaned up. I'll wash up quickly and let them in."

He smacked her ass as she picked up her cutoffs and underwear. He uttered a curse when a text sounded on his cell phone, then thumbed a response as she hurried into the bedroom.

After washing up, she went to join them, and the girls intercepted her on her way into the kitchen.

"A little pregame orgasmic action?" Tiffany asked.

Sophie laughed, feeling her cheeks flame, and quickly decided to derail this runaway train before it went too far. "We were making dip. You look adorable in that jersey, and I love your skinny jeans."

"Nice try." Tiffany leaned closer and said, "Your man's in the kitchen with our men *making* the dip."

Amanda pointed into the kitchen, where Brett was dancing with Adeline, while Mick and Dylan mixed the dip. Sophie's heart stumbled. Brett was talking to Adeline, dancing like she was a little lady, and Adeline was gazing adoringly at him. She hoped that one day, if things got better with his father, maybe he'd be open to having a family. Realizing how far ahead of herself she was jumping, she looked away, and found Carson and Tawny in the living room. They were looking at the picture of Sophie and Brett standing beneath the willow tree in her parents' backyard. The picture had arrived in the mail yesterday with a note from Lindsay that said, *Now you can start your own picture wall.* The second Brett had seen it, he'd gone searching for his hammer.

"Can't blame a girl for trying," Sophie said. "Sorry we made you wait."

"Hey, we're fine, and look at our men. Do they look the littlest bit bothered by the delay?" Amanda asked. "I heard Carson telling Mick that Brett handed over the reins on the upcoming concert to one of his managers, and apparently that's a big thing for him, giving up micromanaging. So you two keep up your lovin', because Brett's needed you in his life for a long time."

Sophie was dying to tell them about his visit with his father, but that wasn't her news to share. They made their way into the kitchen, and Brett reached for her hand, bringing her into the dance with Adeline. The happiness in his eyes made her wonder if he'd already told his brothers.

"Sophie, you look pretty," Adeline said as they twirled around the kitchen. "You're bright pink, like Mommy! Uncle Bretty is bright blue today. I like him bright blue."

Sophie's gaze shot to Brett, and she knew by the wicked look in his eyes he was thinking the same thing she was. They'd already taken care of any chance of *certain parts* of him being blue.

Brett lifted Adeline into his arms and said, "She does look pretty, doesn't she?" He kissed Adeline's cheek and said,

"Almost as pretty as you," earning sweet little-girl giggles. "Adeline, do you think we should tell Sophie our secret?"

Adeline nodded with wide eyes.

"I *love* secrets," Sophie said.

Brett opened his mouth, but Adeline said, "We're going to see a play with music!" so excitedly, all eyes turned to them.

Sophie looked hopefully at Brett, knowing he hadn't gone to see a show since he'd lost his sister. He lifted one shoulder in a shrug that tugged at her heartstrings.

"Who's *we*?" Carson asked as he and Tawny came into the kitchen. Carson glanced at Mick and Dylan, who looked shell-shocked.

"Me and Uncle Bretty, and you and Mommy, and Sophie, and everyone in this room!" Adeline wiggled out of Brett's arms and said, "Can I go color?"

"Sure, honey." Tawny pointed to the coffee table in the living room, where she'd set out coloring books and crayons. "I'll be right in."

AS ADELINE SKIPPED happily into the living room, Brett told himself it was now or never. He'd been avoiding the inevitable, pretending his world might not come crashing down around him.

"You want to take Adeline to a play?" Carson asked.

He met his brothers' surprised expressions, which mirrored his own feelings when he'd mentioned going to see a play to Adeline. But seeing her smile as they'd danced around the kitchen, and hearing her talk about how much she loved music, made him want to take her to see a musical. And when he'd looked across the room at Sophie, he'd known in his heart he was ready to put that part of his past behind him and take another step forward.

He only hoped his brothers and father were ready for the same.

Mick was watching him like a hawk, eyes narrow and serious, as if he could see into Brett's brain and wanted to pick it apart.

"I was thinking I'd take her to a musical. I'd like all of us to go, actually. I think it would be fun." Brett felt Sophie's fingers touch his, and he curled his hand around hers. No more driving around mud puddles. He wanted to plow right through them.

Dylan said, "We'd love to go."

"Us too," Amanda said as she slid an arm around Mick.

"I think it's a wonderful idea," Tawny said with a warm smile. "Thank you for thinking of Adeline."

"I've been doing a lot of thinking lately." Brett met Mick's gaze. "I went to see Dad, and I invited him to stop by today."

Sophie squeezed his hand.

Carson's eyes shot to Adeline. "You invited him *here*? What were you thinking? You knew Addy was going to be here. I don't want him upsetting her."

"It's okay." Tawny reached for his hand. "He didn't cause any issues at our wedding, and I'm sure Brett would have given us a heads-up if he thought there might be problems."

Mick's gaze never wavered. "You should have given us warning."

"I was afraid you guys wouldn't come. I'm not even sure he'll show up," Brett said. "And I was worried about Adeline being here, but not because of Dad. He's been seeing a therapist since the fundraiser, and I'm telling you, he's different. I was worried about how you all would react to him."

"You were right to worry," Carson said. "I won't allow him to make Adeline or Tawny uncomfortable."

"Do you think I'd have asked him here if I thought he'd make Sophie uncomfortable? Or any of your wives?" Brett said in a hushed tone so Adeline wouldn't hear. "Not a chance in hell."

Carson shook his head. "That's not what I meant. I'm just protective of them."

"We all are," Mick said. "You sure he's seeing a therapist?"

"Yes. Definitely. And Mom is the one who hooked him up with the guy."

"Mom?" Mick asked.

"I know. I couldn't believe it either. I was going to call her, but I figured that was between them."

"He did tell me he was proud of me at the fundraiser for the first time since I was a kid," Dylan reminded them. "That was totally out of the ordinary for him."

"He said he hit rock bottom, and he apologized. There were real tears in his eyes, and he's not a guy who can pretend to be anything he's not." They had that in common, too. Brett had been thinking about those tears for days. When he'd told Sophie about their visit, he'd been moved to tears himself, and she'd cried right along with him. It had been as cathartic as it was difficult, and he'd felt freer ever since.

"Look, you guys never thought you'd see the day when I'd want to apologize to him, right?" Brett drew Sophie closer. "I'm proof that people can change. And hell, each one of you are too."

"I think this is great," Amanda said. "That must have been

really hard for both of you, and I'm glad you're taking this step. I've been worried about how we'd explain to our kids why their grandfather was never around."

A pained expression washed over Carson's face. "It's not easy."

"If he shows up, I'm sure we can all be civil." Mick shifted his gaze to each of their brothers, who nodded in agreement.

"That's all I'm asking." Brett sighed with relief. "And, Carson, I'm sorry about not telling you and letting you decide about bringing Adeline. This has been a confusing time for me, and I was worried about the message it would send to Dad if I canceled."

"We can handle it," Carson said. "What's the worst that can happen? He's a prick and we show him the front door."

That brought a little much-needed laughter. They finished making the dip, gave Brett a hard time about not being prepared, and then everyone headed into the living room to watch the game.

Brett drew Sophie against his side on the couch and said, "I saw you stealing glances at me. Just kiss me when you want a kiss. It doesn't matter if my family's here."

"I'm not afraid to kiss you in front of them. I wasn't looking for a kiss. I was just looking at you."

He brushed his scruff along her cheek, the way he knew she loved, and said, "And what did you see?"

"This hot guy who I'm pretty sure is my everything." She climbed into his lap and rested her head on his shoulder. "I love who you are."

He held her tighter and said, "That's good, because you're stuck with me."

"Get a room," Tiffany teased.

"Uncle Bretty has a room. It's right down the hall," Adeline said as she colored in her coloring book.

The doorbell chimed, and Brett's heart rate spiked. Sophie moved from his lap and he pushed to his feet. "I guess he did decide to show up after all."

He went to answer the door, and his brothers followed, standing shoulder to shoulder a few feet away, ready to protect the people they loved most. Brett opened the door, and his stomach pitched at the sight of his father's serious dark eyes and granitelike jaw. *Old habits die hard.*

He pushed those ghosts away and said, "Dad. I'm glad you came."

Brett stepped aside, and their father's lips curled up in the most nervous smile Brett had ever witnessed. It was strange to see his father wearing jeans and a sweater, instead of the suits he wore to the events they both attended, which was the only place they'd seen him in years. He looked much less imposing. Or maybe that was the lack of fierceness in his eyes. Whatever the cause, Brett was glad they were standing on common ground again.

He handed Brett a bottle of wine. "I wasn't sure what you drank these days."

"Thank you. Come in, please."

Brett watched their father's chest rise with a deep inhalation as he stepped inside. His gaze swept across the room, slowing on the faces of each of his sons, their wives standing nervously nearby. Their father nodded curtly, and his gaze caught on Adeline, who was walking around the far side of the couch, watching them with interest. Her little brows knitted, and she fidgeted with the hem of her sweater. Their father's Adam's apple bobbed with a hard swallow. Brett wondered if he was thinking of Lorelei, the way he did every time he saw his niece.

"Dad, can I get you a drink?" he asked to break the tension.

"No, thank you. I'm not drinking these days."

"I would like a drink," Adeline said as she approached.

Carson stepped between his daughter and father so quickly, it was hard not to be embarrassed for them both.

"I'll get you a drink, Addy Girl." Carson lifted her into his arms and gave their father a signature Bad nod. "Good to see you."

Mick offered his hand, giving Carson time to escape into the kitchen with Adeline. "I'm glad you came."

Their father looked at his hand for a long moment before taking it in his own. But he didn't shake it; he simply held it, which spoke volumes for a man who had taught Brett that a firm handshake told the person he was greeting how confident and strong he was. It saddened Brett to see his father giving up that stance, but at the same time, it warmed him to his core.

"It's good to see you," their father said to Mick. He looked at the others and said, "It's nice to see all of you."

Brett led him into the living room to Sophie. "Dad, you remember Sophie Roberts, Mick's assistant."

"Yes, of course. How are you?"

Sophie smiled warmly. "I'm well, thank you."

"Sophie's with me now." Brett put an arm around her.

"Oh," he said with surprise, and a genuine smile lifted his lips. "How wonderful."

"About damn time," Dylan said too animatedly, showing his nervousness, too.

The girls came over to greet him, and then Brett motioned toward the couch. "Have a seat, Dad. Kick back and watch the game."

His father sat on the couch, looking uncomfortable and silently surveying the room. Brett knew that look. His father wanted to bolt. He couldn't blame him. There was so much tension in the room, it practically vibrated off the walls.

When Carson and Adeline returned to the living room, Adeline set her cup of juice down on the coffee table and stood before her grandfather, studying his face. Carson kept a hand on her shoulder, his eyes on their father.

"Hello, Adeline," their father said kindly.

She leaned into Carson's leg. "Hi. You look different than you did at Mommy and Daddy's wedding."

"Do I? I feel different, too." He leaned forward, and she wrapped her arm around Carson's leg. Carson's hand slid down her shoulder, holding her.

"You were gray," Adeline said. "But now you're a yucky blue."

Their father laughed softly, but that laugher didn't reach his sad eyes, which moved to Carson, then returned to Adeline a little warmer. "You're a very smart little girl, aren't you?"

She nodded.

"What color is your daddy?"

She looked up at Carson and gasped. "Daddy! You're lemony!"

Carson smiled. "Am I?"

"Yes!" She let go of Carson and stepped closer to their father. "Now you look kind of gray and yellow and that yucky blue. You have a lot of colors. I haven't seen anyone with as many colors as you." She touched his hand, and Carson's jaw tensed. "I don't want you to be those yucky colors."

She climbed onto their father's lap, and his eyes shot up to Carson, a silent question hanging in the air between them.

266

Carson's nod was nearly imperceptible as Adeline pressed both of her hands to their father's cheeks and said, "Grandpa, please don't be ugly colors."

"Adeline," Carson cautioned her.

She looked over her shoulder at Carson and said, "Ugly *color*, Daddy, not ugly *person*." She focused on their father again. "Do you want to be those ugly colors?"

He swallowed hard again, as if he had a chance of stifling the emotions welling in his eyes. "No, honey, I don't."

She patted his cheeks and said, "Do you see people in colors like me?"

That earned a genuine smile. "No. You're very special."

"I think you're special, too." She climbed off his lap, picked up her juice cup, and went back to her coloring books on the other side of the table.

Brett swore the entire room exhaled.

"I..." Their father rose to his feet by Carson, eyed the door, then asked, "Does she have synesthesia? A cross-wiring of the senses?"

"We believe so," Carson said.

"Fascinating." Their father glanced at Adeline, his expression warming as he shifted his gaze to Carson again. "And terrifying that she could see me so clearly. She saw you, too. *Yellow*, struggling to maintain control. I'm sorry, son. I appreciate the time you've given me with her. I think I'd better take off."

"You don't have to," Carson said.

"Stick around for a while," Brett urged as he and his brothers followed their father to the door.

"I can't, but this was good. Thank you." He held Brett's gaze for a beat before his sharp eyes moved to his other sons, lingering on each of them. "I can't make up for the hurt I've caused. I understand that. But you should know that I've learned how to let some of that anger go, and I never would have if it weren't for the four of you making the decision to bring Lorelei back into the world of the living. I am tremendously grateful for that and for you allowing me to come over tonight. I love you boys, and I'm proud of the men you've become."

He reached for the door, and Dylan reached for him, drawing him into an awkward embrace. His father looked over Dylan's shoulder and mouthed *thank you* to Brett, but Brett knew it wasn't him who deserved the gratitude. He reached for Sophie as his brothers said their goodbyes to their father.

"This is because of you, baby," he said into her ear, taking a step away from the others. "Thank you."

"I didn't do anything but follow my heart." She wrapped her arms around him, her sweet smile lighting up her eyes. "You thought you caused the demise of your family, but look"—she motioned toward his brothers and father—"I think you saved them."

Chapter Twenty-Two

"I *LOVE* THESE heels." Sophie showed Grace a pair of taupe suede pumps that laced up the ankle. "I wish I had them last week." Sophie and Brett had checked off their nooner fantasy when she'd sent him a key to a hotel room with a note that read, *Meet me in room 303 at noon. Bring a special package—or two.* He'd brought a whole box of condoms.

Grace snort-laughed. "If you think Brett would have noticed your heels, then you're dreaming."

"Ha! You're right. You have to admit, he'd go crazy for lace-ups, but they don't go with my dress."

"Then we'll have to find a new dress." Grace ran her finger down the shoe boxes until she found Sophie's size and handed her the box. "Try them on."

She sat on the bench and slipped off her boots. "The musical is *tonight*. I wish we had more time to shop." She couldn't believe it had been almost two weeks since Brett's father came over. She swore Brett and his brothers were closer because of it, and Brett definitely seemed like the weight of the world had lifted off his shoulders.

"Time? I think I've heard of that elusive element." Grace handed her one of the heels.

"I know, right? Thank you for putting all this together for Adeline. I know you have hardly any time between shows, and coordinating the private showing must have been a real pain." Grace had arranged for Brett's family to see a play they'd run last year called the *Magical Musical*, which featured princesses, knights, and friendly dragons. Brett was footing the entire bill, and Grace didn't know it yet, but in return Brett had arranged for an all-expense-paid trip to Hawaii for her on a date of her choosing. Sophie loved that he didn't take anyone for granted.

Grace sank down beside her. "Actually, setting this up for Brett has been the most fun I've had in a long time. I love the cast in this play. They're less divaish than most. And I got to do some creative things this time around. Brett was worried about how long Adeline could sit still, so we modified the show and rewrote the end of the first half to seem like the end of the entire play in case she fizzled out early. If she's doing well and enjoying it, we'll do the second half."

"You're amazing, you know that? Adeline's excited, and I have to say, Brett is, too. He's nervous about it all coming together. You'd think he was the one doing your job. But I guess that's to be expected since he hasn't been to a show in so long and he really wants it to be special for Adeline. We've had dinner with Carson and Tawny four times in the last two weeks, and she was so excited, playing the piano and showing us her new dress." She stood and walked down the aisle and back in the heels. She stopped in front of Grace and said, "What do you think?"

"I think we'd better buy you new lingerie, too, because those heels say forget waiting until we get home; take me at intermission."

"Perfect."

They bought the heels and went in search of a dress to match, weeding through racks of dresses that were either too fancy, too professional, or too sleazy. When they left the third store, Sophie said, "We're never going to find one. Maybe I should save the heels for another event and look for a pair of heels to go with the dress I have instead."

"Absolutely not." Grace pulled her toward a lingerie store. "We just need to change directions a little. Lingerie, lunch, more dress shopping."

Sophie looped her arm with Grace's and said, "Do you know how much I love you?"

"Enough that you didn't blow me off today," Grace teased.

"I love you so much that when I spoke to Nana last night I told her that you needed some matchmaking." Sophie laughed at Grace's deadpan stare as they entered the lingerie shop.

"I'm making a mental note not to be available for their next anniversary party." Grace went directly to a display of thongs. "Pick your poison, baby."

Sophie picked up a beige thong and said, "Who needs underwear?"

"Ew. You're wearing a dress. You need underwear. At least butt floss. But you'd better buy two, because once your man realizes you're wearing a thong and those heels he'll have you wet and wild on the ride over." She handed Sophie another thong and headed for the bras.

"You're such a good friend. You mother me when I want to be a tramp."

"I'm not sure what kind of mother would convince you to buy fuck-me heels and a thong."

Their gazes met and they both said, "Nana," then burst out laughing.

Two thongs and two bras later, they had lunch at a café and caught up on all the things they hadn't discussed over text during the week. Then they hit the pavement again in search of a dress. After going through several shops, trying on at least ten dresses and coming out empty-handed, Sophie was ready to give up.

"We live in the fashion hub of the United States. Finding a dress should not be this hard."

"At least you can fit in all the dresses you try on. I've got nasty cramps, and I swear I'm carrying at least seven pounds of water weight right now."

"Oh *please*, you look great." They went into another store, and as Sophie fished through a rack of dresses, she tried to remember when she'd last had her period. *The Indian restaurant!* She'd had wicked cramps that night and had tried to back out of going.

"How about this one?" Grace held up a beautiful dress almost the exact same color as the heels Sophie had bought. "It's sleeveless, but your man will keep you *hot*."

Sophie was hot now, sweating over how long it had been since she'd had her period, although she'd never been very regular. She told herself not to panic and said, "That's perfect."

They searched the rack for her size, and Sophie asked, "Do you remember when we had dinner at that Indian restaurant?"

Grace handed her the dress in her size. "That was forever ago. Why? Want to go again? It was good."

"Yeah, we should go again sometime." She went into the dressing room, pulled out her phone, and searched her calendar for the date of that dinner. *Shit, shit, shit.* Her period was almost a week late. But she'd been so busy—*humping like bunnies*—and maybe a little stressed, too, with the trip home and then Brett's father's visit.

"Hurry up, Cinderella," Grace called from outside the dressing room.

"Coming." She whipped off her clothes and tried on the dress. The classic sheath-style, sleeveless silhouette dress gathered at one hip and had a high neckline. There was a small slit just above the knee, which Brett would love. She put her hand over her belly and warmed with the idea of carrying her and Brett's baby. She tried to remember if they'd ever had unprotected sex, and their shower tryst came back to her. She closed her eyes as memories of that incredible morning hit, followed by the sound of Brett's voice. *The last thing either of us needs is a kid.*

Committing to a relationship was one thing, but a child?

"Soph, I'm dying out here," Grace said.

Sophie closed her eyes, breathing deeply, and said, "Be right out."

She stared in the mirror, telling herself she was being ridiculous. Her period was always three or four days early or late. She'd probably get it at the event tonight. She made a mental note to put tampons in her purse, smoothed the gorgeous dress over her hips, and decided not to worry unless she had to.

"TONIGHT, THOSE HEELS stay *on*," Brett whispered into Sophie's ear later that evening as they sat in the theater awaiting the start of the musical.

Shivers of anticipation rippled through her. Getting dressed around Brett was as much fun as getting undressed. He was the handsiest, most sensual and loving man Sophie had ever known, which meant getting anywhere on time took advance planning.

But tonight, as they'd dressed for the musical, she'd been running late, and she'd had to deny his advances. They'd made out in the car on the way over, but she'd had to cut that short, too. *We already made your family wait in the hall before the football game. If we're late tonight we'll forever be known as the nymphomaniacs who can't control ourselves.* He'd promptly bit her neck and growled, *What's wrong with that? It'd be true.*

Now, as Adeline bounced excitedly in her seat, chatting about the upcoming show, and Brett's brothers and sisters-in-law surrounded them in the otherwise empty theater, the tips of Brett's fingers moved into the slit on her dress brushing her thigh. She put her hand over his and glared at him. Suddenly Grace's joke didn't seem like such a bad idea.

She leaned closer and whispered, "Maybe we can find a dark corner of the theater at intermission."

His eyes glistened with wicked intent as the theater lights dimmed.

"It's starting!" Adeline said loudly, clapping. She was adorable in a fancy pink dress with white bows in her hair. She leaned closer to Brett and said, "I can't wait to get up onstage! We're going to look pretty up there!"

He put his arm around Adeline and said, "Maybe after the show."

"This was such a great idea," Sophie said to Brett. "You might have inspired a future actress."

"And *you* inspired me to finally live my life to the fullest," he said as the curtains opened and the show began.

THE MUSICAL WAS incredible, clearly designed for children, but with enough humor and vague romantic elements to keep Sophie and everyone else riveted to the stage. When the curtain came down at intermission, everyone clapped, and Adeline jumped up and down in front of her seat, making them all laugh, which made Sophie realize she had to pee.

"I'm going to run to the ladies' room," she said to Brett.

Adeline grabbed Brett's hand and said, "Now, Uncle Bretty? Now can we go up onstage?"

"Give me a second, monkey. Then we'll see if we can find our friend Grace and ask if it's all right to take a peek." He turned to Sophie and said, "Want me to walk you out?"

"No. It's okay. She's so excited. But I don't know if you'll be able to actually take her up there. Usually at intermission Grace and the stage crew are crazed."

Brett hoisted Adeline into his arms. "That's okay. If we can't get onstage, we'll find other things to look at. Right, monkey?"

"This place is so shiny and bright! I want to see it all!" Adeline said. "Daddy, are you coming with us?"

Carson put a hand on her back and said, "You know it, baby."

"Adeline, do you have to use the bathroom first?" Tawny asked.

Adeline shook her head.

Sophie and Brett's sisters-in-law went in search of the ladies' room.

"That was magnificent," Tawny said as they entered the luxurious bathroom. "Did you hear Adeline giggling?"

They each headed for a stall.

"Your daughter kills me," Amanda said. "I can't wait to have babies."

"I can't wait to get Dylan home tonight," Tiffany said. "The man has been feeling me up since the lights went down."

"I thought I heard a few deep sighs," Tawny said.

Four flushes later, they washed their hands and primped in the mirror.

"Did Mick tell the guys he reached out to their father last week?" Amanda pulled a brush from her purse and ran it through her hair.

The girls shrugged and murmured their uncertainty.

"I know Brett's been talking with their father, but he didn't mention anything about Mick doing the same," Sophie said.

"Well, then, don't say anything, please." Amanda put the brush back in her purse. "But I think what Brett did has made a world of difference, at least for Mick."

"For Carson, too," Tawny admitted. "I wasn't going to say anything because Carson's so private, but I know they talked yesterday, and Carson said he thought it was a good beginning."

They all looked at Tiffany, who said, "Do you even have to ask? It's *Dylan*. He went to see his father the very next day, had breakfast with him last weekend, and he talked to him before we left tonight."

All the girls laughed.

"And we have Sophie to thank for it," Amanda pointed out.

"All I did was fall in love. This was all Brett, and I don't think it had as much to do with me as it did with our visit with my family. He definitely changed when we were there. It's like he needed to remember that all families weren't doomed to unhappiness or something. I don't know, really, but I couldn't be happier. He hasn't been to a musical since they lost Lorelei. Have you guys ever thought about how much *love* our guys had for their little sister?" Her eyes teared up, and she tried to blink away the wetness. "Seriously. Their hearts are *so* big."

"Their *love* is so big," Tiffany said.

Sophie fanned her face. "Okay, we need to stop. Seeing Brett with Adeline is enough to make my ovaries explode, but thinking about them with Lorelei is like that old coffee commercial where the kid finally comes home at Christmas. *Instant tears.*"

They hugged and checked their hair one more time before heading back into the theater, which was already dark.

"Did we take that long?" Sophie whispered as they walked down the aisle toward their seats. "Uh-oh. Looks like Brett and Carson got lost with Adeline. Should I go look for them?"

"No. You know Carson. He has to understand every little thing," Tawny said quietly. "They probably stopped to talk to the lighting guy or something."

They took their seats, and Sophie hoped Brett made it back with Adeline in time for her to see the show.

The curtain went up, and the stage was pitch-black. A spotlight bloomed to life, illuminating a piano on the left side of the stage. Carson and Adeline walked out of the darkness, and Sophie gasped. "Tawny! Look!"

Adeline faced the audience and waved. "Hi, Mommy! Hi, Uncle Dylly! Hi, Uncle Micky! Hi, Aunt Tiffany and Aunt Amanda! Hi, Sophie! Look at me! I'm onstage! And I'm gonna play a song!"

Sophie's eyes filled with tears, knowing Adeline had the best uncle in the world for Brett to have set this up for her. Carson looked proud as he guided his daughter over to the piano and sat beside her.

Mick came around to Sophie's side of the aisle and extended

his hand. "Sophie, can you come with me, please?"

Oh no. Is there a work issue? "Sure." She stepped from the aisle, and Mick offered his arm. "What's going on?"

Dylan rose to his feet and placed a bouquet of flowers in her arms with a wink.

Sophie's pulse spiked. "What's this?"

Mick guided her toward the stage. Her pulse spiked anew with every step. "Mick?"

He placed his hand on her back, urging her forward, and said, "Deep breath, Sophie. Breathe."

The lights brightened slowly, bringing life to a weeping willow decorated with yellow lights, a makeshift creek complete with running water and surrounded by plants and flowers like the creek in her parents' backyard. When they reached the stage steps, she saw glittering gold and silver stars hanging from the ceiling, and beneath them Brett waited, looking darkly handsome and nervous in his navy suit and tie.

"Oh my God." Her legs trembled. She was pretty sure she might pass out, and grabbed Mick's arm to stabilize herself.

"Breathe, Sophie. This is your night."

As Mick accompanied her up the steps, a rose-petal path came into view—leading directly to Brett.

Adeline began playing "Twinkle, Twinkle Little Star" and Carson took Sophie by the elbow, as if he knew her legs had turned to jelly.

UNTIL COMING TOGETHER with Sophie, Brett's life had been defined by a handful of happy memories followed by weighty, awful losses and several years of trying not to feel anything at all. As he watched his beautiful girlfriend walking across the stage clutching her bouquet, rose petals puddling at her feet, he wanted to memorize the trembling of her lower lip, the sway of her hips, and the look of love in her eyes. He never wanted to forget the sound of Adeline's piano playing or the rush of emotions coursing through him. It was those all-consuming emotions that sent him forward, unable to wait a second longer to be by Sophie's side.

Carson gave an approving nod as Brett took Sophie's arm and led her up the path to the tree. "Hi, baby."

"Brett...?" Her eyes darted to his family in the audience, then back to him again. "What are we doing?"

"I think you know." He took her hand and got down on one knee.

"Oh God." Tears welled in her eyes.

"I had a whole speech worked out, but now that you're here, I can't remember a word of it."

She smiled as tears slid down her cheeks.

"You're my diamond in the sky, baby. I want to celebrate our highs and be there to pull each other through the lows. I want to go to bed with you in my arms and wake to your smiling face. I want to make all your dreams come true, baby. I want everything with you. Will you marry me? Be my forever kiss?"

He rose to his feet, and she stepped closer, the bouquet of roses crushed between them as she whispered in a shaky voice, "Define *everything*?"

"Everything, baby. White picket fence, a house in Oak Falls for when you feel like going there, babies, sitting on the porch with a shotgun when our girls go to homecoming."

She smiled through her tears, squeezing his hand, and asked, "Are you one hundred percent sure you want children?"

"Absolutely. I want as many as you want, and I promise to love them and provide for them and parent them enough that they'll think I'm a big pain in the ass."

She laughed and whispered, "That's good, because I think I'm pregnant."

Shocked laughter fell from his lips. "Pregnant? Really?"

She nodded. "I took a test before we came, and it was positive."

"Baby!" he shouted. Tears sprang from his eyes as he hauled her against him. "Oh my God. We're going to have a baby!" He kissed her hard, both of them laughing as gasps and cheers rang out around them. "Sophie, is that a yes?"

"Yes!" she said between kisses. "Yes, I'll marry you!"

The lights brightened, and rose petals showered them from above as he slipped the diamond engagement ring on her finger. Then he reached into his pocket and handed her another ring.

"What's this?" She looked at the gold band and read the inscription on the outside of the ring. "Forever Sophie's?"

"You said I could only have a billboard saying you were taken if you had one saying I was." He held up his left hand, and she slid the ring on his finger. "I'm yours, baby. And see that tree over there? That's one of our forever-kiss trees. We'll have two. One in Oak Falls and one in our home here."

"Oh, Brett!" She launched herself into his arms as her entire family, along with Grace and the rest of Brett's family, rushed the stage. "Oh my gosh! My family...?" Tears streamed down her cheeks. "I love you so much."

"Did I hear *baby*?" Nana asked as she pried them apart and hugged Sophie. "I knew all that fierce lovin' would lead to something, but I figured a *ring*. This is so much better!"

They were passed from one loving embrace to the next, and when they finally landed back in each other's arms, Brett saw his father holding Adeline in his arms, standing with his brothers and his mother, and he knew if Lorelei could see them now, she'd be proud of them all. He gazed into Sophie's beautiful eyes, ready to be the husband she deserved and a father to their children she could be proud of.

Sophie went up on her toes and kissed him. "Marrying you was one of my secret fantasies."

"Baby, I have a slew of new fantasies, each involving my gorgeous, pregnant fiancée."

Epilogue

SOPHIE STOOD IN the master bedroom of hers and Brett's new vacation home in Oak Falls, which they'd built on the acreage her parents had subdivided from their own property and given them as an early wedding present. She could see her parents' house from the window, and in the distance, the roof of her grandparents' home. She put her hand on her burgeoning belly and sighed happily. The last six months had not flown by, and she was thankful for that. She wanted to savor every minute, moving her things into Brett's—*their*—home, going together to her doctor appointments, disagreeing on baby names, enjoying Naked Saturdays, and hosting brunch on Sundays. Her gaze traveled to their young weeping willow by the creek. It was too small to carve their initials into just yet, but Lindsay'd had a metal plaque made with their initials inside a heart, which now hung from the lowest branch.

"You're not supposed to see your groom yet," Grace said as she closed the curtains. "It's bad luck, and I'm not taking any chances with my best friend's love life." As the maid of honor, she had been there every step of the way, as had Lindsay, their mother, grandmother, Brett's mother, and all of Brett's sisters-in-law, as they'd planned the wedding.

Then I won't tell you that he snuck in and we made out before everyone arrived. Or how I already peeked at him standing with his

282

family by the creek, and how my knees went weak at the sight of his father with his arm around his shoulder.

Grace's eyes widened. "Oh God. Sophie! Really?"

"What?" She should know better than to think about kissing Brett when she was trying to keep it a secret—especially from Grace.

"As if I can't read that expression? You are wicked!" Her gaze shifted over Sophie's shoulder as Nana approached.

"Wickedness seems to run in our family," Nana said. She fiddled with the chiffon skirt of Sophie's ivory wedding gown and then touched the slim, pink silk bow tied above her baby bump. "You look beautiful, honey."

"Thanks, Nana." Sophie and Grace had set aside several weekends solely for wedding dress shopping, but they'd found her beautiful gown in the first shop they'd gone into. The princess-cut and flowing material left plenty of room for her expanding belly. Only the halter neckline had to be altered to accommodate her bust, which Brett was thoroughly enjoying.

"I still don't know why you two were in such a hurry to build a house when your parents have plenty of room." Nana smoothed her dress over her hips.

"Because they'd like a little privacy," Sophie's mother said.

Nana set a hand on her hip and raised her brows. "As if I won't just walk right in and drag you two out of bed when you need dragging."

"I love you, Nana," Sophie said, "but I'm going to lock my doors until at least eight o'clock in the morning."

Nana patted Sophie's hand. "I'm not worried. Once that baby's woken you up at three a.m. enough times, you'll be begging me to spend the night just to care for the sweet bundle."

Lindsay breezed into the room, and Amanda, Tiffany, and Tawny followed her in. They all looked gorgeous in pink high-low bridesmaid gowns. Amanda and Tiffany had gotten pregnant on or around the night Brett had proposed to Sophie, and they were excited to be having babies so close together.

"Are we ready?" Lindsay asked. "Mr. Not so Pure and Very Immense is waiting."

"Mr. *what*?" Sophie asked.

"I guess you never saw what he wrote in Nana and Poppi's anniversary journal?" Lindsay asked. "You wrote that you hoped you'd get lucky enough to find love as pure and immense as Nana and Poppi's, and Brett wrote 'Happy anniversary' and signed it 'Mr. Not So Pure and Very Immense.'"

Sophie beamed with pride. "That's my man."

"By the looks of you guys, all of y'all have feisty men," Nana said as she surveyed their baby bumps. "You all look like an advertisement for Planned Parenthood. When does Adeline get a sibling?" she asked Tawny.

"Where *is* Adeline?" Sophie asked.

"She's out back with Grace's sisters, whom she found fascinatingly colorful," Tawny said. "They're throwing rose petals on the aisle leading up to the gazebo." Sophie's father and Poppi had built a beautiful gazebo for the wedding, and Lindsay had decorated it with flowers and ivy.

"I bet she found them colorful," Grace mumbled, sharing a knowing smile with Sophie.

"Adeline looks adorable in her frilly dress," Sophie's mother said. "Do you and Carson plan to have more children?"

Tawny put her hand on her nearly flat stomach and said, "You can only hear 'Mommy, I want a baby, too' so many times before you give in."

There was a collective gasp.

"You're pregnant?" Sophie asked.

"We didn't want to tell anyone until after your big day, but..." Tawny's green eyes lit up as she nodded. "Twelve weeks yesterday."

Amanda squealed. "This is so great!"

"Another baby shower to plan!" Lindsay said.

There was a group hug around their burgeoning bellies. Sophie had been close to the girls before she and Brett had come together, but the way they'd accepted Grace and Lindsay into their close-knit circle made her love them even more.

Tawny touched her stomach again. "We're excited. But we haven't told Adeline yet, because we were afraid she'd spill the beans. We'll tell her after the wedding."

"Jackie will be over the moon!" Sophie's mother said. She and Brett's mother had become close while they were planning the wedding.

"She is," Tawny said. "We told her already. She's so happy that her family is finally coming together after all these years."

"Family is everything. And what's this I hear about you coming back home for a few weeks, Grace?" Nana asked.

"I see my mother's been spreading the news," Grace said. "My sister Amber asked me to teach a screenplay writing class at her bookstore, and I could use the break."

"Fresh matchmaking blood!" Nana rubbed her palms together.

"Mom! You'll scare her off before she even arrives." Sophie's mother shook her head. "Sorry, Grace. I'll try to keep her on Lindsay's trail."

"No, thank you," Lindsay snapped. "I do not want to get married. Grace, you and I will have to stick together."

"It's not like I'm moving back or will have oodles of time to try to find a man, Nana, so maybe you should focus on one of my sisters instead."

"How about if we focus on getting this wedding off the ground," Sophie's father said from the doorway. He looked handsome in a dark suit and pink tie, matching all the men in the wedding party.

"Are they ready?" Sophie looked at Grace, who reached for her hand and mouthed, *Breathe.*

Her father said, "I think Brett's about ready to come up here and carry you down over his shoulder. That man's anxious to be your husband, sugarplum."

"Okay, girls, let's go." Lindsay ushered them toward the door.

Sophie's father offered her his arm. "You look gorgeous, sweetheart."

"Thanks, Daddy. And thank you for the land and the beautiful wedding," she said as they made their way downstairs.

Her father stopped on the third step down, and they both looked at the pictures hanging on the wall. There were already so many of them, a copy of the picture of Brett and Sophie at his brothers' wedding, the picture Lindsay had taken of them beneath the willow tree, selfies they'd taken over time, and of course they were all intermixed with pictures of their families and friends.

"Your family is much bigger than mine was when I got married," her father said. "You might need a bigger wall."

Sophie pointed to the bare wall above eye level, which led all the way up to the two-story ceiling. "My brilliant husband-to-be already thought of that."

BRETT FIDGETED NERVOUSLY as each of his brothers and sisters-in-law, and the rest of the wedding party, walked down the aisle. Their family was expanding in leaps and bounds, and he was elated that his and Sophie's baby would have cousins who were close in age. He glanced at his parents, catching his father's eye, and felt a well of gratitude instead of the anger and hurt that used to live inside him. They still had things to work out, hurdles to overcome, but the last six months had brought them together in a way he'd never imagined possible. He'd asked his mother about her friendship with his father, and she'd said that she'd learned long ago not to close the door on anyone she loved. Brett thought that was a good rule of thumb, though he hoped he'd never be given cause to put it to a test.

His gaze swept over Sophie's family and friends smiling as they watched Mick and Amanda walk down the aisle. These were the people who had unknowingly helped change his views and his life. Sophie had opened a door, and everyone here had walked through it, reviving his faith in what could be. What he wanted for Sophie. He knew he should try to remember every detail of their wedding day, but as Adeline skipped down the aisle instead of walking, as they'd practiced, he knew none of it would stick in his head except his stunning bride, pregnant with their first child, standing at the other end of the rose-petal aisle with stars in her beautiful blue eyes. She was a vision in ivory with her long dark hair cascading over her shoulders, holding her father's arm and carrying a bouquet beside her beautiful round belly.

When her smiling eyes landed on Brett, the rest of the world faded away. He didn't think as he stepped forward, closing the distance between them. It wasn't until he was standing before her and Sophie whispered, "You were supposed to wait up there," that he realized what he'd done.

Chuckles came from their friends and family.

Brett gazed into Sophie's eyes and said, "When have I ever done what I was supposed to do?" He glanced at Del, who wore an amused expression. "Sorry, Del."

"Don't ever be sorry for loving my daughter."

Sophie turned and hugged her father. "Thank you, Daddy. I love you."

"I love you too, sugarplum." Del kissed her cheek and went to his wife's side.

Brett took Sophie's hand, unable to stop smiling as he gazed into her loving eyes, and said, "Are you ready, Sexy Sophie?"

Her eyes glittered in the sunlight as she squeezed his hand and said, "For *anything*."

Want More BILLIONAIRES AFTER DARK?

The Billionaires After Dark series includes the Bad Boys After Dark (4 books) and the Wild Boys After Dark (4 books), all of which are now available.

Each of Brett's siblings has their own book, starting with BAD BOYS AFTER DARK: MICK (Mick and Amanda's love story).

Ready for more
Love in Bloom romance?

Join Sophie's friend Grace in her search for her own happily ever after in EMBRACING HER HEART, the first book in the Montgomery series.

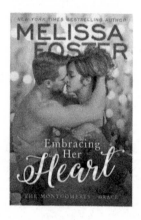

In EMBRACING HER HEART...

Leaving New York City and returning to her hometown to teach a screenplay writing class seems like just the break Grace Montgomery needs. Until her sisters wake her at four thirty in the morning to watch the hottest guys in town train wild horses and she realizes that escaping her sisters' drama-filled lives was a lot easier from hundreds of miles away. To make matters worse, she spots the one man she never wanted to see again—ruggedly handsome Reed Cross.

Reed was one of Michigan's leading historical preservation experts, but on the heels of catching his girlfriend in bed with his business partner, his uncle suffers a heart attack. Reed cuts all ties and returns home to Oak Falls to run his uncle's business. A chance encounter with Grace, his first love, brings back memories he's spent years trying to escape.

Grace is bound and determined not to fall under Reed's spell again—and Reed wants more than another taste of the woman he's never forgotten. When a midnight party brings them together, passion ignites and old wounds are reopened. Grace sets down the ground rules for the next three weeks. No touching, no kissing, and if she has it her way, no breathing, because every breath he takes steals her ability to think. But Reed has other ideas...

New To Melissa's Love in Bloom Big-Family Romance Collection?

The Bad Billionaires After Dark are only one of many family series within Melissa Foster's Love in Bloom big-family romance collection. You have many more love stories featuring loyal, sexy heroes and smart, sassy heroines waiting for you.

Each Love in Bloom book is written to be enjoyed as a stand-alone novel or as part of the larger series. There are no cliffhangers and no unresolved issues. Characters from each series make appearances in future books, so you never miss an engagement, wedding, or birth. Start at the very beginning of the Love in Bloom series absolutely FREE with SISTERS IN LOVE in digital format, or begin with another fun and deeply emotional series like the Bradens, the Remingtons, the Ryders, or Seaside Summers.

A full list of titles are available at the end of this book, or visit Melissa's website for free ebooks, downloadable checklists, family trees, and more.
www.MelissaFoster.com

Below is a link where you can download FIVE first-in-series novels absolutely FREE.
www.MelissaFoster.com/LIBFree

Visit Melissa's Reader Goodies page for FREE downloadable reading order, series checklists, and more.
www.MelissaFoster.com/RG

More Books By Melissa

THE BRADENS at Trusty
Taken by Love
Fated for Love
Romancing My Love
Flirting with Love
Dreaming of Love
Crashing into Love

THE BRADENS at Peaceful Harbor
Healed by Love
Surrender My Love
River of Love
Crushing on Love
Whisper of Love
Thrill of Love

THE BRADENS at Pleasant Hill
Anything For Love

THE BRADEN NOVELLAS
Promise My Love
Our New Love
Daring Her Love
Story of Love
Love at Last

THE REMINGTONS
Game of Love
Stroke of Love
Flames of Love
Slope of Love
Read, Write, Love
Touched by Love

SEASIDE SUMMERS

Seaside Dreams
Seaside Hearts
Seaside Sunsets
Seaside Secrets
Seaside Nights
Seaside Embrace
Seaside Lovers
Seaside Whispers

BAYSIDE SUMMERS

Bayside Desires
Bayside Passions
Bayside Heat

THE RYDERS

Seized by Love
Claimed by Love
Chased by Love
Rescued by Love

SEXY STANDALONE ROMANCE

Tru Blue
Truly, Madly, Whiskey
Driving Whiskey Wild
Wicked Whiskey Love

THE MONTGOMERYS

Embracing Her Heart
Our Wicked Hearts
Wild, Crazy, Heart
Sweet, Sexy, Heart

HARBORSIDE NIGHTS SERIES
Includes characters from the Love in Bloom series
Catching Cassidy
Discovering Delilah
Tempting Tristan

More Books by Melissa
Chasing Amanda (mystery/suspense)
Come Back to Me (mystery/suspense)
Have No Shame (historical fiction/romance)
Love, Lies & Mystery (3-book bundle)
Megan's Way (literary fiction)
Traces of Kara (psychological thriller)
Where Petals Fall (suspense)

Acknowledgments

I had so much fun writing about Brett and Sophie. If this is your first Bad Boys After Dark novel, Mick, Dylan, and Carson's books are also available, as well as all four of the Wild brother's books, and their stories are just as sinfully sexy as Brett's. I hope you'll check out the other series in my big-family romance collection, Love in Bloom, including the Snow Sisters, the Bradens, the Remingtons, Seaside Summers, Bayside Summers, the Ryders, Billionaires After Dark, the Montgomerys, and Harborside Nights. You can find all of my books, publication schedules, reader checklists, and more free reader goodies on my site.
www.MelissaFoster.com

I'd like to thank fan Shelley Maynard for suggesting Axsel Montgomery's band name, Inferno. I love it! Please keep your emails and your posts on social media coming. If you haven't joined my fan club yet, please do! We have loads of fun, chat about books, and members get special sneak peeks of upcoming publications.
facebook.com/groups/MelissaFosterFans

A special thank-you goes to my incredibly talented editorial team. Thank you, Kristen, Penina, Elaini, Juliette, Marlene, Lynn, and Justinn.

As always, heaps of love and gratitude to my amazing family for allowing me to disappear for hours at a time creating these fictional worlds.

Meet Melissa

www.MelissaFoster.com
www.MelissaFoster.com/Newsletter
www.MelissaFoster.com/Reader-Goodies

Having sold more than three million books, Melissa Foster is a *New York Times* and *USA Today* bestselling and award-winning author. Her books have been recommended by *USA Today's* book blog, *Hagerstown* magazine, *The Patriot*, and several other print venues. She is the founder of the World Literary Café and Fostering Success. Melissa has painted and donated several murals to the Hospital for Sick Children in Washington, DC.

Visit Melissa on her website or chat with her on social media. Melissa enjoys discussing her books with book clubs and reader groups and welcomes an invitation to your event.

Melissa's books are available through most online retailers in paperback and digital formats.

CPSIA information can be obtained
at www.ICGtesting.com
Printed in the USA
LVOW03s1927120318
569550LV00003B/833/P